"Adam? Adam Morgan?"

"I'm glad you still know me after all this time. What has it been—seventeen, eighteen years now?"

Maggie felt her smile freeze into place and thanked Adam as she took her place in the passenger seat. He was being very kind to pick her up at the airport; he'd always been kind. There was no reason for her nerves to jangle and spark as if she were a teenager. But that was exactly what she had been the last time she saw him.

"How is your wife, Allison, doing?"

"Oh, Maggie. Didn't your mother tell you? She passed away last April."

Adam murmured something more, but Maggie had no idea what. Her brain had stirred to full awareness sparking with electrical fury. Now she understood why she had been summoned after three years of estrangement. She understood as well as a surveyor reading an old map. She'd journeyed this way before.

MARCY FROEMKE

A native of Winter Haven, Florida, this author wrote her first "book" in fourth grade and bound it in hardcover—the front and back exteriors of a box of tissues. More novels followed throughout elementary school and junior high, after which her love for writing fell prey to the demands of school and careers as elementary school teacher, music specialist, piano teacher, church organist/pianist and piano tuner. Only after receiving her master's of music degree did she return to her first love: fiction.

Marcy has written novels and novellas for inspirational and Regency markets, as well as nonfiction magazine articles. In addition, she currently serves as assistant professor of education at Bryan College in southeast Tennessee. She lives on a hill overlooking that college with her husband, Ken, with whom she recently celebrated their twenty-fifth wedding anniversary. In writing for Love Inspired, she hopes to communicate through laughter and tears the greatest of all love stories: the one between God and humanity.

He hath shown thee, O man, what is good;
and what doth the Lord require of thee, but to do
justly, and to love mercy, and to walk humbly
with thy God?

—*Micah* 6:8

Dedicated to the very special faculty, staff and students of Bryan College and with special thanks to Ruth Green and many others who answered a multitude of questions.

Chapter One

$\backsim$

As the plane glided downward toward Chattanooga, Maggie Gould found the scenery even more striking than she remembered. Twilight was descending over the mountains, and wisps of fog hazed the lights of the city. When the jet banked sharply, she pointed to the distinctive outline of Lookout Mountain, hoping to cheer her four-year-old son, Sam.

"Don't you think it looks a little like a humpback whale?"

"N-nooo," Sam whined tearfully. "Not a whale. Not *anything!*"

She sighed. Through two days of nonstop activity in preparation for their trip, he had fallen from frenzied excitement to pure cussedness. Running an obstacle course of moving walkways, shuttles and escalators to catch their connecting flight in Atlanta hadn't helped. She couldn't blame him, but she felt the annoyance of the passengers around her like blows.

At last the plane landed. With considerable relief she herded Sam through the jetway into the waiting area at their gate. The trepidation she felt over the upcoming reunion with her estranged mother, who'd fallen two weeks ago and broken her hip, had faded in the light of more immediate needs. She must get Sam settled into a warm bed. After this wretched week, which had begun with her losing her job, she was tired, too; although she mustn't delude herself into expecting rest beneath her mother's roof.

Scanning the faces around her, she tightened her hand around Sam's wriggling fingers and stepped to the side. Passengers breezed past. Many walked toward the embraces and welcoming cries of family and friends. A few professionally dressed men and women strode down the terminal, too full of purpose to look lonely.

She frowned. Where was that deacon, who was supposed to meet her? Thanks to her mother, she didn't even know his name. When a graying man dressed in a pin-striped suit met her glance, she walked tentatively toward him; but he brushed past her to greet an elegantly coiffed lady from first class. Maggie backed Sam against the wall, occupying the space the man vacated as if she'd intended that all along.

The surge of passengers began to thin. Airline attendants emerged, crisp and attractive in their dark uniforms, rolling expensive bags behind them. Maggie waited until the cockpit crew exited and there was no one left who could possibly be the missing deacon, unless he was disguised as that pierce-nosed teenager leaning against the window.

Sam's snuffles became sobs. With a grunt she lifted him into her arms. He burrowed his head against her shoulder like a puppy seeking warmth. Rubbing her cheek against his, she patted his curls, then began to walk through the terminal, struggling with the added weight of her carry-on bag.

She should have expected some kind of mix-up. Well, if her ride wasn't waiting outside, she could hire a taxi and charge it to her mother.

The thought cheered her only briefly. Sam's weight dragged at her like a stone; her bag thudded against her knees at every step. When she came to the descending escalator, she eyed it with caution and opted for the stairs. At the baggage area, her spirits fell again. No one was looking for Sam and herself. They had only each other. When had it ever been different?

She tipped the skycap to carry her luggage to the front sidewalk where two taxis waited. Maggie coaxed Sam to the ground and led him to the cleanest-looking one. Just as the driver released the lever to his trunk for her bags, a pink Hyundai cornered the drive and swung into the parking spot in front of the taxi.

The car made her think of cotton candy and bubble gum, but the man who emerged from it shattered the image. He unfolded himself with quick, natural grace while straightening his wrinkled corduroy jacket over a white shirt and jeans. When he offered her a questioning smile, tilting his head slightly, she knew he must be her driver.

She felt unsettled, having expected someone who would wear an expression of bland pleasantness like a mask, which was how she remembered the people in her mother's church. This man's face shouted character from his vulnerable eyes to the lines parenthesizing his mouth. And something about that face looked hauntingly familiar....

He was not handsome precisely, but certainly compelling, which would explain her mother's interest. Rhonda had always been susceptible to masculine charm. *Ah. Mother. You never change.*

Surely he was someone she'd known long ago....

"Hello, Maggie," he called over his idling engine, making no move toward them but holding onto the open door of the Hyundai. *Maybe he's afraid to let go, afraid it will roll off without him*, Maggie thought fleetingly. And then, with a sudden tightening in her stomach, she recognized him.

"Adam? Adam Morgan?"

He paused a fraction of an instant, then bent to turn off the engine and extract the keys. "I'm glad you still know me after all this time. What has it been—seventeen, eighteen years now?"

She felt her smile freeze in place. This was all her mother's doing. Had to be. Things rarely happened by accident with Rhonda. "That sounds about right," she said, hating to hear the false heartiness in her voice.

Slamming the door, he trotted over to them and, to the obvious disappointment of the taxi driver, claimed her luggage. "I'm sorry to be late. My car's in the shop, and I'm in the humbling position of having to use my daughter's. Beth had a play rehearsal at school tonight, and I had to drop her off first."

While Maggie searched for a reply, he crouched in front of Sam, who responded by hiding his face behind Maggie's trousers. "Hello, young man. You must be Sam. Would you allow me to drive you and your mom to your grandmother's house?"

"Don't know any grandmother," Sam blurted, shocking her. Instantly she understood why he had become so cross during the past hours. In the flurry of last-minute details, she hadn't considered her son would be unable to remember his grandmother, that he might be afraid.

"Come on, sweetheart," she said, sliding her hand across Sam's head and down his cheek. "You'll like Grandma." *I hope.* She scoured her brain for inspiration.

"All of her beds are high with tall posters, and you have to climb little baby ladders to get in."

"That's right," Adam said. "And I happen to know she has a yellow silk canopy over yours."

"What's a can-py?" Sam asked faintly, chewing the end of his finger but allowing Maggie to pull him to the car.

"It's a little like a parachute," Adam said, helping the boy climb into the back, then strapping him into a car seat. "You can dream you're floating through the clouds."

Maggie smiled again, briefly, and thanked Adam as she took her place in the passenger seat. He was being very kind; he had always been kind. There was no reason for her nerves to jangle and spark as if she were a teenager. But that was exactly what she had been, the last time she saw him.

Determined to break the uneasy silence that fell as he pulled into traffic, she asked, "You have a daughter old enough to drive?" then winced. So much had passed between them all those years ago, and the first thing she did was remind him of his age. He must be nearing forty; four years older than herself. That had seemed a large gap back then. If she'd only thought about it, she would have been able to figure out how old his daughter was. It wasn't as though her mother had forgotten to tell her about the birth. Rhonda never missed that kind of opportunity.

He gave a little laugh. "I have trouble believing it myself."

"And you have a little one, too?" She nodded toward the back seat.

"Hmm? Oh, you mean because of the car seat. No, Beth is my one and only. She baby-sits frequently, and we keep the kiddie seat in the car all the time."

"I used to do a lot of sitting, too."

"Yes," he said mildly. "I remember."

Of course he remembered. She blinked at her lack of sensitivity, not daring to look at him. A baby-sitting job had provided their first opportunity to be alone together. Adam had been going out with her sister for about a month, if she recalled correctly. One night, Johanna was late getting ready for one of their dates. When rain began to pepper the roof, her father asked the restless young man to drive Maggie to her appointment with the...Millers, wasn't it? Yes. Mr. and Mrs. Miller and their three young terrors, who lived several blocks away. Adam and Maggie had laughed and joked the entire short trip. When they arrived, he held her captive with stories about college life, in particular the antics of his buddies in the dorm. Mrs. Miller had finally opened the door of her house and waved her inside.

That had been the beginning.

"I'm hungry," Sam complained, recalling Maggie to the present. Still, for a lingering instant, she fancied hearing the squeak of windshield wipers. But there was no rain now, only the blazing neon of a small city holding off the dark.

"We'll be at Grandma's soon," she told him. "She'll have something good to eat. She always does."

"I don't know," Adam said after a moment. "She's been laid up for a while, and maybe the pantry's low. We can stop by a drive-thru if you like."

She heard the reluctance in his voice. "We're almost there, honey," she told Sam. "You can wait."

"Oh, let me buy him a burger," Adam said decisively, as though regretting his earlier lapse. "I know you're anxious to get home, but it'll only take a minute. There's one right on the way."

She had little choice but to agree; now that he'd offered, there could be no denying Sam. Besides, she wasn't at all anxious to get home, except for the relief leaving him would bring. Whatever could her mother have been thinking? But that was a question she had never been able to answer.

Moments later, Maggie unwrapped Sam's cheeseburger and carefully divided it into halves, then handed the child his first portion. She nested his container of fries in napkins and placed them on the seat beside him where he could reach them.

"Sure I can't get you something?" Adam asked again, even as they pulled onto Brainerd.

He's as uncomfortable as I am, Maggie decided. The thought relaxed her a little. "I never did care for burgers and fries much." Daringly she added, "But I'm surprised you didn't get one."

Adam laughed. "I did love them, didn't I? Cholesterol finally caught up with me, sorry to say. I still have one every now and then for old times' sake, though."

The ease with which he handled her faint reference to the past encouraged her. They were adults, after all. He wouldn't hold her responsible for something she had done when little more than a child. She had been cruel, but nothing could be gained by going over that again. It was possible to sit beside him without choking out apologies she had stopped rehearsing a decade ago, possible to survive this little ride with him. She would treat him with the same impersonal friendliness she'd give a stranger, for that was what he was to her now, and she to him. Strangers, with a lifetime of other experiences, other loves, a whole other history separating them.

"What do you do now, Adam?" she asked, trying her best to sound urbane. "When did you come back to Chattanooga?"

"You knew I was at Eagleton Hills for twelve years?"

She nodded, not wanting to elaborate on how well her mother had kept her informed on his life during those first years. She knew exactly when he had married, when he'd received his doctorate, and that he'd obtained a dean's position at a small liberal arts college in Virginia almost immediately afterward. All of this was taking place through the bleak years while Zack studied and she cleaned motel rooms to send him through med school. Her mother's gray eyes were always intent upon her when she delivered such messages, and a small smile never failed to tug at her lips. There was no mistaking the unspoken words behind each news update. *This could have been yours. See what you missed by breaking off your engagement?*

"After I left Eagleton, I spent a few years teaching at Texas Tech," he was saying. "We came back to Chattanooga last year. I have a computer business now."

"Do you really?" She couldn't disguise her surprise.

"I know it's a change, but sometimes people need that. I'd liked the area since I first came here to college. My wife, Allison, missed the mountains, and she wanted to be near her folks. And it's not so easy to walk into a college position unless you're willing to go where the openings are. While I was in Texas I became involved in using technology in education, particularly in the training of teachers, and taking a chance on a computer business didn't feel as risky as it might sound. I'm happy to say things have been going pretty well."

She shifted uncomfortably, bumping her knees against the glove compartment in the process. "I'm sure they have."

He looked at her and grinned. They were on the outskirts of the city now, and the widely spaced streetlights only faintly illuminated his face. For an instant his smile made him appear exactly as he had nearly two decades ago. She felt as if she'd slipped into a time pocket, and the feeling took her breath.

"You don't sound all that sure. Don't judge me on the basis of my daughter's car, please. It was what she wanted."

She never could resist one of his smiles. "No one knows what mysteries lurk in the mind of a teenage girl."

Immediately she bit her lip. Everything she said could be taken two ways. She may as well have a twenty-year-old shovel in her mouth, she was digging up the past so much.

He didn't appear to notice. "Amen to that."

"And now you're a deacon, too," she added rapidly. "You *have* been busy."

He cut a glance at her, as if wondering at her teasing tone. "I felt like I owed something back to the church. All those years attending and never doing anything much."

Sam demanded the other half of his hamburger, and she handed it to him, then gave him a few sips of his drink. "I remember how much you enjoyed teaching Sunday school here. The kids really liked you."

"I stopped volunteering after my first year of marriage. Allison and I were only married a few months when she got pregnant. I was in grad school, then there was the new position. It was difficult for her, all those changes. She wanted to stay home with Beth but wanted to work, too. She finally got a part-time job at a horticulturist's and loved it. When we moved to Texas she did some landscape designing. We were all so busy that our time together was precious. To tell you the truth, I was afraid to get involved with the church, other than attending and the few odd things. A church's social life can swallow you whole."

"You're telling me," she said with feeling.

"I know your mom and dad were there every time the doors opened."

"Which meant we were, too." She had best not get into that. "But I think it's good of you to do that—be a deacon, I mean. Even if it does trap you into picking people up at the airport."

"Oh, I wasn't trapped," he said lightly. "I've been trying to visit Rhonda every few weeks or so, more often since she fell. When she told me you were flying in tonight and didn't have anyone to meet you, I volunteered."

Maggie could imagine. Her mother had a way of giving someone no reasonable outlet but to do what she wanted—and without Rhonda's ever actually asking, too. In fact, the person being volunteered would often be left with the impression that Rhonda was the one giving favors, not the other way around.

It was a talent.

"Well, I appreciate it, Adam. We could have taken a taxi, though, and not inconvenienced you."

"Taxis are for visitors, not natives," he said. "And what about you? What have you been up to all this time?"

She gave him a speculative look, wondering why he asked. What could she possibly tell him that her mother hadn't already divulged? "You know Zack and I were divorced over three years ago."

"Yes. I was sorry to hear that."

She believed him. It was less the sincerity in his voice than her knowledge of his character. Unless he had changed drastically, Adam never failed to tell the truth. And he had never been a spiteful person, the kind who would rejoice in someone's failure—even if that someone had hurt him.

"Did she also tell you I just lost my job?"

He flinched sympathetically. "No, she didn't. She only said you were able to take some time off. She did say you'd been teaching in a private school for the past four years."

"Six," Maggie corrected.

"Music?"

"Yes. I taught general music in the elementary classes and directed the junior high chorale."

"I'm not surprised. You always sang beautifully and were a good pianist. Do you also teach privately? Could you build up your clientele until you find another position?"

Now it was her turn to laugh. "Adam, I am not a good pianist. I play Beethoven like a steamroller and do a passable Bach if allowed to go at half tempo. No one would pay me to teach their children beyond the beginning stages, and I can't abide those little pieces. It's the same for teaching voice. There are countless teachers in New York with more talent and degrees than myself. All I could get would be children, and children's voices must be handled so carefully. No, I'd rather look for something else entirely."

She couldn't tell him the real reason, that her love of music had shriveled and died years ago, around the time Zack left. No, that wasn't fair; the song within had begun to fade long before that....

"You'll surely find something soon," he said.

"I hope so." She sounded more disconsolate than she intended, but a surge of anxiety mixed with nostalgia had stolen her concentration. The neighborhood they were driving through pierced her with its familiarity. It was an old, ragtag collection of aging houses, some small, some large, a neighborhood formed in the days before standard subdivision codes. Here a small clapboard house could nestle beside a rambling, multistoried gingerbread; front yards might be generous or no more than a strip of grass. There was no rhyme or reason to the hodgepodge of homes snuggling into the side of the mountain, yet a poetry existed among them nevertheless—a poetry of lives lived safe and well, lives spent loving, fighting, making peace, defending one another through the generations, where neighbors knew one another from birth to death.

They were almost there, almost to her mother's house. Adam's presence, uncomfortable though it made her, seemed infinitely preferable to the meeting ahead. She felt a sudden need to see Sam, and peered over her shoulder. He was asleep, his head bobbing trustingly with every bump and turn.

Halfway up the mountain they passed the old Jefferson homestead, then a patch of poplar and oak trees. Beyond the stretch of woods, the outline of a large, two-story Victorian steadily grew in substance. They had arrived.

Adam entered the circular drive and stopped. Another car was parked in front of the garage; the aide's, Maggie supposed. Someone had turned on the front porch light; several of the interior rooms were lit, as well. Wooden planters overflowing with greenery and late-blooming flowers graced each side of the door. The cane-bottomed rockers on the veranda looked new. She wished she felt welcomed by these signs of expectation and warmth, but she didn't.

When Adam moved to open his door, she reached for his arm as if grabbing a lifeline. He looked at her hand, then at her. She pulled back in embarrassment. She could not delay seeing her mother any longer. Yet she did delay, holding Adam with the only question she could think of, the one hovering in her mind for some time now. She'd felt too awkward to ask about Allison before, since his marriage seemed so connected to their own bad times, but her need to postpone the inevitable burst the words from her like water spilling over a dam.

"You haven't told me how Allison is doing. Is she as happy as she expected to be, returning to Chattanooga?"

A look of desolation entered his eyes, chilling her with premonition.

"Oh, Maggie. Your mother didn't tell you." His gaze shifted from hers. "We came back home because Allison was dying. She passed away last April."

The muscles in Maggie's stomach clenched together painfully, as if she had been brutally kicked. Long seconds passed before she could speak.

"Adam, I'm so sorry."

He nodded and gave a passable attempt at a smile. "We're making it, Beth and I. We'll be okay."

"I know you will," she said swiftly. "I'm sorry I said anything. I didn't want to make you feel sad. I mean, I don't want you to think I—"

"I don't think anything, Maggie. It's a pleasure to speak of Allison. You don't know how hard it is not to talk about her. People try so carefully to avoid the whole subject. I understand why they do it—they're trying not to hurt me or Beth, almost as if we won't grieve so long as they don't remind us. But it's just the opposite. Not talking about Allison is as bad as pretending she never existed. When Beth and I are at home together, Allison is still a part of our family. She always will be."

He opened his car door. Cool air, sweet, light and scented with honeysuckle and rose, drifted over her. She breathed deeply, feeling some measure of solace in the well-loved odors. Unshed tears pricked her eyes. How could Rhonda not have told her?

Adam murmured something, something comforting no

doubt, as he exited and opened Sam's door. He continued to talk, though softly now, directing his comments to her half-asleep son as he gathered him in his arms.

She had no idea what Adam said. Her brain had stirred to full awareness, an awareness sparking with electrical fury. Now she understood why she had not been told the name of the deacon when she'd last spoken with Rhonda, why she'd been summoned after three years of estrangement. She understood as well as a surveyor reading an old map. She'd journeyed this way before.

Mother!

Her earlier reluctance to see Rhonda dissolved completely. Now she burned with anticipation in the need to vent her ire. But, as with so many other needs in relation to her mother, it was doomed to frustration. After Adam unloaded her bags, saw her inside and hurried off, pleading he had to pick up his daughter, Maggie was informed by the nurse's aide that Rhonda had retired for the night.

"Of course she has," she told the young woman, who showed surprise at the edge in Maggie's tone. "Never mind," she told the girl. "Tomorrow will be soon enough."

But when she passed by her mother's downstairs bedroom, Maggie's steps slowed to a halt. Beyond the intricately carved wood, she heard utter silence, the kind only a waiting watchfulness could bring. She nodded, a humorless smile lifting one corner of her mouth. When Sam whined fretfully against her shoulder, she moved on.

Chapter Two

That wasn't so bad, Adam told himself as he drove toward Beth's high school. It could have been a lot worse. Squinting in the glare of oncoming headlights, he merged onto the rocketing traffic of I-75, flooring the gas pedal.

Maggie had hardly changed. The freshness of a young girl had left her, of course. Her cheeks were no longer round, and faint lines had etched into the corners of her eyes. But those eyes still sparked with vitality and warmth. And she moved with the same quick surety she always had, as if nothing could ever crush her. Yet her light form and transparent emotions shouted fragility. She had been hurt, and deeply. Even after all this time he felt himself responding, wanting to help. But she was not his concern now. There was nothing he could do about her situation.

He was well aware that Rhonda had other notions; why else had she trapped him into chauffeuring her daughter? Maggie had realized it, too; he'd seen it in her expression in those last few moments and known enough to beat a hasty retreat. He breathed lighter, knowing she had been horrified at her mother's manipulations. He'd worried she might get the wrong idea at his lending a hand.

It was unthinkable he would betray Allison's memory by looking for a replacement so soon. She had died less than six months ago. He owed his wife far more than that, especially when he'd failed her in so many ways.

He couldn't think about that now.

After a moment, the image of Maggie's indignation restored his good humor, making him chuckle. Her eyes had sparked blue fire. How many times he'd seen them blaze like that, most of the time at her parents, but sometimes at himself.

A fresh wave of relief ran through him at the relative ease of their reunion. He had been afraid seeing her would stir painful memories, but that had not been the case. Enough time had passed, enough days spent with Allison—who in her sweet gentleness had never fired anger toward him, not in all their years together—to mend the claw marks little Miss Maggie had ripped into his soul.

His pulse hammered a few beats, then steadied.

Yes, he felt only a bittersweet nostalgia for his time with Maggie. He had forgiven her long ago. Especially after Beth came along and cemented his relationship with his wife. He sobered and, as he often did, breathed a prayer of thanks for the years God had allowed them together.

Seeing his exit, he veered off the interstate, then began the series of turns through sleepy neighborhoods that led to the high school. When he arrived at the starkly efficient structure his daughter attended, he saw that only a few cars remained in the parking lot. Streetlights illuminated the asphalt decently enough, and the building itself was well lit. There were no dark corners to worry about for his daughter's sake. Nevertheless, the place emitted a locked-up-tight feel and no sign of Beth.

Frowning, he slowly drove the length of the tarmac then back again. At the main entrance, he parked next to the curb and tapped his fingers against the steering wheel for the length of ten seconds, then got out. He walked to the wide double doors and pulled. Locked. Cupping his hands around his eyes, he peered past the mesh-enforced glass to the corridor. Other than trophy cases and pictures of graduating classes lining the hall, he saw nothing except the black-and-white tiled floor. No stragglers lingering after play practice, no lanky schoolgirls with hair the color of damp wheat.

Adam checked his watch: ten-fifteen. He hadn't realized the lateness of the hour, but sometimes their rehearsals went longer than that. Maybe Beth found a ride with a friend. But why hadn't she called him? She was usually considerate in that way.

He strode to the car, jerked open the door and fumbled for her cellular phone. He jabbed his home number, heard it ring five times. Hope surged when Beth's overbright voice came on the line, then fell as he recognized the recording.

He stuffed the phone into his jacket pocket and began to walk along the sidewalk that surrounded the building, prodding at bushes and scanning each inset doorway. In the back, a walkway angled to the track and field complex, which was surrounded by a high chain-link fence. Even from this distance, he could see few objects that might hide any of the thousand horrible things that could happen to a defenseless young girl; no shrubs lined the track; no shadows were heaped beneath the benches. His gaze moved anxiously, then paused at the dark mass of the bleachers. She couldn't be in there.

Please God, no. I can't lose Beth, too.

He ran to the gate, found it locked as he knew it must be. He shook it anyway, but the padlock and chain did not fall helpfully into the grass. Eyeing again the height of the fence—twelve feet at least, and topped with barbed wire—he shrugged off his coat and tossed it to the ground. He paced backward several steps, then ran forward, lunging, clutching and pulling himself upward, his shoes finding toeholds, losing them, then digging in again.

At eye level with the sharp, knotted wire at the top, he paused for breath and courage, clinging like a cat to a screen door. Contemplating the certainty of stitches, Adam's senses returned. He should have brought his jacket to lay over the vicious metal up here. And if his daughter were inside, wouldn't the gate be open?

"Beth?" he called tentatively. Then louder, "Beth? Where are you?"

"Can I help you?" called a voice beneath him.

Adam's head jerked, nearly causing him to fall. The flashlight pointing at his face almost blinded him, but he saw enough to recognize a policeman holding it. On the grass behind him, a squad car idled, its lights off. The officer had been very stealthy. Adam hadn't heard a thing.

"I'm looking for my daughter," Adam called, feeling his face grow hot. "I came to pick her up from play rehearsal and she wasn't here."

The policeman glanced at the field. "They give outdoor performances now?"

"No, of course not." The skepticism in the officer's tone flooded him with indignation. "Can't we go inside and check the bleachers? I'm afraid something might have happened to her.''

"Well, I'll tell you what, sir. You come on down, and we'll talk about it."

Adam's fingers were frozen pincers on the fence. "You don't think I was trying to break in, do you? It's not as if there's anything to steal on a track."

"Well, I don't know about that," said the officer. "We just got a complaint from one of the neighbors about some suspicious activity around the school building. If you'll come down, we'll get it all straightened out."

This was ridiculous. "I don't have time to straighten things out. My daughter could be..." The sound of an approaching motorcycle heightened his indignation. "What did you do, call in reinforcements?" Almost simultaneously, the phone in his pocket began to ring. "That must be her," he said eagerly, scrambling down at last.

The policeman eyed Adam's jacket, picked it up, then put up a restraining hand as Adam reached for it.

"Give me the phone," Adam pleaded. "She never rings long because she thinks I'm either right beside it or away."

"Just a minute, sir." While Adam fumed, the officer tediously patted the jacket and slipped his hand inside every pocket. Finally he handed the cellular to Adam.

Adam snapped it away, glaring his thoughts at the other man. "Beth?"

"No, it's Jackie Parker," bubbled the voice at the other end, dropping his heart to his knees. "Mr. Morgan? Beth told me to call you when I got home, okay? Rehearsal was canceled tonight because Mr. Danbridge got sick, and Beth went for a ride with Jake, all right?"

"Jake?" he repeated. He didn't know any Jake.

"He's a really neat guy," Jackie assured him. "And, Mr. Morgan? I'm sorry I didn't call you before now, because I forgot. Is that okay?"

"Hmm?" The motorcycle was coming into sight now. Two riders were on it, both wearing helmets, thank God. "No, Jackie, that's fine," he mumbled distractedly. "Thank you for calling."

He replaced the phone in his pocket and walked forward, hardly noticing the policeman accompanying him. The motorcycle slowed as it crossed the grass, then pulled to a stop within a few yards of Adam. The glow on his daughter's face lessened as she took in her father's face, the officer and the police car.

"Dad?" she ventured, removing her helmet. "I saw your car parked out front. What's going on?"

Now that he knew Beth was safe, Adam turned his attention to her driver. Colorless eyes, hard as diamond chips, stared back at him behind long strands of hair.

"I might ask you the same thing," Adam said quietly.

Beth dismounted and ruffled her hair with nervous fingers. "Mr. Danbridge canceled our rehearsal after we'd only been here a few minutes. Didn't Jackie call you? She promised she would. So Jake took me for a ride on his bike while I waited for you." Her gaze skittered away from his to the officer's stony face. "Hi," she said tentatively, peering at his name tag, "Officer Tullis."

"This man is your father?" Tullis responded.

A devilish light flit into Beth's eyes as she hesitated just a second too long.

"Of course I'm her father," Adam said, quelling her nonsense with a fierce look. He moved toward her escort, extended a hand and grimly introduced himself, adding, "I like to know who my daughter's friends are."

Caught in the act of removing his helmet, Beth's friend did not hurry himself but carefully propped his headgear on the bike handle before gripping Adam's hand. "Jake Browne," he said, his voice deep and tinged with resentment. He didn't trouble himself to get off his cycle.

"Do you go to school here, Jake?" Adam asked pleasantly, knowing the answer. This was no schoolboy but a man. The well-developed chest and arms outlined by his T-shirt declared it if the sharp, stubbled angles of his jaw did not.

"I'm finished with school," he answered.

"Are you? And what is it you do now, Jake, besides cruising school parking lots and giving rides to little girls?"

"Dad—" Beth said miserably.

"Okay, you're her father," Officer Tullis broke in, his voice unexpectedly light. "If the young man will leave, I'll give you folks a ride back to your car."

Beth bid Jake a shamefaced goodbye. Adam watched the cyclist's retreat with satisfaction as he led his daughter to the cruiser. Except for the blurbs of static from the police dispatcher, the brief ride to her car was silent. Adam forced himself to thank the officer for his trouble, then tried not to lose his temper when Tullis followed them all the way to the interstate.

Finally Beth broke the taut silence. "I'm sorry, Dad. I didn't mean to cause all this trouble."

Her apology served to release his anger. "I don't know why you didn't call me as soon as you found out about the rehearsal."

"Well, you had my phone," she said reasonably.

"There aren't any pay phones in the building?"

"Yes, but you don't usually carry the cellular with you, and I figured you'd be inside the airport and wouldn't hear it."

"You figured." He shook his head. "You could have tried."

Beth's tone grew more irritated. "I *did* ask Jackie to keep calling until she reached you. I thought I'd done everything I could."

"You know what I think, Beth? I think you were afraid to phone, afraid to ask permission to ride with your new friend, because you knew I wouldn't give it."

"Do you think I'm a sneak?" she cried, with what Adam felt was just a little too much righteous indignation.

In spite of the heavy traffic on the interstate, Adam risked a lengthy stare at his daughter's profile. She met his gaze, her wide green eyes incensed. Her resemblance to Allison was so strong that for an instant, a lump caught in his throat. Like her mother, Beth possessed a quiet beauty. She was all muted colors, not striking contrasts like Maggie with her dark hair and fair skin, but no less pleasing.

Beyond a doubt, Jake Browne had been pleased. Adam steeled himself not to soften at the resemblance. Allison had never looked at him with scorn, not like his daughter was doing.

"No, Beth, I don't think you're a sneak," he said tiredly. "But I do believe a young girl's head can be turned by a tough-looking guy who flouts authority. Who is he, anyway? Does he have a job? How old is he?"

"I don't know how old he is. I don't go around asking people how old they are, do you?"

"Watch your tone, Beth."

"Well, I'm sorry, but it's not polite to ask personal questions, is it?" She hesitated. "I think he works at Sally's Garage."

"Hmm," he said, inflecting the syllable with meaning.

"I know what you're thinking, but he's saving for college."

"I'm impressed. What does he plan to study, leather jackets and chains?"

Beth's mouth dropped. "Daddy, you're a snob!"

"I don't think so, baby. I just know there's something appealing about danger to those too young to know better."

"But I'm sixteen years old!"

"My point exactly," he said, turning off the interstate and taking the long, winding road that led to home.

"Mom never treated me this way," she mumbled, stabbing him with a flare of pain.

"Your mother trusted everyone. I don't."

"Tell me something I don't know," she said, just loudly enough for him to hear.

In Maggie's dream, she and Carter and Johanna were children again. They raced through an endless field of daisies, Johanna far in front, Carter and herself lagging behind. Gasping, she struggled to pass him. Every time she edged forward, he matched her pace effortlessly. She cast a desperate look at her brother, but he kept his face turned forward. No one smiled. Johanna drew farther and farther ahead, a spindly shadow running along the horizon. Abruptly Carter stopped and raised triumphant arms.

"I won!" he declared.

Maggie glared at him. "You did *not!*"

"Yes, he *did!*" Johanna cried, appearing suddenly, incomprehensibly, behind them. Her face had aged to the adult Johanna, becoming rounder, matronly, then older still, looking shockingly like Rhonda.

A thump sounded, and all three of them shattered into crystal splinters.

Maggie jerked to wakefulness, her heart racing. She raised herself on her elbows, bewildered at first by unfamiliar surroundings. No, not unfamiliar, she thought as moonlight, slatting through the miniblinds, aided her vision. The same Sheraton furnishings she had known all her life were still here, from the mahogany four-poster beneath her to the bow-fronted chest of drawers. Two identical chairs with carved backs and cherry-striped upholstered seats nestled into the corner. Nothing had changed.

Buy quality antiques and you will never be out of style, Rhonda often said. Maggie had to admit she found the classical furniture more appealing now than she had as a teenager, when most of her friends enjoyed more trendy looks.

She slanted her eyes at Sam. Thankfully her sudden wakening hadn't disturbed him. He had refused to sleep in the yellow room—Johanna's old bedroom—despite, or maybe because of, Adam's description of the canopy as a parachute. Excitement could rapidly change to fear in a four-year-old, especially an exhausted one. Now he lay curled toward her, his arms reaching for her side of the bed, she noted with tenderness.

No wonder she had awakened. Her arms were cold. Always the restless sleeper, Sam had twisted the coverlet and sheet into a heap between his ankles. Softly she pulled the bedcovers over them both and settled back.

The bedside clock displayed 4:10. Maybe she could catch a couple more hours' sleep.

A noise broke the quiet, sounding oddly like the one in her dream and coming from downstairs. She sat up immediately and slipped from the bed, throwing her robe around her shoulders. Burglars? She could only wish. *Please, God, don't let it be that Mom has fallen again.*

She frowned as she hurried down the stairs. Was that a prayer her mind had formed? Had the association of home made her retreat into patterns of thought she'd long felt were useless?

Prayers were for children. She encouraged Sam to pray every night because she wanted him to grow up with values and a sense of wonder. He believed in Santa Claus and the Easter Bunny, too. Reality would intrude soon enough.

Besides, even if God did trouble himself to meddle in every one of the billions of lives on the planet—a concept that staggered her imagination—that sort of prayer was ridiculous. "There are certain things we just don't pray for," a visiting pastor had counseled her youth group aeons ago. "Never ask God to change the past, for instance. He still does miracles, but even He won't go that far. Don't be like the seventeen-year-old who thought he'd found the best way to tell his dad about wrecking the family car. He took his chance while saying grace. After thanking God for the food, he finished with, 'And please, Lord, help me to not have run into Linda Berkley's car this afternoon.'"

They had laughed at this absurdity, but she wasn't laughing now. Reaching the hall, she flicked on the lights and hurried toward the master suite, her bare feet freezing on the hardwood floor. She could hear Rhonda muttering angrily behind the door. Without allowing herself to hesitate, she turned the knob.

"Are you all right, Mom?"

Rhonda Covington's head twisted toward Maggie. Standing a few feet from the bed, she tightened her grip on her walker, the network of blue veins on the back of her hands darkening. Her knee-length gown and matching robe, made of the finest pink silk, clung damply to the front of her thighs. An overturned pitcher of ice water, a tray and a shattered glass lay at her feet on the floor.

"Haven't you learned to knock yet?" Rhonda answered crisply.

Maggie curbed a flare of anger. "I heard something and thought you might need help."

"As you can see, I'm fine. I was on my way to the bathroom and braced my hand on the nightstand. I didn't know the girl had set the tray so close to the bed."

"You should have called me." Averting her eyes from the cold angles of the walker, Maggie hurried to straighten the mess.

"What, with you and the baby all the way upstairs? I've never been one to yell like a fishwife. Besides, I'm perfectly capable of taking care of myself."

"I'm sure you are," Maggie murmured as she gingerly placed glass shards on the tray. "Don't walk another step. You'll cut your feet or slip on the water." She glanced up, saw the slight tremor in her mother's arms. "I'll finish this in a second, but let me get you a dry gown first."

"All right." Rhonda sounded weary suddenly, and turned slowly back to the bed. "My nightwear is hanging where it always did."

Maggie went to the right-hand side of her parents'

large walk-in closet. Her eyes gleamed at the rich colors and variety of clothing hanging from the wooden rods. With a stab of sadness, she saw her father's suits, shirts and trousers still hung on the left. She had played here as a child on a few daring occasions, when her parents were away and the baby-sitter was careless. She remembered rubbing the soft fabrics of her mother's dresses against her cheek, sniffing the faint perfume that clung there. She remembered wondering if she would ever grow into such a beautiful, elegant woman as her mother was.

The youthful vitality of the bent old lady in the bedroom may have gone, but beauty still lurked behind the sagging, crinkled skin. As did her generations-old Southern aristocratic spirit. Certainly her irritability toward her younger daughter hadn't faded. The unexpected rush of softness she had felt on seeing her mother's frailty dissolved. This was the woman who had refused to help her when she needed it most. Why had she come?

"What's taking so long?" called Rhonda.

Maggie breathed deeply. "Just waiting for you to tell me which gown you want to wear."

"Oh, it doesn't matter. The green, I think. No, the apricot."

Maggie brought the required ensemble to her mother and began helping her change. "You still have the best wardrobe in Chattanooga," she said, making small talk to overcome her awkwardness. Would her own arms be this shriveled one day? After struggling for years with infertility, Rhonda had given birth to Johanna when she was forty. Maggie and Carter had followed at two-year intervals. Yet Rhonda had remained astonishingly youthful through her fifties and sixties. Now, at seventy-six, she finally looked her age.

"Your father always wanted me to dress like a lady." The older woman's gray eyes raked over Maggie's sweatpants and T- shirt. "I tried to pass that on to my daughters, but one can't be successful every time, I suppose."

"My clothing budget has never been up to your standards."

"When you buy quality and classic designs, you save money. Some of my outfits are nearly thirty years old. Your father always said you could tell more about a woman by what she wears in her leisure moments than how she looks when everybody's watching."

"It never mattered to Zack what I wore, especially around the house." She threw the words as a challenge and was not disappointed when Rhonda's expression became scornful.

"*Zack.* I'm surprised you'd even mention his name in my home."

"Really? Well, I'm surprised you invited *me* to your home after what you said the last time I was here. Why did you, Mother?" When the older woman didn't answer immediately, fire burned through Maggie's body. "Was it some misguided attempt to throw Adam Morgan and me together? That's why you had him meet me at the airport, isn't it? But that doesn't make any sense. You told me it was my duty to stay with Zack no matter what he'd done, even though you've always disliked him."

For the first time, Rhonda looked uncomfortable. "I needed help and so did you. Let's leave it at that. Don't hover, Maggie. I still have to go to the bathroom. You go on up to bed now."

Swallowing her exasperation, Maggie stepped back but followed until Rhonda closed the bathroom door firmly in her face. She turned to clean the last of the broken glass and water from the floor. Not until her mother was safely tucked into bed again did she move to the threshold.

"Maggie," Rhonda said when she reached the door.

"Yes?" She balanced the tray on her hip, thinking how cold her own voice sounded. Somehow she would have to gain better control of herself.

"I..." The older woman met her eyes briefly, then glanced away. "I'm glad you came."

Maggie was too astonished to say anything. She only stared while her mother reached to turn off the bedside lamp.

Chapter Three

Adam glanced through the glass walls of his office to the small showroom floor and stifled a smile. Mrs. Gabbert was back for the second time this week. That made at least six visits during the past month to his store. Harry Gretencord, his sole employee other than a part-time accountant, answered her questions with admirable patience, though Adam could see the strain in his eyes. And no wonder. When a customer debated this long about a purchase, he or she rarely bought anything.

Mrs. Gabbert might be different, though, if she could ever decide what it was she wanted. Like a number of lively elderly customers he'd met, she longed to understand what all the fuss was about over computers. But her undeniably sharp intellect could not grasp more than the edges of technology. That didn't surprise him. He knew computers inside and out but still found them a miracle.

The clock read half-past twelve. Finally lunchtime, and he couldn't decide what to do: grab a salad or yield to the impulse to visit Rhonda Covington and find out how she was getting along.

Oh, he might as well be honest. It had been almost a week since he had brought Maggie home from the airport and he hadn't enjoyed a decent night's sleep since. Although he'd assured himself her long-ago abandonment no longer hurt, there must be an explanation why her sensitive face and low voice kept intruding into his thoughts. Maybe some small part of him refused to forgive her. He couldn't live with that. God had forgiven him too many times for him to hold a grudge.

The parts catalog blurred as he tapped his pen on the desk blotter. Surely the old attraction wasn't pulling at him again. He had to see her one more time to find out, because if that was the case, now would be a good time to schedule that long-postponed buying trip to Nashville. And he wouldn't use his friend John Clatchett's plane, either. He could take a leisurely drive up Monteagle Mountain and make a two-hour journey last four. He'd have to stay more than a couple of days to get everything he needed. Maybe a week. Beth had friends who were always asking her to stay overnight, so she'd be all right.

But if he suddenly appeared on Maggie's doorstep, what would she think? She'd be bound to misinterpret. If she didn't, her mother would.

He recalled the expression on Maggie's face when he'd last seen her, the promise of trouble in her eyes. Maybe he should do a Good Samaritan check, just to make sure everything was all right between them.... No. None of his business.

A sudden thought tipped his mind to a decision. With more eagerness than he cared to admit, he slipped on his sports coat, flicked Harry an encouraging wave, opened his office door and walked into the corridor that led to the parking lot.

"You feed that boy too much sugar," Rhonda said as she cautiously lowered herself onto one of the chairs at the kitchen table. Sam, chomping on a hastily made peanut butter and honey sandwich, watched her move the walker to the side with cautious eyes. After six days, he'd grown very comfortable with Grandma but still hadn't made peace with her walker.

Maggie stared daggers at the strawberry-dotted wallpaper above the kitchen range as she steadily stirred a pot of her mother's homemade soup. Rhonda had insisted she thaw it after rejecting Maggie's suggestion of sandwiches for lunch. Chunks of beef remained frozen, however, and she dared not leave it a second for fear of scorching.

"He's going through a stage, I think," she said carefully, wishing her mother would stop telling her how to raise her child. "Right now he's a very picky eater."

"You'd better widen his palate, then. I expected my children to eat what was set before them, and I made sure every meal was nutritious."

"I give him vitamins, and he eats plenty of cereal and fruit."

Rhonda shook her head. "Sugar and more sugar. No wonder he looks so pale." Suddenly she put one hand to her forehead.

Maggie viewed her with concern. "Another dizzy spell?"

"I've stayed in bed too long, that's all. Anyway," Rhonda added, lifting her head, "mealtimes are to be shared with family and friends. Now Sammy won't want to sit at Grandma's table and enjoy her good soup." She tilted playful eyes at him.

"I'll sit with you, Grandma."

"That's my big boy. But will you eat my soup?"

When Sam smiled at her mischievously, she waved him closer. "Come let me see your elbow, child." After a few seconds' examination, she looked at her daughter with worry. "Maggie, this cut hasn't healed. Maybe you should take him to the doctor."

"No doctor!" Sam declared immediately.

Maggie sighed. On the morning after they arrived, Sam had tripped on the sidewalk and fallen into her mother's rosebushes, scraping his arm on the bricks bordering the flower bed. Little pearls of blood had outlined the nasty scratch, but it was hardly worthy of expensive medical treatment.

"It's healing fine, Mom. Don't scare him."

"When was the last time he had a physical?"

"He had a virus about six months ago. The pediatrician checked him over then and said he was fine."

"I mean a *real* physical—blood work and everything. Some things aren't visible to the eye in the beginning. Any caring parent would want to do everything in her power to ensure her child stays well."

Her mother's tone was imperial; gone was the small lapse into good-naturedness. The entire week had been like that—moments fraught with friction interlaced with tantalizing glimpses of a different Rhonda. Someone softer, more approachable. But those kinder moments were most often saved for her grandson.

Rhonda had always been a charming woman and gracious hostess to others. Their home often rang with the laughter of guests and relatives during Maggie's childhood, and Rhonda treated her husband, Philip, like a

king, scurrying to serve his every wish, always deferring
to his judgment. Even Carter's misdeeds netted more
smiles than scolds. But with her daughters, Rhonda had
acted more like a drill sergeant, and with Maggie most
of all. *Because I wasn't as compliant as Johanna,* she
thought with the old ache. *I wanted reasons for rules
and answers to my questions. I still do.*

But she never got them. Not from her mother, and not
from God. But that was a whole other matter. Or maybe
not.

Maggie's thoughts churned fretfully. She felt the need
to talk about their estrangement, maybe even reach some
kind of resolution if that were possible, but they were
falling into their old roles: arguing about trivial matters
while the important issues waited like a dragon in a cave,
its fierce eyes watchful in the dark.

Rhonda had not quite finished. "Have you noticed
how often he's thirsty?"

"Oh, Mom, children are always clamoring for a
drink." A sudden memory struck her, and she turned
sharply, lifting the pot from the burner and setting it
aside. "You're not starting *that* again, are you?"

Sliding her eyes from her daughter's, Rhonda stroked
Sam's tousled curls with an expression of disinterest. "I
have no idea what you're talking about."

"I think you do. The diabetes thing." Her childhood
had been haunted by her mother's firm conviction that
one of them would contract juvenile diabetes. Every year
each of the children was forced to endure what seemed
like torture to them—complete physicals, including
scary blood tests. Few of their friends had such consci-
entious mothers. How odd it had seemed then. It seemed
odd now. Rhonda had not otherwise been an overpro-
tective worrier. Why that one phobia?

Maggie couldn't help voicing the question, adding, "It's not as if anyone in our family ever had it. And to reassure you about Sam, no one in Zack's family has it, either."

Rhonda's mouth set into a stubborn line. "There's always a first time."

A movement outside the window drew Maggie's resentful eyes. A silver Riviera was pulling into the drive. "Looks like we have company." When the driver emerged and slammed the door, her heart lurched sickeningly. "Oh, no."

"Who is it?" queried Rhonda.

"Adam Morgan. Did you ask him to come?"

"Of course I didn't." But she looked pleased all the same.

Seconds later, Maggie composed her face into a pleasant mask before opening the door. "Why, Adam," she said in welcoming, but carefully detached, tones. "How nice to see you."

"You too, Maggie." He glanced past her with an uncomfortable-looking smile.

She widened the door and stepped aside. "Oh. Please come in. Mom will be happy to see you." It was important he know right away that she didn't think he'd come to see *her*.

"I hope so," he said, walking past. "But she's not the only one I came to visit." When her eyes widened, he added hurriedly, "I especially wanted to see Sam."

"You did?"

She didn't know whether to be relieved or more worried. He said nothing further as she led the way to the kitchen. After greeting her mother with a hug and giving Sam a handshake, he accepted, without the slightest hesitation, Rhonda's demand to share their lunch.

While Adam and her mother talked companionably, Maggie ladled three bowls of soup into the everyday china, then set each one on a plate, adding buttered slices of steaming French bread on the side. Her fingers trembled, she noticed with irritation. On a fourth plate for Sam, she cut a small portion of potatoes and beef into bite-sized pieces onto a piece of bread, drizzling gravy over all. She was reaching for the drinking glasses when Adam suddenly appeared at her side.

"I'm sorry, Maggie. Let me help you. What can I do?"

"Sit down, Adam Morgan," Rhonda demanded. "Guests don't work in my house."

Maggie said quickly. "It's all right. There's nothing to be done except for putting ice in the glasses and pouring the tea."

Adam rinsed his hands at the sink and opened the freezer door. While she echoed her mother's protests, he ignored them both and filled the glasses. Maggie carried the plates to the table feeling absurdly pleased at his little act of masculine rebellion. She tried and failed to imagine Zack helping in the kitchen. But it was silly to make comparisons.

When they were seated, Rhonda asked Adam to say grace. Maggie couldn't resist slitting her eyes toward him as the words flowed golden and smooth from his mouth. His face seemed to glow with sincerity and affection, as if he were talking with a close friend. *Dear Adam,* she thought, and did not criticize herself for calling him *dear.* She would think so of anyone who could so sweetly and simply hold on to their childhood beliefs. But Adam was not simple or a child. Her brow creased in puzzlement. He had suffered a devastating loss, worse than her own. How had he held on to his faith?

It was probably genetics, she decided. Hadn't scientists discovered a gene for aestheticism? Maybe there was a faith gene, and you either had it or you didn't. Maybe the ones who believed in predestination were right after all, only God foreordained his chosen ones by stamping himself right into their cells. It was just her luck to be born without the brand.

The meal proceeded with much banter between Adam and Rhonda. Gradually feeling more comfortable, Maggie ventured into the conversation now and then. She felt gratified when Adam made consistent efforts to include Sam, who had never been a very talkative child.

While Maggie served cookies and milk, Rhonda said, "I'm so glad you came to see us, Adam. You always make me feel thirty years younger."

"You mean I make you feel like a baby?" he teased.

"You flatterer," Rhonda said, laughing flirtatiously. Maggie thought wryly, *Some women never grow out of it*. "Why didn't you come sooner?"

"I didn't want to intrude on the two of you getting reacquainted. But I couldn't wait any longer when I realized it was Wednesday and youth night at church. Do you think Sam would like to attend?" He glanced at Maggie. "Beth teaches his age group, and I know she'd love to have him. It would give him a chance to meet some children his own age."

"Well, I don't know—" She hated to make that first step toward her mother's church again. In New York it had been easy to take Sam occasionally in her effort to provide him with a foundation of good, moral values. There she'd carefully avoided visiting the same church twice in a row. But here in the South, if you ventured a toe into the vestibule, it was like being a fly and catching your wing in a spider's net. The more you struggled, the tighter you got caught.

"Oh, let him," Rhonda said. "He's been lonesome without playmates. You know that."

Rhonda was right; he had been lonely. "Would you like to go, Sam?" Maggie asked reluctantly. They weren't going to be here long, after all, and he was accustomed to daycare and the company of other children.

"Do they play games? Will they have snacks?"

Adam chuckled. "Yes and yes. And with my daughter there, you can count on drama, too. She likes to have the children act out the Bible stories. With costumes!"

The phone on the kitchen wall rang. Maggie hurried to answer it as Sam spoke his willingness to go if Adam went, too. This disquieting sign of attachment made her "hello" sound distracted. She *was* distracted. Adam was promising to pick Sam up himself when the voice on the other end of the line caught her complete attention and nearly stopped her heart.

"Hello, Miss Margaret," said Zack, his inflection as breezy as if they talked twice a day instead of once in three years.

She immediately hunched over the phone, one hand cupping the receiver as if to prevent his words from intruding into the kitchen. "Why are you—how did you know I was here?" At the sound of the tension in her voice, Rhonda and Adam fell silent behind her.

"I'm just fine, and how are you?" her ex-husband drawled lightly. "Social amenities are important in every situation. Didn't you learn anything from me? But that's something you knew already, being a Southern belle and all."

"Would you call me right back, please?" she said with steel in her voice. "I want to go to another phone."

"Why, sure—"

She slammed down the receiver before he could say anything else. Without meeting the two pairs of eyes she felt drilling her, she excused herself, walked to the gossip bench in the hall and waited for the phone to ring. She didn't have long to sit.

"How did you get my number?" she demanded.

"Take it easy, Miss Margaret. When I couldn't get you at your apartment, I called our old friend, Suzy. She told me you'd gone to help your poor little old mama. How is the old bat? Still praying me into an early grave?"

"What do you want, Zack?

"All right, be that way. I've been meaning to call you for a while, and when I heard you were just up the road it seemed too good to be true. You're less than two hours away on Interstate 75, did you know that?"

"I didn't live half my life in Chattanooga without knowing where Atlanta is. I have no desire to see you, Zack."

"That's cold, Maggie." The teasing note dropped, as did the exaggerated curves of his accent. Like her, Zack was born and raised in the South but years in New York had narrowed his vowels, and hurried his delivery. Evidently moving to Atlanta with his new wife had led him to revert to his old, dripping-with-honey speech patterns. Zack could always adapt when it suited his purposes. "I'm not going to retaliate in kind, because I wouldn't mind seeing you again. We were married a long time, and I still think of you as a friend." Seething, Maggie was eloquent in her silence. "But the main reason I called is because I want to see my son."

"You want to see your son," she repeated, knuckles turning white around the receiver. "After three years."

"You're the reason I haven't seen him in all that time. He's too young to travel on planes, remember telling me that?"

"I'm not the one who moved nearly a thousand miles away."

"Is that supposed to mean I can't ever see him?"

"The judge gave me total custody."

"With my consent." His voice lowered. "I couldn't leave you all alone."

"Don't pretend you felt guilty for your sordid little affair. Sam was inconvenient. Not many child brides want to tend to one-year-olds."

He snorted. "I have my rights. I pay child support."

"Not nearly enough."

"That's one of the reasons I'm coming to see you. We have to talk. Sam is growing up without his father, and that's something I don't want to happen."

"No." She could not prevent the wobble in her voice.

"I want to be a part of his life. Don't make me get nasty, Margaret. I can afford the best legal advice in Atlanta."

Tears welled in her eyes. "Don't do this, Zack. Even you can't be that cruel."

"You're overreacting. I'm not trying to take him away from you. I just want to be part of his life."

"Zack," she choked pleadingly.

He sighed impatiently. "Look. We can't do this over the phone. Let me come up there. I'll get you out of that house and away from your mother. Let me take you out to dinner. The sooner the better. Tomorrow night?"

Maggie could imagine her mind exploding into a thousand tiny fragments. She turned toward the kitchen door, through which she could see the table where Adam and her mother and Sam were still seated. At her glance, the two adults immediately stopped their quiet conversation and looked at her. Rhonda's eyes sharpened into a frown; Adam's sympathetic expression nearly undid her. And there sat her baby, oblivious to everything as he nibbled a cookie.

"Tonight," she said suddenly, recalling that Sam had been invited out. If she timed things well, maybe she could avoid letting Zack see him at all.

"Sorry. I have a function to attend this evening, but tomor—"

"Cancel it," she said firmly. "Come tonight or not at all."

"All right," he said after a second's pause. "Is seven okay?"

As she recalled, most youth activities began about that time. She agreed and replaced the receiver without saying goodbye. Snatching a tissue from the dispenser beside the phone, she wiped the tears from her cheeks and blew her nose. Then, squaring her shoulders, she put on a bright face and returned to the kitchen.

Chapter Four

That evening after dinner, Adam covered the remains of Jane Garrison's lasagna with aluminum foil—she'd made enough for a football team—and placed it in the refrigerator beside the mixed salad greens and a gooey chocolate-pudding-and-graham-cracker-crumb thing that Beth loved. Nearly half a year after Allison's death, the ladies' society at church still thought he and Beth couldn't make it on their own, and at least twice a week someone brought a full meal. He appreciated it but sometimes wished they'd leave them alone. Especially since most of the contributors were single women with hopeful smiles that Beth never failed to point out after they left.

After loading the dishwasher, he exited the kitchen and walked to the foot of the stairs. "Are you about ready?" he called, then heard the whine of the blow dryer. He jogged upstairs and through Beth's open bedroom door saw her sitting on the edge of the bed in the pink robe Allison had given her, her long pale hair tossed overhead as she waved the dryer back and forth. "Hey!"

Startled, she looked up and shut off the motor. "What?"

"Time to go. Aren't you done yet?"

She grimaced. "We'll be there before the church is open, Dad."

"Not by the time we pick up Rhonda's grandson. Come on, now. You promised you'd be ready if I took your turn at kitchen duty."

"I guess I can go with wet hair," she said with a distasteful glance at the mirror above her dresser.

"You look beautiful to me," he said, smiling.

"You only say that to make me hurry."

"Whatever works."

One side of her mouth lifted. "Just give me five minutes, okay?"

"Make sure it's only five. I'll be waiting in the car."

In less than ten, she slipped into the seat beside him, wearing jeans and a pale yellow sweater, filling the car with the fresh herbal scent of her shampoo. He was unmoved.

"It's a good thing I'm not ice cream or I'd be melted by now," he said tightly, cranking the engine and clicking the garage opener. As he reversed down the drive, he added, "I don't know why you had to wash your hair again anyway. Don't you do it every morning? It's going to fall out."

"No, it won't," she said with a half giggle. "I happen to like clean hair, that's all." Now she sounded defensive. As he drove down Evergreen Street, he slanted a curious glance at her. "Some of us went hiking after school. We piled up leaves and jumped around and got a little dirty."

He was quiet as he merged onto I-24. "Who's *we?*" he asked carefully.

"Just a few friends. Jackie and Leslie and some others."

"Hmm. That Jake guy wouldn't be one of those others, would he?"

She faced him swiftly. "What if he was? It's not like we were sneaking off by ourselves or anything. I don't know why you don't like him. He's really nice."

Adam cut her a look that said, *I'll bet.*

"Well, he *is.* You act like he's some kind of sex maniac or something, but he's not."

He's playing it slow. That makes him craftier than I thought. "I'm relieved to hear it. How is he spiritually?"

Beth displayed a sudden interest in the passing scenery. "I'm trying to talk him into going to church," she said finally.

"That's a good place to see him. Other than that, I don't want you hanging around him anymore."

"That's not fair!"

"He's too old for you."

She did not respond, but from the corner of his eye he could see the firm set of her jaw against the outline of the darkening sky. The silence remained tense until Adam's Riviera began to labor against the slope of Dogwood Mountain. Time to change the subject, he decided.

"You'll like Sam Gould. He's a good kid."

"I'm sure he is," she said in a pleased-to-meet-you-stranger kind of voice. And then, thawing a little, she continued, "You said his dad was coming to see him tonight?"

"Well, Maggie was kind of hoping to avoid that until she can prepare the child better. That's why I wanted to get there early. Sam hasn't seen his father since tod-dlerhood, and she doesn't want to traumatize him.''

"That's too bad," Beth said, her protective instincts stirring as he knew they would. She had a natural love for children; that must have come from Allison. For the first two years of Beth's life, Adam had been half-afraid of his daughter. He'd taken every cry and tantrum per-sonally and thought she would break if he didn't handle her like glass. All that changed, though, when she could walk and talk. "Divorce stinks," Beth added.

"That's for sure."

"You knew his mom when you were young, didn't you?"

Adam winced. "Yes, I did, many long years ago, back when the world was new and people drove chariots and wore togas.''

"Poor old Dad. Hope I didn't hurt your feelings or anything.''

"Nothing I won't get over."

Her grin widened. "Mrs. Thrasher said you two dated awhile?''

Some people had long memories, he thought, moving uncomfortably. Mrs. Thrasher went to his church and had been one of Maggie's teachers in high school. Adam felt her interest in the personal lives of her students was a little too well developed. "Yes, we did. Two years, actually.'' Before Beth could drill him further, he slid the car into the Covington driveway, pulling carefully beside a black BMW. "Looks like we didn't quite make it.''

"Oh, no. My fault."

"No, baby, it isn't."

Adam's heartbeat sped as he turned off the ignition. *Don't get involved,* he told himself as they climbed the veranda steps. But he knew he already was. The shattered look in Maggie's eyes after talking with her exhusband had haunted him all afternoon.

When she opened the door, her expression was almost as wild as before, though relief flickered in her eyes at their presence. "You're here," she said, her voice taut. "And this must be Beth."

While Adam introduced them, he tried to avoid staring. Maggie wore a rose silk dress that set off her dark hair dramatically. She looked incredibly beautiful. Why would she dress so appealingly for dinner with an ex-husband? Maybe fixing herself up gave her more courage. Surely it didn't mean she still had feelings for Zackary Gould. He was disturbed at the surge of jealousy this idea brought.

Maggie escorted them inside and to the parlor. Adam and Beth greeted Rhonda, who sat stiffly in a wing chair, her walker poised in front of her like a shield. Sam was sitting on the floor opening a large package while a man looked on from the sofa. At their entrance, the man stood and paced toward Adam, hand outstretched.

"Zackary Gould," he said, brimming with confidence. *And why shouldn't he be?* Adam thought, shaking his hand and introducing himself and his daughter while Maggie went to hover protectively near Sam. Gould's dark blond hair shone with the talents of an expensive stylist, his well-tailored suit probably cost more than Adam made in a week and he was good-looking enough to pose for a postage stamp, if the post office ever did a series on Greek gods. In his jeans and I Did See Rock City sweatshirt that Beth had given him, Adam felt like a tourist.

"I've heard a lot about you, Adam," Gould said affably.

"Have you? I've heard quite a bit about you, too."
Adam's voice was equally pleasant. He couldn't fail to
notice his daughter's interest as she looked back and
forth between them. Before the silence could grow, he
added, "You're early, aren't you? Must have had good
traffic."

"Well, now, I left in plenty of time. I had a feeling
Miss Margaret might be a little worried about Sam seeing his daddy again. It's a good thing I came before you
took him to church, or I might have missed seeing him
entirely." His summer-sky eyes narrowed in Maggie's
direction.

Beth walked to the boy and knelt beside him on the
floor. "Hi, I'm Beth. What have you got there, big
guy?"

The boy lifted a tomato-red, yard-long truck from the
box. "A fire truck!" he said, awed. He glanced shyly at
Zack. "Daddy gave it to me." Quickly he looked back
at the truck and began to roll it across the Persian rug.

Rhonda cleared her voice. "Take it to your room now,
Sammy. Mr. Morgan and Beth are waiting for you."

"Do I have to?" Sam asked.

"Yes," Maggie answered. "You promised to go, remember? They came all the way here to get you."

"We'll have lots of fun," Beth chimed. "Let me help
you put your truck away. Will you show me your
room?"

While Sam hesitated and looked from the toy to his
newfound father, Zack approached and stooped to his
level. "Go ahead, fella. You'll see Daddy another time."

Adam felt as much as saw Maggie's reaction to this
statement. But the words worked like magic on the child,
who began to move toward the stairs with Beth follow-

ing. When he had climbed halfway up, he paused.
"Bye...Daddy."

"Goodbye, Sam."

Adam heard vulnerability in Gould's tones and felt
unexpected sympathy. It dissolved when the doctor
urged Maggie, in commanding tones, to hurry. She
grabbed her purse from the desk and threw him a desperate look as Zack hastened her toward the door.

"Thank you, Adam," she murmured.

"Yes, thank you, Adam," Zack repeated. "You saved
me the price of a baby-sitter. Oh, and goodbye, Miz
Rhonda. It's always a pleasure."

Rhonda responded with a solemn inclination of her
head. When the latch closed behind the couple, Adam
gave Mrs. Covington a long look. She returned his stare
and sighed.

While they traveled, Zack kept up a running com-
mentary about the changes in Chattanooga since his last
visit, and the dangers of preferred healthcare provider
networks. *He could always talk,* Maggie thought. If left
to her, the car would have remained silent as a tomb.
But when he pulled into the parking lot of The Barn,
anger stirred her to life.

"Not here," she said.

"Why not? It's one of Chattanooga's finest." He
parked and tried to race around the BMW in time to
open her door, but she was already striding toward the
entrance. He chuckled, hurriedly locked the car and followed.

The hostess led them through the candlelit room past
other well-dressed diners to a table beside the fireplace.
While Maggie frowned, Zack gallantly seated her in a
heavy, tapestried wing chair. She studied the expensive

silver and china, then lifted her eyes to the roughly pan-
eled walls. The contrast of elegance and simplicity here
had always caught her imagination; and the food was
good and plentiful, too. None of that fancy New York/
French cuisine that left you hungrier after the meal than
before.

She glanced at the menu and ordered lobster, the most
expensive item she could find.

Without so much as a blink, Zack dittoed her choice,
then grinned as the waitress gathered the menus. "This
place brings back sweet memories, doesn't it?"

"My memories of you aren't sweet anymore." But
that was not entirely true. While they were dating, Zack
couldn't often afford the rich ambience of The Barn, but
he proposed to her here, his words accompanied by a
popping fire and soft classical music, just like now. "Did
you reserve this table for any special reason?" she
snapped.

"To be frank, I hoped it would put you in a better
frame of mind than you were in this afternoon. I guess
it's not working."

"Does that surprise you? You brought me here under
duress, not because I wanted to come. Nothing will—"
She stopped as the waitress served a fragrant French
onion soup, accompanied by tiny round crackers. "Nothing will put me in a good frame of mind. Just say what
you have to say and be done."

"Fiery Miss Margaret. Always causing trouble with
that independent streak of yours. Couldn't even hang on
to a job because of it."

"What's that supposed to mean?"

"You know," he said, his smile becoming strained.
He swallowed a couple of mouthfuls of cracker-filled
soup. "If you'd had your students sing the kind of music

your supervisor demanded instead of giving in to the kids and letting them do what they wanted, you wouldn't be on the unemployed list.''

She tasted her soup, then set down the spoon. It was delicious, but it might as well be rice cake as far as her appetite was concerned. "We performed more than enough Handel and Mozart. The children were losing interest. There was no harm in singing the occasional show tune and movie theme song. And they especially loved the spirituals.''

Zack shrugged charmingly. "Well, you can take the girl out of the South, but you can't take the grits out of the girl.''

She noticed that an attractive, middle-aged lady at the next table, a woman with suspiciously yellow hair and a perfectly presentable escort sitting across from her, could hardly keep her eyes off him. At least Maggie didn't have to worry about that anymore. And then a sudden realization struck.

"Wait a minute. How did you know about my job?''

"What? Oh, I'm not sure. Your friend Suzy told me probably. She's the one who told me where you were.''

"She knew I lost my job, but she didn't know why. No one knows except Carter, and he wouldn't tell you a train was coming if you were stuck on the tracks.''

"All right, you've got me. One of the new trustees at your school is married to a patient of mine. When they moved up north, I called in a favor.''

Maggie leaned back in disbelief. Taking it as a sign she was done, the waitress swept away their soup bowls and replaced them with salads.

"*You're* the reason I lost my position?'' she whispered.

"Well, you helped, Miss Margaret. It wasn't the first

time you'd been boiled in oil for going against the department head. I couldn't have done it if you hadn't made an enemy of her first.''

"I can't—I can't believe you would do this to me. Even you couldn't be so low.''

He plunged his salad fork into the mass of greens and took a huge bite. "Aw, what's the big problem?'' he said, a spot of blue cheese dressing appearing at the corner of his mouth. "You don't like New York. The whole time we lived there you complained about all the people and the noise.''

She pushed her salad away. "That doesn't matter. I'd made a life there for Sam and me. How dare you interfere!''

Wiping his mouth with his napkin, he leaned toward her, all levity gone. "I dare because I want my son. Margaret, I can get you a position in one of the finest private schools in Atlanta. And I have contacts in Chattanooga if you'd prefer to live here. I'm a reasonable man.''

There were no words that could express her rage. "I don't want your help. I want you to leave me alone.''

"If you lived nearby, we could share custody without making it too hard on our child,'' he said earnestly. "I don't want to divide his life into six-month increments, do you? I'm only asking for weekends, and that's not possible unless we live fairly close. We have to consider what's best for Sam.''

"You should have considered Sam long before this.'' Mindlessly she clenched her napkin in her fist. "You belong in another century, Zack. No court of law is going to listen to you, especially when they find out you made me lose my job. People can't be manipulated to suit your convenience. What happens when you decide to move from Atlanta to—to California or somewhere else?''

"I won't. I'm settled now."

"That's what you said when you married me," she said between gritted teeth, rising. "Enjoy your dinner. I'm calling a cab."

"Sit down." The hard edge in his voice made her hesitate. But she didn't have to listen to him, not anymore. She reached for her purse. "There's something you don't know." She heard a note of pleading. "Please, Margaret. Let me explain. Rayne was in a car accident last spring. A bad one. Her pelvis was crushed, and she had to have an emergency hysterectomy."

For an instant she was so shocked, she couldn't speak. "I'm terribly sorry. You never told me."

"We'd only begun to think about having children when it happened. We hadn't made any provisions. None of her eggs could be saved, Margaret. We won't be able to have a child together."

She absorbed this for a moment. "I'm sorry, Zack. I really am."

It was the truth, she realized. Childlessness was not something she wished on them. She had no interest in revenge. But he was asking too much. Clutching her purse to her middle, she stood again. "Even so, you can't expect me to hand over my son like a consolation prize. You and Rayne can afford to adopt. Or you could hire a surrogate mother. But you can't have my baby."

Zack gave her a grave look. "We'll have to see about that," he replied.

"You can't deny him his son," Rhonda said later that evening, after Maggie had tucked a tired but happy Sam into bed. Adam had returned the boy alone while Beth went for pizza with her youth group. When Maggie saw the warmth and curiosity in her old friend's expression, she encouraged him to stay. The three of them had taken seats in the parlor while she related the story of her disastrous dinner. She felt little reluctance in telling Adam; there was more understanding in his eyes than her mother's. "You should never have gotten divorced," the older woman continued. "This is what comes from broken families."

"Yes, I remember your saying that when Daddy died." Maggie could no longer keep back the bitter words she'd imprisoned in her heart since her father's funeral. "Do you remember what you told me? 'What did you expect to happen? From the instant I set eyes on him, I knew Zackary Gould was worthless. But worthless or not, you're bound to him in the eyes of God.' The words are branded in my brain." She looked at Adam and stopped. This was family business, and she was making him uneasy. "Well, that doesn't matter now. But knowing how you felt—how you feel—about him, I can't believe you're saying it would be good for Sam to shuffle back and forth between us."

"I'm not saying it would be good, but Sam is half Gould. He needs to know who his father is." Rhonda closed her mouth and looked thoughtful, then added faintly, "It won't be the first time the sins of the father hurt the children...."

"You're tired, Mom. You should go to bed."

"And I should be going," Adam said, springing to his feet. After bidding good-night to Rhonda, he asked Maggie to accompany him to his car. "I forgot to bring in Sam's cap."

Willingly Maggie followed Adam past the lighted veranda and down the steps to the shadowed driveway.

While he opened the car door and retrieved the forgotten item from the front seat, she stood back, shivering a little in the cool night air. The cloudless sky stretched endlessly above her. When she was a child, she'd been fascinated to learn that the stars were suns with planets of their own. Now astronomers declared that many of the points of light were faraway galaxies. Such vastness...

She became aware that Adam was watching her. With an embarrassed smile, she took the items and thanked him.

Apparently in no hurry to leave, he said softly, "It's a beautiful world."

For an instant she feared he would quote Scripture at her; she could almost hear him saying, "The heavens declare the glory of God, and the firmament showeth his handiwork" or some such. When they were engaged, he was always doing that. His religiosity had overwhelmed and frightened her, which was part of the reason she couldn't go through with their marriage. But he said nothing more.

"Sometimes it's hard to remember that," she said at last.

"I'm sorry you're having such a rough time, Maggie."

His voice was gentle and his expression so kind that her eyes clouded. "Am I wrong, Adam? Should I share custody with Zack?"

He shook his head. "That's a tough one. I'd say it depends on whether you can trust your ex-husband to take good care of the boy."

"Trust Zack?" She laughed humorlessly. "As a husband, definitely not. But as a father...I don't know. When Sam was a baby, he hardly bothered with him. And where has he been for the past three years?" Hugging her arms to herself for warmth, she shook her head when Adam offered his jacket. "With Zack's high-society life-style as a plastic surgeon, I picture him treating Sam as a convenience—someone to show off to his friends, his one claim for immortality. You saw that expensive fire truck. I'm afraid Zack is the kind of man who'll try to win his child's affection with money, not time. I don't want Sam to become so materialistic that he plays one parent against the other."

"Are you talking about the same little boy I took to church tonight? The one who won first prize for coloring and gave his award to the second-place winner because she was crying?"

"Did he?" She smiled radiantly, then sobered. "Oh, Adam. When I was a little girl, I didn't dream the life of an adult was so complex, so...sad. I thought grown-ups owned the world. Had I known—"

"You'd have refused to grow up?" he suggested lightly.

"I wish that had been an option." She studied his features in the dim light. "How do you do it, Adam? You've been through so much, and yet you aren't bitter. Or if you are, it doesn't show. You still believe, don't you? Or do you go through the motions for Beth's sake, continuing to attend church, playing the game?"

"Faith isn't a game, Maggie. It's a choice."

"A choice," she repeated dully. She shouldn't have said anything. Now he would deliver a sermon.

She saw pain in his eyes. "Maggie, you're a parent. A great part of your essence is within Sam. Do you want good things for him? Do you want him to love you because he chooses to or because you've forced him? And is it possible to force love?"

For several seconds she remained silent, then smiled

gently. "You know, Adam, I am cold. I'd better go inside."

He watched her until she reached the door. "Sleep well," he told her softly.

"You, too," she answered, and entered the house.

She was surprised and disappointed to find her mother hadn't moved from the chair. After this terrible evening, she needed to be alone to sift through her thoughts. How strange to have spent time with both Zack and Adam on the same day. She wasn't sure which man had disturbed her more.

"I thought you'd gone to bed."

Rhonda laid her magazine on the end table. "I feel as though we have unfinished business."

"Oh?" Maggie reluctantly took a seat opposite her.

"What you said earlier made me realize how angry you've been. That's why you haven't contacted me in all this time, isn't it?"

"I haven't contacted *you?* You were the one who told me to leave."

"I suppose I did." Rhonda smoothed the afghan lying across her knees with one tremulous hand. "People say a lot of things they don't mean. I was grieving over your father and worried to death about you. I guess you didn't understand that."

"No, but I'd like to." She leaned forward, softened by her mother's words. Rhonda had never come so close to apologizing, and she couldn't let this moment slip away. "Why *didn't* you help me, Mom? I needed you. All I wanted was a place to stay, to heal, while Zack and I worked out the details of the divorce. You can't imagine how painful it was having to find a smaller apartment, being forced to pack and move with a baby while I was hurting inside."

Rhonda's gaze dropped. "I wanted you to go back to him. It was your duty to stay with your husband."

"Even though you never approved of him in the first place? Or did you figure I'd made my bed and had to lie in it?"

The older woman breathed quietly for a moment. "'What God has joined together, let no man tear asunder.'"

"Oh, great." *When in doubt, blame your selfishness on God,* Maggie thought coldly. "Even the most conservative fundamentalist would admit I had Biblical grounds for a divorce." Not that she needed permission from anyone or any being who had never shown her He existed in the first place.

For an instant, Adam's voice drifted into her mind. *Is it possible to force love?*

"For centuries women have stood by their men for worse things than adultery," Rhonda argued.

"But you don't understand what I went through. You *never* understand." The echo of her own words startled her. She could almost see the ghost of teenager past. Next she'd be running to her bedroom in a torrent of tears. "Rayne Gray wasn't his first affair. There were others through the years. I'm not sure I knew about all of them." She spoke more softly as the words grew more difficult. "But Rayne was the first he wanted to marry. The divorce was Zack's idea, not mine."

Rhonda's tones were correspondingly quiet, almost consoling. "But if you'd forced him to wait, maybe he would have come back to you and his child."

"But he didn't." The floodgates had opened; there was no way to contain her outrage. "Even you have to concede there's no chance for reconciliation now, so you're hoping Adam and I will get back together, aren't you? Well, I'm sorry to disappoint you again, but I'm perfectly happy with things as they are."

"It would be good for the child to have a full-time father," Rhonda said, coming closer to admitting her desire than Maggie expected.

"You need to stop manipulating people," she fired. "You don't know anything about how I feel. I don't want to risk my heart and life with a man again. You can't relate because you had a wonderful marriage. Daddy was perfect."

A long silence filled the room, broken only by the ticking of the clock on the mantel. "No one is perfect," Rhonda said finally.

"Well, of course no one is completely perfect. But Daddy was the steadiest man I ever knew." And though he forced all of his children to go to church and demanded obedience, he could also be charming and giving. If there was laughter in the house, it usually began with him. Her lips curved upward in remembrance. He was always there for her, especially when he noticed Rhonda's coldness. He'd made up for a lot of bad things in her childhood. How she missed him, missed his being there for Sam.

Rhonda appeared to be in distress, her breaths quickening, her hands moving restlessly in her lap. "I don't know what to do," she whispered. "You have a right to know. I'm not going to live forever, and Sam..."

After a moment, Maggie moved to her mother's side, crouching beside her chair. "What is it, Mom? Don't upset yourself."

"Help me, Lord." Rhonda's bloodless lips worked soundlessly for an instant. "I never wanted to tell you this. Your father disagreed with me, but I felt it would be better this way. Better for everyone." She gave her a quick, direct glance, then stared downward. "Perhaps I was wrong."

"Go on," Maggie whispered, her pulse racing. "Whatever it is, you can tell me."

Rhonda swallowed noisily. "Maggie. You're…you're not my daughter."

Maggie flinched. "Why do you always try to hurt me?" Suddenly the sight of her mother's pallor alarmed her. "I was only expressing myself earlier. I didn't mean to make you angry."

"No…no. Listen." Rhonda lifted trembling hands to her temples. "I always felt the same toward you as I did my biological children, I promise you that. I've always loved you. But…you're not my daughter."

Maggie stared at her without comprehension. "What are you saying? That I'm adopted?"

"No." Rhonda pulled the walker to her, struggled upright and began tottering toward her bedroom, her vision directed straight ahead. "You are Philip's child with another woman who died at your birth." And now she did look pointedly into Maggie's eyes, obviously struggling to maintain her composure. "She died of complications due to diabetes."

Speechlessly Maggie watched Rhonda enter her room. As the door began to close, a thousand questions bubbled to her lips; but Rhonda held up a restraining hand.

"That's enough for now, child. We'll talk more tomorrow when I have my doctor's appointment. I'll call Beth in the morning and ask her to stay with Sam. That way you and I can be alone, and I'll answer your questions. Right now I have to rest." Her mouth moved in an attempt at a smile. "Giving up lifelong secrets is hard work."

When the latch clicked, Maggie pressed her back to

the door and slid downward until she reached the floor. Unmindful of the fine fabric of her dress, she remained seated, staring at nothing, until her knees grew stiff and a chill swept over her shoulders. Then, without feeling her shoes touch the treads, she drifted upstairs like a wraith, like someone who had never existed.

Chapter Five

Maggie's smile wavered as she opened the front door the following afternoon. She tried to keep her expression smooth as she looked inquiringly past the tall, haggard man standing on the porch.

"I'm the pinch hitter," Adam said. "Beth called me to say she has an honor society meeting after school. They're planning a fund-raiser and she couldn't get away."

"Where's Beth?" came Sam's disappointed voice behind her.

Maggie sent a swift frown in the boy's direction. "Oh, no, Adam, I wouldn't dream of imposing on you after a hard day at work." *A real hard day from the look of him,* she thought with concern, dismissing for a moment how intensely she'd waited for this opportunity to be alone with Rhonda. "We'll take Sam with us."

"What, and spoil my plans for an early supper at the Burger Palace with the big guy?"

Maggie felt Sam push past her skirt to peer up at

Adam. "The Burger Palace?" There was no missing the eagerness in his voice.

Maggie motioned him in. "This is very good of you."

"The pleasure's all mine, ma'am," he drawled, putting a hand to his forehead as if tipping a hat.

Maggie's eyes met his in sudden amusement as years flowed backward, and she was seventeen again. The summer after her junior year, she'd found a job at a dude ranch in Arizona through a friend of her pastor's. She leapt at the chance to escape the restrictions of home, even though it meant leaving Adam after he'd decided to stay in Chattanooga for the summer to be near her. Part of the reason she went was to put distance between them. He had begun to talk marriage, and from one moment to the next she alternated between joy and panic.

But after a couple of weeks, the novelty of waitressing tables, grooming horses and cleaning stables diminished. She grew tired of the heat and sore muscles and found herself longing for home and Adam. Her letters, and then Adam's, became increasingly warm and probably in her own case, she thought fleetingly, full of self-pity.

And then came the day in July when Adam, having booked an entire week as a guest at the expensive ranch, arrived to surprise her. Adam, who never had money for anything and worked forty-hour weeks to pay his way through college. Yet somehow he managed to come. And what a visit it had been: him acting the cowboy—an act he often repeated during the following year—and her the hired hand. With Adam to help her do the chores, they spent long, contented hours riding, taking walks and sitting in the shade on the porch swing.

On the final day of his stay, he asked her to marry him; and she had said yes.

Waves of shame washed over Maggie as she remembered the sacrifice he made and all she had done afterward. He recalled it, too; she saw it in the way his gaze skittered from hers and by the sudden rise of color in his cheeks.

My goodness, she thought, sinking even further. A man who can still *blush!*

His vulnerability twisted her heart. She found herself staring at him as he stooped to Sam's eye level and began to talk about where they might go after getting burgers.

She suddenly became aware that Rhonda was watching her from the doorway. "Are we going or not?" the older woman asked crisply. Yet Maggie couldn't miss the gleam of satisfaction in her eyes. Irritated, she snatched her purse from the hall table, gave Sam a peck on the top of his head and hurried across the threshold.

"We might be back later than you," Adam said, following. "Sam and I've agreed to go to Point Park."

"It's on the top of Lookout Mountain," Sam explained as Maggie locked the door. "I can look down on Grandma's house from up there. It's the mountain that looks like a whale, isn't it, Mommy?"

A tense silence fell inside Rhonda's Mercury Marquis. Although almost a decade old, the car had little more than thirty thousand miles on the odometer. Maggie had driven it a couple of times since she'd come home, but she still couldn't get used to it. Negotiating the downward curves of Dogwood Mountain made her think of threading a needle with a houseboat. It didn't help that she hadn't driven during her years in New York.

"Okay, we're alone," she said finally, risking a look at Rhonda, then hitting the brakes hard when a dog trotted across the road. The older woman jerked violently forward against her seat belt—unnecessarily so, Maggie thought.

"Maggie! You shouldn't ride the brakes like that. You'll burn them out. That's what your father always said."

"Did you want me to run over that puppy?" she cried. "No, of course you didn't. You're just trying to talk about anything except what I need to hear." Maggie thought back to her mother's revelation—no, *not* her mother. Oh, please, let it all have been a nightmare, but she knew it was not. And to the long, sleepless night afterward: the tears, the wandering through the house to stare at family photographs on the wall, but not her family, not her family in the way she'd always thought; the long minutes crawling past as she stared at Sam as he slept; Sam, with his unknown heritage that might endanger him, might already have endangered him; her mother's—*Rhonda's*—fears concerning diabetes now explained, although she'd tried to mask it by making her own children subject to the same tests, all in the effort to deceive.... How could she, how *could* she!

"Tell me about my real mother," Maggie finally said.

Rhonda stiffened. "Maggie, you may call that woman your birth mother or your genetic parent if you want, but your *real* mother is sitting beside you in the front seat of this car. At least I feel real enough. Those million diapers I changed were real, or they surely did smell it. That was real food I cooked three times a day and served to you, and so was my body real that ached with tiredness all those nights I sat up waiting for you to come home—"

"Tell me about *her*, then," Maggie interrupted, her lips tight.

For a moment Maggie feared she would try further

delaying tactics, but finally she said, "Philip met her in Orlando during one of those conferences where he was always reading papers or giving lectures—and I don't know much more than that. I never wanted to know the details. She was a young girl, a graduate student, younger than I was and single. I suppose you can relate to how that made me feel."

Maggie could, and for a moment sympathy twinged for Rhonda, who played the older woman's role, the taken-for-granted-wife, in the love triangle that was as old as man. Then she remembered Rhonda's lies, and her empathy leaked away.

"What was her name?"

"Emily Rose Wilkerson," Rhonda replied after a slight hesitation.

Emily Rose, Maggie repeated to herself, liking the simple sound of it, the feel of the syllables sliding off her tongue. Her mother...had she been as beautiful as her name? Was her nose small and straight, like Maggie's? In a family of prominent noses, she had always wondered why hers was different.

She negotiated a turn onto the main thoroughfare despite Rhonda's protests that the interstate would be faster. Maggie was in no hurry to arrive at the doctor's office, where she knew Rhonda would seal her lips in case anyone might overhear their family secrets. Besides, Maggie hated to merge onto interstates. It felt like a suicide attempt every time.

The afternoon sun, angled and distant with the approach of winter, painted the sky with lost dreams. It was the kind of day she knew would fill her memory with mellow tones, so that ever after, when autumn's melancholy beauty drew round again, she would recall the day she learned about her mother and identify it with the sound of the Mercury's incurable dashboard rattle, the sight of an achingly blue sky and below it, old houses converted to lawyer's offices and used car lots snuggled beside chain restaurants and strip malls.

"Does anyone else know?" The possibility that someone might have known her beginnings when she hadn't filled her with indignation. "How did you explain my arrival?"

Rhonda sighed. "We moved. You'll recall we spent the early years of our marriage in Florida and that you and Johanna were born there. She was too young to remember how suddenly you came to us. Naturally a few of our Florida friends found out, but we lost touch with them through the years. My mother was the only one of our parents still living at the time, but she was always good at keeping things close."

Like mother, like daughter, Maggie thought, simmering. "What about my—Emily Rose's family?"

"According to Philip, she came from good stock. But her folks wouldn't have anything to do with her once they found out about—once they discovered she was expecting a married man's baby."

"Me," whispered Maggie. "They threw her out because of me."

"No, child." Rhonda's voice gentled. "They disowned her because they didn't approve of what she had done. It had nothing to do with you."

Maggie gave her a look. "I'm a grown woman, not a child. It had everything to do with me." Rhonda turned her head to gaze out the window. "What was she like?" Maggie added wistfully.

"I never asked your father that sort of question. And he knew better than to volunteer anything I didn't inquire about."

Glancing at Rhonda's profile, Maggie wondered how any woman could take her husband's illegitimate child into her home to raise. Maybe she liked having Maggie around to remind Philip of his biggest mistake.

"How could you—you must have been so angry at Dad. Why were you willing to do it—to pretend I was your own?"

"Because you were Philip's child, and there was no one else. And as to blabbing to everybody about where you came from, why, there was nothing to be gained by stigmatizing you or him. In those days that…particular sort of dilemma wasn't so common or acceptable as it is now. Which says something about the state of the world today, I must say."

"My own family wouldn't claim me."

"Your own family *did* claim you. Stop being so dramatic. It's not as though you were ever in danger of being sent to Oliver Twist's orphanage."

"But if my mother had lived…"

"You would have been raised by her, I imagine."

"All alone? Did she have a job? Would Dad have supported us?"

"He would have fulfilled his responsibility—there's no doubt about that. Your father was a good man other than that one lapse. He swore to me that he'd never sinned in that way before, and he wouldn't do so again. I believed him then and I still do now."

But I'll bet you never let him forget it, either, Maggie thought. Yet Rhonda had always appeared to be a supportive, happy wife, at least in public. One could almost think she worshiped him. *Maybe I'm being unfair.*

And maybe I'm not. Rhonda had lied, had forced Maggie to live a lie all her life without knowing it.

"Too bad that sin resulted in me," she said, and the

bitterness in her voice mirrored only a shadow of what she felt in her heart. Rhonda had hurt her before, but nothing could match this. Maggie wondered if she would ever be able to forgive her. She wanted to turn the car around, grab Sam and fly back to New York. And that's what she would do, just as soon as her commitment to her mother—*Rhonda*—was done. She would not run out on her promise, nor answer betrayal with betrayal.

"There you go again with your melodramatics. You should have been an actress instead of a musician." Rhonda shook her head and leaned tiredly against the armrest. "Adultery is a sin and you know it. Not your sin, of course, but theirs. Still, God can bring good from any circumstance."

"Oh, please. What if Dad had decided to leave you for my mother? Would that have been a good circumstance?"

"My husband never would have done such a thing."

"Mine did."

"And that," Rhonda said triumphantly, "explains the difference between your father and Zackary Gould."

"Does it? All it says to me is that no man can be trusted."

"For all have sinned and fallen short of the glory of God, Maggie. If you say that about men, you have to include women, too."

"Gladly," Maggie said, sending her a cutting glance.

"If you're referring to me, what I did was with the best of intentions." She reminded Maggie to turn right at the next light. "I suppose you've never done anything in your life that didn't turn out as you hoped, never told a lie or hurt anyone, never been unkind."

Maggie opened her mouth to protest, but a sudden

flash of Adam's face stilled her words. *Yes, I have. Oh, yes.*

She made the right, then almost immediately, another right to enter the crowded parking lot of the medical complex. Following Rhonda's directives, she searched for a handicapped spot but couldn't find one.

"I'll have to drop you off at the front," Maggie said.

"But I have a handicapped sticker," Rhonda argued, sounding unexpectedly childish.

"Apparently so does everyone else. Do you see a space I don't?"

After a fractional hesitation, Rhonda said quietly, "No. But you'd better walk inside with me before you park."

"What's wrong, Mom?" Maggie asked with an immediate rush of anxiety, then frowned at how easily she'd reverted to Rhonda's familial name. Well, she had to call her something, and the older woman had certainly filled the maternal role in her life; she was not too angry to admit that. But she would not think of this woman as her real mother, not ever again, no matter what Rhonda said.

"My head hurts a little, that's all."

"Are you dizzy, too?"

"Slightly. It's nothing to worry about."

"We'll have to tell Dr. Stallbart."

Nearly an hour of waiting passed in a series of luxuriously appointed chambers before they were ushered into the examining room. The nurse, a solemn, lovely woman, allowed Rhonda to sit on one of the two straight chairs instead of straining her leg to climb on the table, then took her blood pressure.

"How is it?" Maggie asked the nurse. "She's been experiencing dizziness and headaches lately."

"Not bad—one-forty over ninety—but Mrs. Covington always has a good pressure. She's been dizzy and has headaches? I'll tell the doctor."

A few minutes later, Dr. Stallbart came in to examine Rhonda. He suggested her dizziness might be caused by an inner-ear infection and left after writing a prescription. Maggie thought how much lighter Rhonda seemed after being reassured by her doctor. For herself, she still had questions. Yet Dr. Stallbart seemed unconcerned. Was it possible Rhonda's symptoms had *a psychological* base as the doctor had also suggested? Did they result from stress? Perhaps Maggie's presence had actually aggravated and delayed her recovery instead of helping it?

After leaving the doctor's office, Rhonda and Maggie took the elevator to the basement, turned left several times and finally asked an orderly for directions. The cafeteria, a large, square, windowless room, was partly filled with casually dressed people who appeared to be patients and their families. Here and there Maggie spotted members of the staff. After seating Rhonda at an isolated table near the kitchen, she went through the line to order tea for Rhonda and coffee for herself.

"I want to know everything you can tell me about Emily Rose," Maggie said as she placed Rhonda's beverage in front of her and sat.

Rhonda stirred two scant teaspoons of sugar into her tea. "Before we talk about your birth mother, I want to clarify what we were speaking of earlier. You said something about not trusting men. I want you to know they're not all like your ex-husband. You can't let that one experience leave you jaded, nor your daddy's failure, either. Philip was a good man, a godly man. There are many like him. I'm thinking of one right now."

Cynical sparks lighted Maggie's eyes. "Hmm, let me

guess... Can it be Adam you're talking about? You always thought he hung the moon. When I was a teenager, sometimes I believed you preferred him over me. You constantly used him as an example for me to imitate."

"Don't be absurd." She blew across the top of her cup, then sipped cautiously. "There is a steadiness at the core of Adam. A strength. I've sensed it in him from the time he was a college boy and loved him for it. You couldn't have found anybody more different when you took up with Zack Gould."

"Maybe that was the point."

"What did you say?"

"Nothing." Maggie lowered her gaze to the black depths of her coffee.

Rhonda's pensive glance moved to a woman reading a newspaper on the far side of the room. "Even Philip, much as I loved him, was not the rock Adam is." She lowered her cup and cradled it in her fingers. "He was moody, your father."

"Dad? Moody?"

"He was susceptible to depression, although he made an effort to hide it from you children. I tried to help him through his bad patches and make things easier for him when I could. He was especially down before he went to Orlando that time, I remember that. I don't believe he would have given in to temptation under other circumstances."

"Are you implying my mother tempted him?"

"I'm sorry, I shouldn't have said that. You're taking it the wrong way."

"Was that why you were always so strict with me? You thought I'd turn out like her, a siren who steals husbands?"

Rhonda remained quiet a moment before speaking.

"Mothers always worry about their daughters. I hope you have a daughter someday, so you can understand. Little girls are vulnerable and very, very precious. You want to raise them to be trusting, to feel the world is a safe place. But it's not. Therefore you guard them as best you can, for of all human creatures, girls are the most fragile. Not only physically, but emotionally. To the unscrupulous, that's what makes them so desirable."

A retort immediately rose to Maggie's lips, but the solemn look on Rhonda's face made her pause. After a moment she said softly, "I may not have a daughter, but I have a son. And I'll tell you this. He is infinitely precious to me. And fragile. And vulnerable?" Tears salting her eyes, she gave a humorless laugh. "Dear God. A million horrible things could happen to him, and sometimes, when I can't sleep at night, that list of horrors runs through my mind—"

Rhonda reached across the table and covered Maggie's hand with her own. "That's when you pray, my dear. Everyone has those nights, but God can help you through them."

Maggie shook her head. "You always have an answer, don't you, Mom? You make it sound so easy."

"Nothing is easy. But you don't have to go it alone." She tightened her fingers around Maggie's. "That's not what you're trying to do, is it? Go it alone? Without God, without anyone?"

Maggie sensed the depth of Rhonda's concern, and her own emotions struggled upward. For an instant, she wished she had a faith like her mom's. In that moment, disillusionment over Rhonda's deception faded, and she felt closer to her than ever before. But whatever it was that allowed Rhonda to override the doubts of an educated mind seemed to be missing in her.

She searched for words. "I need to know about my mother," she said finally.

"I've told you all I can, Maggie!" Rhonda placed her other hand over Maggie's in a pleading gesture. "I didn't want to know about her. Can you understand that? Sometimes I preferred to think she never existed, and that you were my daughter in the flesh as well as spirit. I never asked for nor wanted these complications in my life.

"But that's what sin does, don't you see?" Rhonda continued, the yearning in her voice touching Maggie deeply. "It complicates everything, robs the pure joy that should color every breath we take. I want it to be enough that *I* love you, that your *father* loved you and most of all, God loves you, the same God who has directed your path from the very beginning."

"But it's not enough, Mom." Maggie slowly withdrew her hand from Rhonda's and sat back. "I appreciate all you've done for me, I really do. I know we've had our differences, but..." She paused to wipe her eyes with a napkin, then took a deep breath. "Thank you for raising me as your own. I'd like to think I would've done the same, but I don't believe I have it in me. So..."

Without comprehension, she watched a man and woman put their trays in the dish return. She swallowed, then looked directly at Rhonda.

"So, I want you to know how much I appreciate everything, and that I—I love you—" she had not dreamed how hard it would be to utter those words after so long "—but I need to know more. I want to find my family— my other family—not just for me, but for Sam."

"I understand," Rhonda said quietly. But she didn't, Maggie saw. She only looked hurt. "You do what you have to, child, but I've told you all I know. From here on out on this subject, you're on your own.''

Maggie nodded, then slowly rose to return their dishes.

Chapter Six

Adam merged onto I-24 East, glided smoothly into the center lane, then glanced at Sam, who was sitting with his head tilted back, glazed eyes staring at nothing. The boy was almost asleep, but not quite.

The same, he thought with a tired chuckle, could be said for him.

He had forgotten the energy required to keep up with a four-year-old. At the park, Sam had run down one paved pathway after the other, exploring monuments, scaling park benches and venturing partway down the hazardous trail that snaked along the girth of the mountain. Three times the child had climbed on top of the Civil War cannon poised at the mountain's edge, and three times Adam had discreetly rushed to his side before he tumbled off the barrel and rolled thousands of feet into the Tennessee Valley.

Passing on the left of a beautifully restored Studebaker, Adam recalled a child development course he had taken in college. The professor had claimed four-year-olds were more likely to be found in emergency rooms than any other age group. It was the time when children began to outgrow clumsiness and gain mastery of such functions as running and jumping. The result, Dr. Bradshaw had said, was utter fearlessness.

Adam believed it.

By the time he pulled into the Covington driveway, the sun had disappeared behind the mountains, and Sam's head was bobbing at an alarming angle suggestive of a broken neck. The boy came to life with amazing quickness, however, when he saw the parlor glowing warmly through the sheers. He flew out of the car, up the steps and inside before Adam set a foot on the sidewalk.

"Did you see me waving, Grandma?" he heard Sam shouting. "I was sitting on the cannon."

Adam entered the kitchen in time to observe Rhonda rest one hand on the boy's shoulder. "Did you, darling? That was *you?*"

"It was! And everything looked real tiny up there, and I couldn't tell which one was your house. And we rode straight up Lookout Mountain in a train!"

The kitchen smelled pleasantly of roasted chicken. Maggie was standing at the counter chopping apples and pears, her face turned toward her son. She smiled faintly at Sam's enthusiasm, then raised her gaze to his.

Adam felt as if he had been hit by a truck.

Something must have shown in his face, because in the instant she started to glance away, her eyes caught his again and held. Curiosity melted to discomfort in her expression. Appalled but helpless to stop himself, he continued to stare as she ducked her head and resumed chopping with a vengeance, the juice from the apples spurting in all directions.

Who had he been kidding? he asked himself. He was

as in love with Maggie as he had ever been. Maybe even more: for the complex woman she had grown up to be, for her stark need of something to anchor her.

That would not be him, he told himself as he forced his gaze to Rhonda and leaned casually against the doorway. Listening to Maggie's mother tell about her visit to the doctor, responding with socially correct comments from an interior autopilot he didn't know was there, he was unable to rein in his mind as it raced with painful thoughts.

No way. There was no way this could work.

Saying Maggie was willing to give them a second chance—a possibility he doubted, given her bad marriage experience—he would not dishonor the memory of his wife, not like this. He had never loved Allison in the way he loved Maggie. He had known it going into the marriage, known he was cheating his wife by offering only half a heart.

He tried to make it up to her. Little by little, he learned to adore Allison for her own special qualities. That had been easy. Everyone who met Allison loved her. She was so good, so gentle, harmless and soft as a lamb. But she had never been Maggie.

He prayed to God Allison never suspected she was his second choice. But he had known it, and that was enough.

To give in to what he wanted now would be the final insult.

But there was another reason why he could not yield; an even more important one.

Maggie had apparently lost her belief in God, or thought she had. He remembered a different time when her faith was young, strong and idealistic. But now she was confused, conflicted in the worst way a person could be. Until she settled her philosophy one way or another, she would wander without direction.

He was not a man who expected his wife to parrot his every thought and feeling; in fact, the differences between Maggie and him had years ago sparked fire into their relationship. But this one matter—his faith—was more crucial and sacred to him than any other in life. If forced to define himself in one sentence, he would have to say, "I am a follower of Christ." His belief formed the heart and soul of him. Maggie and he were not of the same mind, and he would not subject Beth to the inevitable strain that would cause in their home.

When he finally realized Rhonda was asking him to stay for dinner, he refused as kindly as he could. She insisted.

"Don't put pressure on him," Maggie said, reaching for celery stalks and chopping, chopping. "He must be very tired, and I'm sure he wants to go home."

"I can hear my recliner calling me now," Adam said.

Rhonda waved a hand dismissively. "Nonsense. You have to eat, so sit for a few moments and then you can go. It's the least we can do for you after the treat you gave Sam today."

"Actually, I need to be sure Beth's fed. Or she may be home by now. If she's started dinner and I don't show up..." He smiled and began to edge backward.

"I'm sure she's able to take care of herself. Beth is a very responsible young woman."

Maggie scraped the apple and pear chunks and celery slices into a bowl, then added a handful of raisins. "Mom, he needs to see about his daughter. Don't make him feel guilty."

"Well," Rhonda said in reasoning tones, "why don't you call and find out what she's doing?"

Adam eyed the phone on the wall, then looked at Maggie. She was sprinkling chopped walnuts into the mixture. As she reached for the jar of mayonnaise, she glanced at him briefly. He saw color spring to her cheeks.

"Okay," he said, and wondered who was speaking. "I'll call her."

Rhonda nodded and gave him a cat-licking-cream smile. He tried not to think what that meant as he dialed his telephone number. He let the phone ring ten times before giving up. The face of Jake Browne flitted like a monster in a horror movie across Rhonda's refrigerator.

He remembered his visit earlier in the day to Sally's Garage where Jake worked. The visit hadn't gone well, and Adam had left, knowing he'd made a mess of things.

On the way out of the garage, he'd noticed the scaffolding with buckets of paint resting on boards at the top. His eyes had moved slowly upward to a larger-than-life painting covering the back wall. The painting was made by Browne himself and showed Jake riding his Harley through stormy, lightning-split clouds; only the front wheel remained partially unfinished. Behind him rode a sprite of a girl, her delighted face tilted upward, her hair whipping fetchingly in the wind.

Recognizing Beth, Adam had felt his heart knot into a fist.

"I guess she's not home yet," he said finally, trying not to let his anxiety show. "I'll dial her cellular." When his daughter's chipper voice answered on the second ring, he relaxed slightly. "Hi, where are you? I thought you'd be home by now."

"I'm in my car, Dad." She laughed delightedly, her *I've-got-a-secret-and-I'm-not-telling-you* laugh. Ordinarily he loved to hear it. Tonight he was not so sure. "Where are *you?*" she added.

"I'm still at the Covingtons'." He managed to keep his voice pleasant, even sent Maggie a brief smile as she passed by him with the bowl of Waldorf salad, all the while imagining Beth cruising through town with Jake and enjoying her disobedience to the hilt. "Is someone riding with you?"

Beth laughed again. What could possibly be so funny?

"I think you hear the radio playing."

The background noises faded. Something slammed. The front doorbell rang, and Maggie crossed in front of him to answer it. A sudden suspicion made him walk to the kitchen entrance, the telephone coil stretching dangerously. Peering into the hallway, he saw Maggie open the door and admit Beth.

"Hi, Dad," she said into her phone, grinning mischievously.

"Well, aren't you just the cutest thing," he responded, relief pouring through him.

"I thought I'd drop by to see if you still needed my help, but I guess everyone's back. Sorry I couldn't get here sooner."

"We're glad you're here now," Rhonda said. "You're just in time for dinner!"

The valley held the day's warmth long after twilight, and the breeze whispering through the kitchen curtains was mild. Gradually during the meal, the lively ordinariness of Beth and Sam's chatter made Adam relax. Maggie seemed more comfortable, too, and conversation flowed normally among them all.

After supper, Rhonda suggested Beth search the hall closet for Carter's old telescope and show Sam the stars.

Maggie and her mother disappeared into Rhonda's bedroom. Adam quietly washed the dishes, hoping Rhonda wouldn't scold him for it. When he finished, he draped the dish towel across the faucet to dry and walked through the hall to the front porch.

Beth had set up the telescope at the far edge of the garage, where there were fewer trees to block the view. Sam stood on a block, one eye pressed to the eyepiece, both hands fiddling with the focus. Adam sat in one of the rockers and listened to their muted talk, hearing little difference in the pitch and enthusiasm of their voices.

His daughter was still a little girl in many ways. Not grown-up, not mature. He sighed contentedly and leaned back to watch the stars as they were meant to be watched: faraway, twinkling and mysterious as God.

When the door opened quietly and Maggie exited, his heart thumped like a young boy's. He lowered his arms from behind his head and tried to look unaffected.

"Mom said to give you her apologies," Maggie said as she stepped down one step, leaning out to see Sam and Beth. "She's gone to bed."

"Oh, already? Then Beth and I should be going, too."

"If you leave so soon, Sam will expect me to find the Big Dipper for him, and I never could."

Adam laughed. "That's right, I remember. It's easier during the summer. This time of year the Dipper is closer to the horizon and usually behind the trees." He saw her looking skyward and couldn't resist coming to stand beside her on the steps. "Look, there's Cassiopeia. It's simple to find anytime." He pointed upward. "See it? The star pattern looks like the letter *M*. Or *W*, during certain times of the year."

"I never could find that, either."

"Yes, you could, when you tried. You just weren't

interested. It was always music that put the stars in your eyes.''

She fell silent for a moment, her gaze continuing to search the sky. ''I remember how you used to tell me about the constellation myths. It surprises me a little that you've always been interested in those old stories. What convinces you Christianity isn't simply another myth?''

While his heart drummed, he prayed for guidance. Finally he said, ''I can't tell you that I was a depraved drug addict whose life was dramatically changed when I decided to follow Christ. I was just an average kid, getting into trouble sometimes, but mostly trying to do the right thing. My parents and I never had major conflicts. There was nothing traumatic in my life to make me rebellious or bitter. But I can tell you this. When I made the choice, there was a difference. In here.'' He touched his chest briefly. ''The law of His love is written in my heart, just as I believe it is in yours.'' He stared at her profile, hoping he had not sounded too preachy. He sensed how delicately poised she was, teetering on the precipice of belief.

She was quiet, seeming to consider his answer. ''I think I'm astronomically challenged,'' she said suddenly with a stiff little laugh.

I'm some kind of challenged, too, he thought, studying her face with misery as his pulse raced. He had never wanted to kiss anyone so badly in his life.

When a movement caught the corner of his vision, he turned with relief to see Beth and Sam standing at the bottom of the steps. He eased farther away from Maggie, coming to rest against the opposite rail.

''Can Beth and me go for a walk?'' Sam asked.

''Are you all done looking through the telescope?'' Maggie asked in an overbright voice.

"I can't see anything. Beth says I will when I'm taller. Can we go to the dead-end street and back?"

"You'll have to be careful walking alongside the main road. It's pretty dark tonight and there are always cars."

Adam looked at Maggie, trying to gauge her feelings. "Maybe we should run along. Beth probably has homework."

"No, she doesn't," Sam protested. "She told me she didn't. And it's just a little way to the street, Mommy, remember? I want to show her that funny old tree we saw."

Maggie glanced briefly at Adam. "It's not far," she explained. "Sam and I walk there almost every day. We found a tree split by lightning, and some squirrels have made their home in it."

"Sure." He turned to his daughter, wondering why she was being so quiet. "We'll have to leave right after, Beth."

"Okay," she said with little enthusiasm, her solemn gaze moving slowly from him to Maggie, then back.

"Yes!" Sam jumped spiritedly. "Come on, Beth!" He grabbed her hand and pulled, a tiny boat tugging a larger, more sluggish one.

They stood watching their children for a moment. When Sam and Beth disappeared from sight, Maggie gave him a perfunctory smile and went to sit in one of the rockers. Adam followed, settling beside her.

"We could go inside if you like," Maggie said abruptly.

"I'd rather not take a chance on disturbing Rhonda, if it's all the same to you. Unless you're chilly."

"No, I'm fine. You're probably right."

An awkward silence fell. She leaned slightly forward, putting her rocker into motion. The faint creak of wood pressing against wood joined the other night rhythms of crickets, frogs and a lonely sounding owl. A car glided smoothly past, its high beams cutting across the bordering woods like a searchlight.

"Did I tell you what a great time Sam and I had this afternoon?" Adam said, finally. "You've done a wonderful job raising him."

"And you have a fantastic daughter. Not only is she beautiful, but she has an adorable personality. I keep thinking of myself at that age. Compared to what I remember being like, she seems so...well-balanced, I guess you'd say. Not full of angst and self-doubt like I was."

"That was mainly Allison's doing."

She looked at him, her expression soft. "You must miss her terribly."

"Every day."

She shook her head, then leaned back and closed her eyes briefly. "I can't imagine what you and Beth must be going through."

"I don't suppose your divorce has been any picnic, either," he said softly.

A lightning frown creased her forehead. "No. Definitely not."

She stared blindly into the night, her expression so fragile that he found he could not look away.

"Is something wrong, Maggie?"

"No, of course not." The words spilled from her lips as easily as any social lie.

He grunted, a humorless chuckle. "You've just reminded me of a conversation Allison and I had a few months before her death. She told me that people kept asking her how she was, and she would automatically tell them she was fine—even though cancer was stealing

her life cell by cell. She said she couldn't tell them the
truth because they didn't really want to hear it.'' He gave
her an intent look. ''But I do, Maggie. If something is
bothering you—if I can help in any way—let me know.''

Wearing a lost expression, Maggie turned to read his
face. ''Thank you, Adam.'' She stood suddenly and
stepped to the rail. Crossing her arms and leaning against
the thick wooden banister, she said quietly, ''I won't lie
to you. Frankly it would be a relief to talk to someone
I can trust.''

Pleasure shot through him. He forced himself not to
smile, then tasted dismay at his overreaction to her faint
praise.

''Yesterday I found out something that's shaken my
entire world,'' she continued.

''I think I understand how you feel.''

Her eyes sharpened. ''How could you possibly?''

Why did she look so suspicious? ''The custody issue
with your ex-husband over Sam,'' he explained quickly.
''I won't presume to know the depth of your feelings,
but having spent a little more time with the boy today,
I can empathize better. Your son is a prize.''

She blinked, then gave a short laugh. ''I've hardly
thought about that all day. Mom used to accuse me of
being self-centered, and I guess she was right.'' He
waited, curiosity and concern mixed in his eyes. ''Imagine if all your life you thought you were one person,
then suddenly found out differently,'' she went on.
''Suppose you were told your whole existence began
with a lie.''

She seemed to expect him to say something. He
spread his fingers helplessly. ''Sorry, Maggie, I'm not
following you.''

Fingering the pocket of her skirt, Maggie pulled out

a yellowing document. "This evening after supper, Mom and I slipped into her bedroom for a minute. She gave me this."

He accepted the paper from her hand and unfolded it, holding it closer to the feeble porch light. "Your birth certificate?"

"It's my only clue to who I am."

Adam glanced down without comprehension, then up. "Maggie—"

"Just read it carefully—every line. Please."

His gaze moved over the blanks a second time, then suddenly caught. "They got your mother's name wrong," he said.

"No." Her voice was strained, her lips tight. "My mother's name is correct. This is my real birth certificate, not the false one Mom and Dad used to identify me when applying for school and vaccinations."

She continued her explanation while he listened in growing disbelief. As she spoke of her father's affair and her mother's death, disbelief changed to pity. When she finished, he pressed her hand briefly. The jolt he felt at the touch of her skin was the shock of compassion, he assured himself.

"I'm so sorry," he said. "I'm…astounded, as a matter of fact."

"I know. I didn't think this sort of thing happened to real people."

He wanted to ask her if she was very angry with her parents, but he didn't dare. She looked on the verge of tears now. If she wept, he'd be forced to take her in his arms to give comfort. He didn't want to risk that, not tonight.

"What are you going to do?" he asked at last.

"I'm almost crazy with the need to know about my

genetic family. Not only for my own satisfaction, but for knowledge that might affect Sam's health.''

''Where will you begin? There's no address on the certificate. Do you have any information about Emily Rose at all?''

''Just that she and Dad met at Bellen University in Orlando, where she was a student. Hopefully I can start there.''

''If they'll release her records.''

''Right. But they have to.'' She ran her hand along the rail as she thought. ''I'm going to make some calls tomorrow and see how far I can get. I feel like I'll accomplish more if I go in person, though. Sometimes it's harder to deny a face across the counter than it is an anonymous voice on the phone. And if I'm there—if I'm successful in finding information about my mother—I might be able to meet some of my relatives. I can't tell you how driven I feel to go to Florida, even if I only walk some of the same paths she walked. Breathe the same air.'' She gave an embarrassed laugh. ''I hope I don't sound obsessed.''

He regarded her with compassion. ''I think I understand how you feel.''

He could hear Sam talking behind the trees; the children were returning. Plans flew through Adam's mind. ''Rhonda seemed to be getting around pretty well tonight.''

''She's had a few problems, but I believe she'll be able to be on her own in a week or two. The doctor was very positive this afternoon.''

''What if you could leave right away—say the first of next week—and were only gone a few days? Beth could stay with her at night. Maybe you could get someone to look in on Rhonda during the day while Beth's in school.''

"Oh, no," she said quickly. "That would be too much of an imposition on Beth. Besides, I doubt I could get a flight so quickly without paying full fare. I'm embarrassed to say finances are a problem right now."

"Beth would love it." And not only that, he thought with the glee of one swatting two flies with the same swatter, it would put the Jake Browne question on ice. "And I could fly you down."

"*You* could fly me down," she repeated in surprise.

"I have a friend who has a Cessna. He lets his friends use it every now and then. Even with one stop for refueling, we could get to Orlando in almost the time it would take a jet, because you wouldn't have to change planes in Atlanta."

He was only being compassionate, he tried to tell himself. A friend helping a friend. He knew better than to invent ways to spend time with Maggie.

"But your business—"

"It would only take me a day. I can drop you off, then you could book a return flight when you're done."

"I wouldn't dream of putting you to that kind of trouble."

He could see she was tempted. "If you knew how I welcomed every chance to pilot John's Cessna, you wouldn't call it trouble."

She tilted her head. "So you finally learned to fly. I'm impressed."

Beth and Sam were walking up the drive, their cheeks painted pink by the cooling air. Sam called to her and waved, and Maggie waved back. "Thanks for the offer," she told Adam. "Let me think about it, okay? And are you *sure* Beth wouldn't mind?"

"I'm positive she'd enjoy it." But he felt a momentary twinge as he watched Beth guide Sam onto the sidewalk beneath the porch. She returned his stare, and he thought he had never seen her look so guarded, or so knowing.

Chapter Seven

~

"Bellen University, Office of the Registrar."

"Yes, hello. I'm trying to track down the address of someone who attended there about thirty-five years ago. Do your records go that far back?"

"Ma'am, we've kept records since the university was founded in 1936."

"Wonderful! Do you have an address for a student named Emily Rose Wilkerson? She would have been in the graduate school in 1963 or 1964, I think."

"I'm sorry, the Privacy Act of 1974 won't let us give that information to the general public."

"Oh." Maggie twisted the phone cord around her index finger. She had expected this, but she still felt disappointed. She pulled her feet closer to the bench as Sam pushed his fire truck past. With his cheeks puffed out, he was imitating a muffled fire alarm, but not muffled enough. Maggie covered one ear and pressed the phone tighter to the other. "Actually," she said, lowering her voice, "I'm not the general public, I'm her—a family member trying to trace a relative."

"Ma'am, as far as I know, you could be a crazed killer looking to send a mail bomb. I can't help you."

The beveled glass in the front door splintered the morning light across the oak floor. Sam squinted, temporarily blinded. The truck rolled from his grasp and, unbalanced, he landed hard on his elbow, then gave a bellow of rage. Though she knew he was more angry than hurt, Maggie dropped the phone to soothe him.

"Hush, baby. You'll disturb Grandma."

"Too late," Rhonda said dryly, emerging walker-first from her bedroom and wearing a pink flowered housedress with snaps down the front and fuzzy scuffs. Maggie felt a moment's surprise at how old she looked, though part of it was the elderly ambience of her clothes. Rhonda usually dressed for style, not comfort. "What's going on with Sammy?"

She examined his elbow, found only a small red spot and patted it reassuringly. "He's all right."

"I'm not all right! I want my daddy!"

"He didn't get much sleep last night," Maggie explained, her heart dipping. "I think he was too excited from his outing with Adam yesterday."

"That makes two of us who didn't sleep," Rhonda replied, her gaze moving from Maggie to the bench. "Is someone on the phone?"

"Oh! Long distance!" Maggie rushed back. "Are you still on the line?"

"Still hanging," replied the voice. "I've decided you're not a female Unabomber after all. Sounds too much like my house over there."

"That's good," Maggie said, hope growing as she waved frantically at Sam. He responded by pressing pouted lips together, but at least he stopped crying.

"I still can't give you the lady's records," the voice

continued, "but you might try calling the alumni office. They publish directories every year and sell them. If your relative wanted to be listed, her address should be in there."

"Thank you very much," Maggie said warmly, hanging up.

"Any luck?" Rhonda asked, her eyebrows lifting, though her face remained expressionless.

"Some. I need to make a few more calls after I get you something to eat. Sam and I already had breakfast."

"Maggie, I am perfectly capable of getting a bowl and cereal myself, since that is apparently your idea of a morning meal."

Casting aside a familiar feeling of irritation, she said, "I can make you something else if you like."

"No, you're too busy. You never could flip an egg without breaking the yolk anyhow." She turned slowly, the walker pumping up and down. In an undertone, she added, "I'm going to try to use that cane with the three legs today and stop being such an old woman."

"Is your dizziness gone, then?"

"Just about."

Rhonda clumped on toward the kitchen. Compassion sweeping through her, Maggie followed. "You'd be surprised at what I've learned to do with an egg," she said, and moved toward the cabinet that held Rhonda's cast-iron skillet.

Minutes later, Maggie set a plate containing one egg, overmedium, raisin bread toast and two crisp pieces of bacon in front of Rhonda.

"Well, well," the older lady said appreciatively. "You even remembered how I like my bacon."

Feeling absurdly proud, Maggie said, "How could I

not? Dad always used to make a fuss about your burning it every morning."

"I cooked the trichinae out of it, you mean. Unlike your father, I grew up on a farm and know what hogs do in their spare time."

Maggie smiled and lifted the curtain at the window. Sam was playing in the wide back yard, pushing his fire truck across the rocks bordering the flower beds. The truck went everywhere with him now; it was as though he didn't own another toy. Feeling ten pounds heavier, she released the curtain.

"Go ahead and make your calls," Rhonda instructed as she buttered her toast. "I'll keep an eye on Sammy."

Maggie murmured her thanks and tried not to run to the gossip bench. In a few moments, she returned to the kitchen, considerably less enthusiastic.

"The alumni office didn't have her address. Apparently she didn't want to be listed in the directory."

"What about the Orlando hospital where you were born? It's on your birth certificate. Wouldn't they have records?"

"I'm sure they do, but I doubt they would give them to me without a court order."

"And that would take time."

"Right." Maggie sank into the chair opposite Rhonda, propped her elbow on the table and cupped her chin. She met the older woman's eyes. "Looks like I'm going to have to go down there."

Rhonda forked a last bite of egg to her mouth, then pushed her plate forward. "Don't let me stop you. I'm doing fine."

"I wouldn't leave you without someone. Yesterday Adam said he thought Beth would be willing to stay here at night."

Lowering her eyes to the table, Rhonda pressed a napkin to her lips. "You told Adam, then."

Maggie hesitated. "I hope that's not a problem."

"No. Adam is discreet—he'll know better than to spread rumors."

She gave Rhonda an intent look. "Mom, are you still wanting to keep this quiet?"

"Is that so hard to understand? Even if you don't care what people say, I do. I don't want them talking about Philip."

"In other words, I'm a dirty little secret."

"No, Maggie! You twist everything around. There is simply no reason to set people's tongues wagging after all this time."

"All right." She glanced away, hiding the cynicism she knew must be in her eyes. Rhonda could protest all she wanted about preserving Philip's good name, but Maggie thought it was her mom's own pride that was being saved.

Rhonda struggled to her feet and glanced out the window. "When will you leave?"

"As soon as I can arrange things, if you're sure it's okay."

"It's all right with me. I already told you that. But I hope you're not planning on taking Sammy with you. It would be better if you let him stay with Zackary."

Maggie could not believe her ears. "It would be better if I did *what?*"

"You've been plain about letting me know I made a mistake in not telling you about your birth mother. Thinking as you do, how can you deny your son his true father?"

"The situation is not anywhere near the same, Mom. Zack caused me to lose my job. If he's willing to go that far, he would take Sam away from me if he could. I'm not giving him the chance.''

The look Rhonda gave Maggie made her feel twelve years old. ''You never were a sensible child. What will you do, then? Drag Sammy all over Florida or leave him with me? I'd be delighted if I were able to keep up with him.''

''Of course you're not well enough to watch him. Johanna can, though. She could leave early Sunday morning, visit awhile with you, then be back home in Murfreesboro by evening. It would be a great opportunity for Sam to get to know his cousins better.'' A second later she added, ''Half-cousins.''

''Johanna's very active in her church. She won't want to miss a whole day.''

''Saturday, then.''

''Have you asked Johanna if she's willing to do this?''

''She'd better be. She owes me.'' Maggie rose, took her mother's plate to the sink and washed it.

Rhonda leaned against the walker. ''And the reason you're giving her for this sudden trip is…?''

Maggie felt a headache coming on. She set the plate in the dish drainer, then turned to face the older woman. ''You can't be serious. Do you expect me not to tell Johanna and Carter?''

''Why would you want to do that?'' Rhonda queried, her distress so profound that Maggie's heart did a slow tumble. ''What could possibly be gained?''

''What could be gained?'' The anger that swelled inside her was frightening. She delayed answering, looking out the kitchen window to check on Sam while imagining a giant hand pushing the anger down, like a baker kneading dough. ''You're always talking about God and doing the right thing. Is living a lie the right thing?''

She was mad, mad as a hissing snake, and she felt the words slithering hot and steaming from her mouth. "How can you reconcile your faith with deceiving your own children?"

Rhonda flinched and remained silent a moment before speaking. "You're doing this to punish me. You're hurt that I never told you about your birth mother until now, and this is your way of getting back. I never should have said anything. I should have taken the secret to my grave. Now nothing is ever going to be the same again!"

Adam's mind was running in a thousand directions that afternoon as he turned into his driveway. Had he been thinking more clearly, he would have noticed Jane Garrison's maroon Crown Victoria parked out front and kept on going. But it was too late now. She had seen him.

"Adam!" she cried as she emerged from her car and held up an oblong casserole dish. "I've brought something for your supper tonight!"

Parking beside her, he pressed his lips into a smile and stepped from the Riviera. "Jane, you shouldn't have." Really, *really*, you shouldn't have, he thought, then scolded himself for his unkindness. "You're way too busy to be cooking for Beth and me so often. I don't want you running yourself down."

"Oh, good heavens," she said with a laugh, and tossed her head in a fruitless effort to dislodge feathery bangs from her eyes. "You make me sound a hundred years old. I have nothing *but* energy. And real estate doesn't tire me out, it invigorates! Now take this pan of Italian pork and rice so I can get the wind out of my hair. I just had it cut today. Do you like?"

Adam forced himself to focus. Her shining chestnut

hair was cropped closely to her scalp, reminding him of a cap. The style revealed her small, perfect ears, from which hung large, dangly earrings—red ones, to match her business suit. She was a slender woman, but too tall for the short cut. She often declared she was younger than he, but in the harsh afternoon light he wondered.

"You look very nice," he said.

"Well, thank you, gallant gentleman! Now, let's go inside and I'll show you what to do with that casserole."

He subdued an impulse to laugh. "Jane, don't trouble yourself. I think I can handle it. Warm it in the oven at three hundred and fifty degrees, right?"

"It's no trouble at all," she said, and walked expectantly to the door.

Sighing inwardly, Adam shifted the dish to his left hand and searched his right pocket for the keys. When he opened the door, he walked determinedly toward the kitchen, even though Jane lingered at the living room sofa.

"This is such a beautiful room," she called after him. "I love the antiques, especially this mahogany sideboard—is it a Duncan Phyfe? The high ceilings make the room spacious, and the beams are a perfectly quaint touch. Sure you don't want to sell? I could get you a great price!"

"No, thanks," he said loudly. "I'm putting the dish in the oven now."

"Allison had exquisite taste," she said, lowering her voice as she joined him. "In everything."

"Well, thank you." He nodded toward the eye-level oven. "There it is, baking away. Did I do that right?"

She laughed delicately. "Adam, you have such a delightful sense of humor." With a sinking feeling, he watched her pull out a stool from the kitchen bar and sit. "Now aren't you going to offer me a cup of tea for all my hard work? I'm so thirsty I could die!"

"Sure," he said, and jerked the teapot from the back burner to the sink, turning the water on full blast. "I'm afraid I have to hurry though. Got to make some arrangements tonight for a trip I'll be taking next week."

"Oh? Business or pleasure?"

"I enjoy every chance I get to fly," he answered cryptically.

He thought of Maggie's call at lunchtime today and could hardly keep from smiling in spite of his misgivings that he was walking into trouble. She had decided to take him up on his offer; she sounded desperate to do so, in fact. A hurried call to John had assured him the Cessna was his on Monday. All that remained was for Beth to give her assent to stay with Rhonda, and they would be set. He was sure she'd be willing, or pretty sure. She had seemed sullen at breakfast this morning, though. Hopefully she wasn't coming down with anything.

He wouldn't permit himself to think about what might really be wrong, or remember the expression he had seen on her face when she surprised him on the porch steps last night, standing too close to Maggie and no doubt looking like a moonstruck tomcat.

"All right, don't tell me, Mr. Mysterious," Jane said with a little smile. "By the way, I've been hearing rumors about you."

"Is that right?" Adam removed a carton of skim milk from the refrigerator and put it in front of his guest. He slid the canister of sugar toward her and gave her a spoon.

Her gaze flickered over the condiments with a superior amusement that irked him. "I hear that Maggie Covington, or whatever her last name is now, is back in town with her small child, and that you've been seeing her.''

His lips tightened as he grabbed a hot pad to remove the screaming kettle from the stove. He clanked a flowered mug to the counter, plopped a tea bag in it and poured. "Rhonda Covington has been recovering from a broken hip. I've been trying to help out with the family.''

She gave him a glance heavy with irony. "That's good of you. You're a very kind person.'' After dipping the tea bag in her cup, she took a slow, cautious sip. "I don't remember if I ever told you, but Johanna was either in my class at school or a year or two behind. I'm not sure after all this time. I didn't know her very well, but I remember when you dropped her for her little sister. Everybody talked about it—the high school sophomore who landed a college guy.''

"Johanna started dating someone else,'' he said. "I didn't drop her.''

"Oh, Adam, you're such a gentleman. Anyhow, I think it's just awful how Maggie treated you after all that. Have you ever been able to forgive her?''

Adam braced his hands on the counter and stared steadily at Jane, his eyes narrowing. "Now, Jane,'' he said.

Her lips twitched coyly. "Now, Adam,'' she echoed in the same tone of voice.

The door to the garage opened. Beth walked in, glanced at the adults and swung her backpack to the top of the low shelves lining the mudroom. Adam greeted her effusively, as did Jane. Beth was less enthusiastic in her pleasantries.

"I couldn't put the Hyundai in the garage because

there were too many cars in front of the door," she said. "I had to park in the street."

"That's my fault, dear," Jane said, sliding to her feet and draining the mug. "I'd better be going and get that car out of your way. I brought you and your dad a casserole."

"Thanks." Beth showed her teeth in a grimace of a smile and loped toward the living room.

Jane's brows arched behind her bangs. "Well. Goodbye, Adam."

Adam saw her to the door, thanked her again for the food and returned to his daughter, who was stretched facedown on the sofa, one arm trailing on the carpet, the other cradling her head. He sat opposite her in one of the armchairs flanking the large picture window that overlooked their sharply sloping lawn and a heart-stopping view of Needle's Cove across the street.

"Bad day?" he asked.

She mumbled something into the cushions.

"I'm sorry, I don't speak sofa," he said pleasantly.

Beth rolled over, her hair half covering her face. "I said the day was all right, okay? I'm just tired."

"Oh." He drew back, hoping it wasn't some woman thing. Allison had known what to do when their daughter got moody, but his favorite method of coping was to get out of her way. "Did your speech go well?"

"It went. I placed second."

"Beth, how fantastic!" His daughter's sophomore honors English class had staged an essay competition with the juniors and seniors. Today the finalists—four in each grade—had delivered their papers orally in an after-school assembly. Beth had worked for weeks on her topic, a study of the social life of single women in Jane Austen's novels. To place at all when competing against upperclassmen was a true accomplishment. "I'm really proud of you."

She closed her eyes. "Yeah. Thanks."

Adam waited a moment, frowning. "What's the matter?"

"Nothing." Her lashes flickered open, and she stared at the ceiling. "Not a thing."

He had played long enough, he decided. "I'm glad to hear it," he said jovially. "Especially since I have a favor to ask of you."

Her eyes swung toward him, two lasers taking aim.

"I was wondering if you'd be willing to stay a few nights with Mrs. Covington next week while her daughter is out of town," he said, all in a rush.

Beth's legs slid to the floor, and she sat up. "Where's she going?"

"Maggie? She's flying down to Florida."

"Why?"

"Some family business she needs to take care of quickly."

"She can't wait until her mother's better?"

"Rhonda *is* better. You wouldn't have to do much— just be there after school and cook dinner like you do here at home sometimes. Mrs. Covington would probably be all right on her own, but you'd be there just in case."

Beth stared at him intently. "I don't know, Dad. I have lots of things to do after school."

"Your club meetings and play practice? Mrs. Covington will understand that. Just let her know each night when to expect you."

"Check in with her like a baby, you mean."

"That's not it at all, Beth. Naturally she would need to know when you're coming."

"I'd have to tell her everything I was going to do, every minute of the day."

"Not every minute of the day, just after school. I'm not quite sure I understand the problem." He was afraid he did, though. "Is there something you plan to do that you don't want anyone knowing about?"

They eyed one another for a moment, the air between them heavy with unspoken thoughts.

"No," she said finally. "I just don't like being monitored."

"You haven't been monitored since you were in fourth grade." He grinned encouragingly and added, "I could make it worth your while."

"How much?"

Feeling a sharp pang of disappointment, he named a figure.

"That sounds good." Her mood seemed to be brightening. "I saw a blouse I wanted at the mall the other day. So how long is Mrs. Gould going to be gone?"

"She doesn't know for sure, but I doubt it will be longer than three or four days. We're planning to leave on Monday."

Beth became very still. "We?"

Adam swallowed. "I'm flying her down in John Clatchett's plane, but I'm planning on coming back the same day. That way, I'll be here if you need me."

With dismay he watched the color fade from his daughter's cheeks. Her shoulders began to rise and fall slightly as her breathing increased.

"I can't believe it," she whispered.

"Believe what, Beth?" he whispered back, his heart thudding.

"I thought you loved my mother." Tears pooled in her eyes.

He went to her immediately, his own lashes growing wet. "I loved her more than my own life."

"No you didn't. You couldn't have. Not if you've forgotten her so soon."

"How can you say that?" He slipped an arm around her shoulders. "You know what she meant to me."

"Oh, really?" she cried, and shrugged off his arm to stand over him. "Then why are you hanging around your old girlfriend so much, Dad? I saw the way you looked at her last night. I'm not a child, you know. I'm not stupid!"

"I think you're making too much of my trying to help an old friend in trouble," he protested weakly.

"Oh, am I? Then why haven't you thought about the date today, Dad? Why haven't you once thought about it?"

Her words hit him like daggers. He felt his mouth drop, his eyes round. Seeing his belated comprehension, Beth sobbed and ran from the room.

Allison had died on April sixteenth, six months ago. He and Beth had agreed to put a rose on her grave on that date every month for the first year. Today was the sixteenth, and he had forgotten.

"Oh, Beth," he groaned, and put his head in his hands.

Chapter Eight

❧

"What I can't understand is how Dad could have done this," Johanna said, looking at Maggie. It was Saturday afternoon. Johanna had brought her two boys with her to pick up Sam, and the cousins were playing outside while she visited with Maggie and her mother at the kitchen table. Her broad, pleasant face was troubled as she turned to Rhonda. "Both of you seemed so happy together. Tell me about this mystery surrounding Maggie's birth. Maggie, you only gave me enough information to whet my appetite."

Rhonda slammed her cane on the floor and started to stand. "You two can talk about it. I'm going to lie down."

"No, you don't, Mom." Johanna gently eased the older woman back into her chair. "I know how you think. You believe I'll be disappointed in Daddy and mad at you for not being up-front about everything. Well, I'll admit I *am* disappointed in Dad. I don't know how he could get so far from the Lord that he'd do such a thing, but I believe he must have gotten right with

Him. He sure seemed straightened out when he raised us.''

It seemed to be a question, and Rhonda, blinking quickly, said, ''Yes, he loved God with all his heart. And he was determined that we bring up our children in the Lord's way.''

This seemed to be as good a time as any to clear the table, and Maggie got up and started scraping plates. Johanna sent her a mildly annoyed look and made no effort to help, which was typical, Maggie remembered, growing warmer.

''What I can't understand,'' Johanna said, ''is how you forgave him. I've tried to put myself in your shoes, and I don't know if I could do what you did. If Sid betrayed me like that, I doubt I'd ever get over it. But you must have. You were so good to Daddy.''

''He was good to me,'' Rhonda said after a moment's fumbling in her pocket for a tissue. ''In some ways, our marriage grew stronger after Maggie was born.'' She wiped her eyes. ''Girls, your father was not a philanderer. I believe he really loved that young woman, but I'm certain he loved me, as well. After she died...''

Eyes riveted on Rhonda, Maggie set the stack of dishes in the sink and slipped back into her chair.

''After she died,'' Rhonda repeated, her voice growing hushed, ''there were nights when I'd wake up to find his side of the bed empty. Sometimes I'd simply lie there and wait for him to come back. I was still angry, then. Other times I'd follow. Sometimes I'd find him standing over Maggie's crib watching her, or tucking the blanket over her feet.'' Her gaze locked with Maggie's. ''And once I found him downstairs in the parlor, sitting in his favorite armchair and weeping. That's when everything changed between us. I felt my own hurt and resentment melting away. I took him in my arms and we held each other through all that long night.''

Maggie's eyes filled. She could not look away from Rhonda.

The older lady took a long, shuddering breath. ''After that he never left my side. Not at night, nor any other time.''

Johanna slid her hand across the table and wrapped her fingers around her mother's. In an uncharacteristically gentle voice, she said, ''I always thought you were a great mother. Now I know it.''

After the kitchen was cleaned, the women gathered in the parlor and paged through aging photograph albums while the boys charged in and out of the house. When the time came for Johanna to leave—she didn't want to drive after dark, she said—Maggie felt a deep rift opening in her heart. She had never spent a night away from Sam. She fought tears as she placed his suitcase in the back of the van. Sam was too involved with his cousins to be sad. After giving her a swift hug, which she determinedly prolonged, he climbed into the vehicle beside Andrew with undisguised eagerness.

Flooded with misgivings, she said, ''Johanna, I've been thinking that maybe this isn't the best time—''

''I've been thinking, too,'' her sister interrupted. She lowered her voice, though the boys were talking to each other and not listening to them. ''I've been thinking about how God can bring good from any circumstance, even sin. Dad was wrong to do what he did. But if things had gone another way—if your mother had chosen to abort you, or if her diabetes had caused her to miscarry, or if Mom hadn't been as forgiving as she was—I never would have had you for my sister.'' She reached for Maggie's hand, and Maggie readily responded, linking her fingers with Johanna's and trying not to flinch when she squeezed hard. "Now you go on and find out what you have to. And don't worry about Sam, for crying out loud. I think I know how to take care of children."

"I believe you," Maggie said with a shaky laugh.

And there was nothing to be done except stand away from the van and wave until her world diminished to a dot on the horizon and disappeared.

The next morning Rhonda announced that if she was well enough to visit the doctor, she certainly could attend morning worship. Maggie, feeling hollow from the amputation of Sam, wearily dressed in a fitted navy dress and submitted to the inevitable.

Parson's Ridge Bible Church was a fifteen-minute drive from her mother's house. As Maggie rounded the last curve and turned up the steep drive that led to both front and rear parking lots, she studied the familiar old structure, feeling a riot of emotions. Built of mountain stone with a high steeple in front and rows of stained-glass windows on each side, the building blended into its wooded surroundings better than many newer churches she had seen. In back and perpendicular to it was the Family Life Center, which had been a new addition at the time of her father's funeral. The annex was beginning to age nicely; lichen could be spotted on some of the lower stones. She had no idea if the green fuzz was good or bad for the rock, but it looked as though it belonged.

She parked in a handicapped space near the back entrance and escorted her mother inside, steeling herself for the onslaught.

She smiled and smiled at familiar faces she could no longer name, shook hands with beaming men in suits, exchanged pleasantries with women wearing floral print dresses, stared levelly into the eyes of children who used to be no taller than her waist. She was finally able to lead Rhonda into the sanctuary, where they sat in the pew long deeded to the Covington family: third row, pulpit side.

Maggie breathed deeply and told herself to relax. The organist was well into a Bach fugue and having a hard go of it. Maggie tried not to notice and let her gaze wander across the eggshell-plastered walls to the high cedar ceiling, then to the tall, arched, stained-glass windows, each depicting a recognizable scene from the Bible. She seemed to have a memory attached to each one. Noah's ark made her think of a favorite Sunday school teacher, Mrs. O'Neill, who had spent an entire three-month quarter on the story. The old lady—long gone, now—had been patient with her fourth-grade girls as they giggled over their meticulously drawn mural week after week.

The pastor and music director entered from the side door, jarring her to the present. Reverend James Dixon looked only vaguely familiar; he had presided at her father's funeral, and she did not recognize the other man at all. Reverend Dixon seemed too young, too unstamped with worries to be a pastor, his handsome features contented and optimistic as he gazed at his flock.

The choir entered, filed into the loft that faced the congregation, and began the introit. Beth Morgan, she saw with a start, stood on the first row. With a sense of the inevitable, she moved her gaze upward and found Adam in the bass section. When the choir sat, Adam's eyes locked with hers almost instantly, as if she had drawn them. He looked surprised for a fraction of a second, then gave her a small smile. She returned it until she felt Beth's humorless stare. When the girl did not respond to her friendly grin, Maggie shifted uncomfortably and fixed her attention on the pastor.

The service moved on. When the time came for the sermon, Reverend Dixon began dramatically. "If it be possible, as much as lieth in you, live peaceably with all men." He went on to say that Romans twelve offered more instruction in Christ-like living than the average person could handle in a lifetime. "If Christians only read and adopted that one chapter," he said persuasively, "their lives and society would be transformed."

Maggie listened, finding his gentle voice and simple words a refreshing change from the sermons she had heard in her childhood. Still, she was relieved when the postlude began, and she moved Rhonda through the crowd as quickly as possible. They were almost to the back door when Adam, his choir robe unzipped over a striped shirt, tie and jeans, found them. Beth trailed behind, looking as if she'd rather be anywhere else.

After greetings were exchanged, Adam said, "Well, how did we do, music lady? Not quite as polished as your New York choirs, I'm afraid."

Maggie assured him they sounded fine. She could not prevent herself from glancing curiously at his daughter, who seemed different from the bubbly girl she had come to expect.

"Are you feeling all right, Beth?" she asked pointedly.

"I'm okay." When Adam gave the girl a sharp look, she returned it.

Rhonda leaned against the wall. "She's probably worried that I'll bore her to death during the next few days."

"Oh, no, Mrs. Covington," Beth declared immediately. "That's no problem. Really." She turned to her father. "I thought you were going to tell Mrs. Gould when you're picking her up tomorrow."

"Right," he said with a cautious look. "Is seven too early, Maggie?"

"Seven's fine, but I could save you some time by taking a cab and meeting you at the airport."

Beth said, "Oh, no. Dad will be *happy* to pick you up, won't you, Dad?"

"Yes, I will," he said firmly, and took Beth's elbow, leading her away as he said his goodbyes.

"You guys have a *great* time," Beth said, dragging against his arm.

Maggie stepped closer, feeling a deep need to reassure her. "It's not really a pleasure trip."

"Sure," the girl said knowingly. "Whatever you say."

"I'll see you tomorrow," Adam said evenly, his face pinched with anger as he pulled his daughter down the corridor.

Rhonda and Maggie exchanged glances. "Oh, dear. Looks like a little possessiveness at work." Rhonda made no effort to hide her pleasure. "I wonder why that should be?"

"Give it a rest, Mom." In a movement similar to Adam's, Maggie grabbed Rhonda's arm and shuffled her toward the exit.

Chapter Nine

Maggie was awake by five Monday morning and ready to leave by six, her suitcase and overnight bag stationed by the door. All that remained was to choke down breakfast; her pulse was racing too fast for her to have an appetite, her stomach too unsettled, but she had to eat something. She walked softly past her mom's room toward the kitchen, not wanting to wake her until the last moment. She was debating whether to wake her at all; the home-health care aide would not arrive until after ten. It seemed silly to disturb her sleep merely to say goodbye, but Rhonda had been insistent last night.

She was spared further vacillation when she entered the kitchen and found her mom at the range. Only the hood light over the stove was on, and the burner beneath the kettle was glowing cherry red. Rhonda wore blue silk pajamas and a matching duster, but her disarrayed hair marred the elegant picture she made in the shadowed room.

"Let me watch that for you," Maggie said, hurrying toward her. "I wish you hadn't got up."

Rhonda sat at the table. "I was awake anyway. I didn't want you leaving without saying goodbye."

"I'll only be gone a few days." Maggie glanced at the woman who had raised her, registering the dark shadows under her eyes and her faintly troubled expression. "You're not worrying about the plane, are you?"

"Not particularly, but when you get to my age, you don't take any farewells lightly."

The kettle began to whistle. Maggie brought two mugs, silverware, Rhonda's tea caddy and a jar of instant coffee to the table, then set the kettle on a hot pad. She sat, filled their cups with hot water and began to stir in coffee crystals in one cup.

"You're feeling all right, aren't you, Mom?"

"I'm getting better every day." She dipped an orange spice tea bag several times into her cup, brought the mug to her mouth, then placed it back on the table without drinking. "Last night I was thinking about how things are going to change if you're successful in your search."

Yes, Maggie thought, *things will be put right, finally.* But she could not say that to the solemn woman across from her.

Rhonda continued. "If you're lucky, you may add a few relatives to our family tree. But don't expect too much, Maggie. I'd hate for you to be hurt."

The barriers in Maggie's heart softened. "I appreciate that. Since Emily Rose's family rejected her, I know they may not be willing to accept me." Something more needed to be said; she could sense it as Rhonda's gaze dropped to her cup. Maggie slid her hand across the table. "I'm just looking for answers, Mom. Not a new family to replace the one I have."

For an instant, she wondered if she spoke truth. But

she owed a lot to this woman, no matter how troubled their history.

Rhonda pressed her daughter's fingers. "I hope one day you'll understand what I did, and I'm not only talking about the circumstances of your birth." A look of intense concentration crossed her face, as if she searched for words she could not find. "I know I hurt you badly when you and Zackary divorced." Her mouth moved soundlessly for a moment. "That was not my intention."

Maggie pushed down a flare of anger. "You meant it for the best." She slowly withdrew her hand. "I'm making toast. Do you want some?"

The minutes of breakfast and clean-up dragged by, but at last Adam rang the doorbell. A flurry of greetings, farewells and brief hugs followed. Maggie felt caught in a dream as she walked beside Adam down the sidewalk. They really were going.

While he put her bags in the trunk, she opened the passenger door, then turned a final time to see her mom outlined in the open doorway. Maggie waved and tried to raise a foot to step in the car. Though her calf muscles tensed, her body would not respond.

Something within whispered, *Go to her.*

I've already said goodbye, she answered. There's no reason to overdo it.

Go to her.

No, she thought. *Rhonda is not a sentimental woman and never was. Remember all those times I ran to her as a little girl, eager to give her a handful of wildflowers or a special drawing? What did she do but brush me aside?*

Look at her. Really, really look.

While Maggie's hand trembled on the car door, she looked. She saw a woman small and frail who once was strong. A maddening, imperfect woman full of contradictions, not unlike herself.

Hardly realizing what her feet were doing, she raced up the sidewalk, paused an instant to study Rhonda's hopeful eyes and swept her into a strong embrace.

"Thank you, Mom," she whispered. "Thank you for everything. I love you."

"I love you, too, Maggie," Rhonda said through tears. "I always will."

Maggie kissed her mom's cheek and hurried back to Adam.

Compared to the commercial jets Maggie had ridden in the past, John Clatchett's plane looked like a toy. It was a single-engine, high-wing Cessna 172, Adam told her, proud as if it belonged to him.

"Have you flown a lot?" she asked as Adam, radio headphones clamped over his ears, accelerated the aircraft down the Lovell Field runway. She felt every bump and crack in the pavement. *This must be what it's like to ride in a blender.*

"You're not worried, are you?" He flashed a grin, spoke again to the tower and pulled back on the controls. Suddenly the roughness smoothed; they were airborne. Fingering her seat belt as she looked down at the shrinking airport and rapidly passing terrain, Maggie held her breath until she felt the Cessna level.

"Better?" he asked, his voice sounding tinny in her headphones. Adam had given her a set before they took off, explaining the engine would be too loud for conversation otherwise. He was right; she could hear it roaring in spite of the headphones.

"Much," she said. The plane hit an air pocket and bucked. "What was that?"

His grin widened. "Nothing to be alarmed about. We're bound to get air turbulence flying between the mountains." He peered happily through the windows, looking at scenery thousands and thousands of feet below.

"How long will we be in the air?"

"About four hours, not counting one stop for fuel."

He appeared disappointed the journey would not take longer. In spite of her fears, she smiled. Her concerns that this trip might prove awkward were fading. It amazed her how comfortable she felt with him, or would once they were on the ground.

"I really appreciate your doing this for me," she said.

"It's John you can thank. He keeps saying somebody needs to take his plane for a spin so it'll stay in good working order, but I know he's being kind to a fellow addict. I learned to fly at Eagleton Hills and had unlimited access to the college plane while I was there. Once you get started, it's hard to quit."

"I'd be happy to thank him. Oh, and I've brought my checkbook to pay for the fuel."

He looked obstinate for an instant, then appeared to reconsider. "I'll tell you what. Let's split it. I'm overdue a turn at the cockpit and would have flown in the next week or so anyway. To tell you the truth, it's good to have a real destination."

"I'm afraid I've caused more trouble than you're admitting. Beth didn't seem too happy you were leaving."

For a few seconds she thought he hadn't heard her. "Beth is having some problems right now," he said finally.

"That seems to go with the territory of being a teenager." She hesitated, wondering if she should press on. In the end, she could not prevent herself. "Yesterday after church, I had the impression she resented our trip. She seemed angry at me.''

His jaw set. ''She was rude, and she will apologize.''

''No, don't force her. Not on my account.''

''Sometimes children have to be forced to do the right thing.''

''I doubt she thinks of herself as a child anymore. I know I didn't at sixteen.''

How adeptly they avoided exploring the reason for Beth's anger, Maggie thought with discomfort. No doubt it was a subject best left alone.

''She's not too old to need guidance.'' After a swift glance, he began to tell her about Jake Browne and the painting on back of Sally's Garage. ''This jaunt to Florida has been for me as well as you. I've forbidden her to see him again, and Beth will stay out of trouble at Rhonda's house.''

''Oh.'' Maggie stared ahead, adding nothing more.

Adam darted surreptitious looks her way. ''Do you disapprove?''

''I have no business approving or disapproving, Adam,'' she reminded him.

''But you think I'm being too strict.''

''Sometimes girls that age find the word *no* as challenging as a red flag. If she's able to drive a car, she thinks she's an adult. She might be more attracted to making her own decisions than she is to that young man. When you give ultimatums, she thinks you don't trust her judgment.''

''I don't.''

She wanted to laugh at his emphatic tone but didn't dare. ''You can't let her know that, Adam. You'll make her determined to prove you wrong.''

He stared. ''You sound very knowledgeable about

someone you barely know. Are you talking about Beth or yourself?"

She squirmed at his direct hit. "You're right," she said finally. "I don't know much about Beth and shouldn't try to give advice. Sorry. I'll be quiet from now on."

"It will be a long, dull trip if you do that. I did ask for your opinion."

His expression was as apologetic as a puppy caught chewing a slipper. She could no more resist his smile than she ever could. The thought brought a surprising pang.

"Just for the sake of argument," Adam went on, "what *would* you recommend in this situation? You believe I should let her see him whenever she wants?"

Maggie thought a moment. "My only child is a little boy. I don't think I have any words of wisdom for you and Beth."

"Oh, come on. I can almost guarantee I won't take your advice. I'm too set in my ways. But I'm interested in what you'd suggest."

"Okay." She peered past the wing, saw they were passing a sizable-looking city and wondered where they were. "I'd try to work out a compromise. Allow them to see each other, but only when chaperoned. My guess is, the biker will lose interest quickly."

"I did tell her she could invite him to church."

"That's admirable, Adam, but do you think he would be comfortable with that? I was thinking more along the lines of having him over for pizza and a rented video." She smiled, her enthusiasm building. "Something rated G. He'll either pull a disappearing act or adopt the conservative approach and trade his leather for button-down shirts."

He grunted. "Very diabolical, but you've forgotten the third option. He's more likely to shoot the television and set the house on fire."

"Yes, there is always that." One corner of her mouth raised. "You're a hard sell, Morgan."

"Told you."

They exchanged smiles until Maggie, feeling her face warm, tore her gaze away. She strained to keep the conversation on a less personal level for the next hour. Almost before she knew it, she heard Adam communicating with the control tower at the Valdosta airport. Minutes later, they landed to refuel.

Maggie took that opportunity to run to the ladies' room. When she emerged, she found Adam conversing with what was apparently a family group waiting near the observation window. A thin, middle-aged lady wearing a faded cotton dress was speaking loudly in a thick Southern accent about her husband's pending arrival from Tampa. The three children flanking her, all dressed in worn T-shirts and shorts, seemed equally eager to talk with him and interrupted each other frequently. One of them, a small boy, constantly dipped his hand into a large bag of jelly beans he clutched. When the child offered a palmful of candy to Adam, he hesitated, then accepted the sticky gift with thanks. Maggie laughed.

Adam made friends everywhere he went, she remembered. Zack extended his best persona only when around people who could socially or professionally advance him. When at college, she had found his arrogance exciting, had believed it thrilling to be able to attract the notice of one of the most popular and hard-to-please men on campus. Later, after their marriage, she came to know his discrimination for what it was: self-serving snobbery.

She had seen him in action, dinner after dinner, party after party.

Why am I comparing Adam and Zack again? she asked herself. *I have more important things to think about.*

When they were airborne again, Adam gave her tightly interlaced fingers a sideways glance. "Still nervous about my driving?"

"No," she answered, and thought with surprise how this second takeoff had not disturbed her at all. "Just...nervous."

Adam nodded with understanding. "Since you couldn't get your mother's address from the alumni office, where will you begin?"

"The campus library should have copies of old yearbooks. Sometimes student and faculty addresses are listed in the back. At least I can photocopy her picture."

If nothing else comes of this trip, she thought, *I'll find out what my mother looked like.* She felt a shock of longing for even this small link. *Surely Emily Rose hadn't been sick the day the photographer was there; surely she hadn't been camera shy!*

"If that doesn't work, what next?" Adam persisted.

She wished he wouldn't ask so many questions, as though he sensed her investigation was doomed to failure before she began.

"Probably the hospital, then social services. If I hit brick walls everywhere, I intend to start legal action to force the hospital to release their records." She looked at him. "Why? Do you have any ideas?"

"Only that you might consider a private investigator."

"If I don't have any luck on my own, maybe."

The problem was, private investigators were expensive, and she would die before she mentioned her financial difficulties to Adam again. The possibility that she would be counting pennies in her thirties had never entered her head in younger days, when hope sprung as endlessly as a fountain. Zack and she had labored years for a comfortable way of life and found it, for a little while.

Maybe she should have sued for alimony after all, she thought, staring down at acres of pine trees and a terrain increasingly dotted with glittering lakes. But it hadn't felt right. She wanted to cut all ties with Zack. Even though he helped support Sam, she cringed at accepting his money for herself. But that had been when she had a decent job, of course. Had she known Zack intended to make her lose that as well as everything else…

She made an effort to relax and unhooked her fingers, splaying them across her knees. A comfortable silence fell between Adam and herself. In the landscape below, pine trees gave way to orange groves interrupted by square after square of houses. The sunlight pouring in the windows warmed her skin. Closing her eyes, she allowed the drone of the engine to drown her thoughts. She leaned back and began to drift.

Sometime later, the sound of Adam's voice jerked her to awareness.

"Orlando control, this is November-nine-six-two-one-Romeo. We're at fifty-one-hundred feet on a heading of one-seventy-five, requesting landing at Orlando Executive."

Seconds later, she heard a voice respond, "November-nine-six-two-one-Romeo, squawk four-two-one-seven. Maintain heading and speed."

Eyelids still drooping, she watched Adam twist a dial.

"November-nine-six-two-one-Romeo, squawking," he said.

She sighed peacefully. Adam sounded confident and professional. It was comforting to know she was in good hands.

"November-nine-six-two-one-Romeo," said the voice, "we do not have you on our radar."

Maggie came fully awake, her gaze flying to Adam. "Is everything all right?"

He held up a hand, silencing her. "I don't think the transponder's working."

"The *what?*" She heard the hysteria in her tone and bit her lip.

"The transponder locates us on radar. We should be fine, if nothing else is wrong."

"If nothing else is wrong!" she cried. "If they don't know where we are, how will they keep us out of the path of other planes?"

"They won't have *that* much traffic. It's not as though we're landing at Orlando International."

"But...anything could happen." She waited for him to reassure her, but he was pressing the transmitter button again.

"November-nine-six-two-one-Romeo, may I continue to land?"

She heard the control tower voice giving him permission. *Oh, Sam.*

"God help us," she whispered as they began to descend.

Adam's gaze met hers, a strange spark lighting his eyes. "Calm down, Maggie. We'll be okay."

"Aren't you going to pray?" she heard herself ask. If God really were there, He'd surely be more interested in faithful Adam's prayers than hers.

"I've been praying ever since we left Chattanooga," he told her.

And a lot of good it's done, too! she thought, forgetting all logic in her panic. She could not stop herself from asking, "The possibility of crashing is really remote, right?"

Caught in the complexities of landing, he did not answer. She squeezed her eyes shut. *Please, God, please, my baby needs me.*

Pictures flashed against her closed lids; scattered wreckage spread across singed earth; a closed coffin with Rhonda, Carter and Johanna and her brood gathered around. Zack would be there—Zack and Rayne. And poor little Sam. He wouldn't understand why Mommy was never coming home. Zack would take him for ice cream after the funeral, then a toy store and she would fade to a memory connected to the one photo her ex-husband would allow Sam to have on his nightstand. When next autumn came, would Sam remember their sunny walks in Central Park, where they kicked golden leaves into little piles?

There were so many things left undone: Sam's raising; the discovery of her real mother. And this valiant man beside her; she owed him something, too. An explanation, at least. No. A long, overdue apology.

Adam couldn't die! Beth needed him, even more than Sam needed her. How could she survive a second tragedy at this critical time in her life?

He was a good man, a shaft of sunshine in a dark world. She should have recognized that long ago. What a loss his death would be to everyone who knew him.

And who would weep for Maggie?

After an agonizing interval, she felt the wheels touch ground. The Cessna bounced up, then down again, followed by that paradoxical sense of increased speed that bridged flight and earth-bound travel. She strained forward, then back as the plane began to slow down.

She watched the muscles in Adam's jaw relax and sat up, dizzy with relief. Moments later, they taxied toward a hangar, and Adam brought the Cessna to a stop. Dipping a couple of fingers into his shirt pocket, he turned and extended his hand.

"Would you care for a melted jelly bean?" he asked.

She laughed, as she knew he meant for her to do. But her thoughts were troubled. Why had she automatically called on God when she believed they might crash? And why had doing so seemed as natural to her as breathing?

Chapter Ten

Maggie waited in the airport cafeteria while Adam talked to the mechanics. She was ravenous after their morning's adventure and ordered grilled cheese and vegetable soup. By the time Adam joined her, she was sipping a second cup of coffee and enjoying the memory of a wide slice of cherry pie.

"Thanks for staying," he said, sliding into the chair opposite her and signaling the waitress. "I know how anxious you are to get started."

"I couldn't leave without finding out what was happening with you and that plane. Hopefully you're not going to try and fly it back."

"Not right away I'm not." The waitress, who looked too young to be out of school, came over, and Adam ordered a hamburger and fries. As she walked away scribbling on her pad, he noticed Maggie's lifted brows. "Tomorrow I'll eat low-fat. Right now I'm giving myself a reward."

"You won't get any argument from me. Were the mechanics able to find out what was wrong?"

"They're going to go over the whole plane, but the transponder definitely needs to be replaced. You can't land at certain airports without it. I called John, and he said to do whatever's necessary." He paused as the waitress brought coffee, then stirred in a drip of cream. "There's a problem. They think it'll take a couple of days to order the part and install it."

"Oh, Adam. What will you do?"

"Take a minivacation, I guess. Someone has to return the plane."

"But your business!" Her heart skipped a beat. "And Beth."

"Harry is capable of running things without me." He moved uncomfortably. "As to Beth...I'll call her this evening after school. She'll understand." He did not look convinced.

"I hope so." She studied him with worried eyes. "This is all my fault."

He gave her a stern look. "And why is that? Did you sabotage the Cessna?"

"I couldn't sabotage a flashlight. But you wouldn't have come to Florida if it weren't for me."

"I'm here because I want to be, Maggie. No one put a gun to my head."

She lowered her eyes, then glanced around the sparsely populated room, with its plain white walls and patterned commercial carpet. Anything to avoid the warmth in his stare and the reluctant response it brought.

"You're very considerate," she said finally.

"That's what you think." Quickly returning her gaze to his, Maggie was surprised at his expression. He looked mischievous, yet oddly strained. "Wait until I ask if I can tag along with you."

"Tag along? With me?" Her voice sounded hollow.

"What else can I do down here? If Beth found out I visited the tourist traps without her, she'd change the locks on the house."

The waitress appeared with Adam's meal, then glided away. When Adam bowed his head for a moment, Maggie leveled uncomfortable glances right and left. No one seemed to notice them. After opening his eyes, he squirted a pool of ketchup on his plate, then mustard, and swirled the mixture with a French fry.

"Do you still do that?" she asked, appalled and amused.

Carefully avoiding her gaze, he popped the morsel in his mouth. "Only when I'm nervous about whether my presence is welcome or not."

"You know it has nothing to do with that."

Still not raising his eyes, he nodded. "Don't tell me. You want to investigate on your own. You're looking for your mother, and naturally you feel it's a private search."

"Well...yes."

"That's fine. I understand." He took a large bite of his hamburger and chewed while the silence lengthened. Tearing a napkin from the dispenser, he wiped his mouth. "I'll rent a motel room and catch up on the news." He dipped a couple of fries in the streaked sauce. "Maybe watch a few soaps and get hooked. I've wanted to do that for a long time."

Maggie eyed him suspiciously. He continued to eat without looking at her. She fought the melting but knew it was useless.

"All right, Adam. You can come with me, if that's what you want."

"Only if you're sure. I don't want to be in the way."

Their gazes locked. Struggling to keep down a smile, she said, "Don't push it."

While Adam finished his lunch, Maggie rented a Ford Escort, the only vehicle her budget would allow. She refused to worry about what Adam would think. When he arrived at the rental pick-up, he made no comment other than to ask if he could drive, an offer she accepted willingly. Her driving skills were still rusty, and she did not know Florida highways at all.

Adam absorbed the rental agent's directions to Bellen University without question, and minutes later they glided onto the East-West Expressway.

"A toll road through the city?" Maggie asked indignantly.

"You'd be surprised how many they have down here."

"You seem to know your way around. I guess you've driven in Florida before."

"We visited one of Allison's aunts in Altamonte Springs a few times during the early years of our marriage, but Aunt Bobbi died a long time ago."

Everywhere they went seemed to spur memories of Allison.

Maggie stared at the passing scenery, more scrubland and lonesome pines than she had imagined. The blue sky appeared low, weighted down with mountains of clouds. The sun burned through the windows, waging war with the Escort's hissing air conditioner.

When Adam exited and paid the toll, she viewed with astonishment the two-lane road he turned on. Lining the street were block homes not much larger than her apartment in New York, many of them painted shocking colors: pink nestled beside orchid, green next to brown.

Many were bordered by chain-link fences sheltering children, dogs, toys and the occasional plastic flamingo or daisy pinwheel. Gradually the pastel rectangles gave way to older, ramshackle frame homes, some with wide front porches, a few with thick columns that bespoke prosperous days long past.

"Are you sure we're going the right way?" she asked.

"I'm sure." He cocked an eyebrow. "You don't have the tourist's mentality about Florida, do you? The ad agencies would have you believe the state is wall-to-wall beaches, fancy night spots, family resorts, ritzy shopping malls lined with palm trees. That's down here, all right, but Florida is still largely rural and small-town. There's a lot of poverty."

She grew quiet, wondering if her mother had grown up in one of these graceless little houses. Not that it would matter.

"Would you like to hear some music?" he asked after a moment, fingering the radio dial.

"No." He looked surprised at her vehemence. "I mean, not particularly. Go ahead if you want to hear something."

"I'm sure there must be a classical station some-where."

"That's all right. Play whatever you want. I don't care."

"You don't? I remember a girl who demanded jazz if Mozart couldn't be found."

"People change. I seldom listen to music anymore."

"You don't listen to music?" he echoed in disbelief.

"Look, a sign to Bellen!" she exclaimed. The subject of the radio was dropped as Adam braked at an inter-section and turned onto a four-lane crowded with fast-food places and the usual jumble of businesses that could be found in any American city. Following a series of signs, he drove until they reached the campus.

Well-kept lawns, stately hardwood trees and old brick buildings lent a welcome air of age and tradition. Brilliant tulips lined the pathways crisscrossing the grounds, and students, backpacks slung over shoulders, ambled in all directions. Adam followed the signs to the library and parked.

The library reminded Maggie of a church with its wide row of steps, Corinthian pillars and a large double wing at the back, reminiscent of a cross. With Adam beside her, she ascended the stairs and walked through the lobby into the main room, hardly seeing the rich wood posts holding the exposed balconies on three sides or the intricate design of the balustrades. The librarian's desk was her sole destination, as if her entire life had been leading to this moment.

Arriving at the counter, she caught the attention of a young male librarian and tried to speak, only to discover her mouth was dry as a wasteland. It was Adam who asked where the old annuals were stored.

"What year?" the librarian asked, his brown eyes drawn to Maggie.

She found her voice and told him.

"Anything that far back is stored in the archives. People don't often ask to see the really old yearbooks, so we lock them behind glass for preservation. Let me get my keys, and I'll take you down."

After a quick elevator ride to the basement, the librarian led them past a row of glass-fronted bookshelves until he paused at one, selected a small key from an impressively crowded ring and opened the doors.

"Take as long as you need," he said. "My name is

David. Call me if I can help. Let me know when you're done so I'll remember to lock up."

Maggie, her gaze running along the spines, thanked him absently. With trembling hands, she pulled the volumes from 1960-1965 and set them on a nearby table. Adam slid one of the yearbooks from the pile and began to check the index as Maggie sat beside him, greedily turning the pages of 1963.

"This one doesn't have addresses, although the names are listed." Adam said softly, "The only Wilkerson I've found is a Samantha."

"Look up her picture. There's a chance she's a relative."

"Um, I don't think so," Adam said seconds later, pointing out a photo of a freshman girl, her pretty eyes slanting distinctively.

"Japanese-American. I don't think we can rule anything out at this point."

Adam smiled as if amused at her dictatorial attitude, and set the open book aside.

"This index doesn't have addresses, either," Maggie said, her heart falling. "But her name is here!" Holding her breath, she turned to the section on graduate students, her eyes moving rapidly across rows of youthful faces.

"There she is," Adam said gently, and pointed to a young woman halfway down the left-hand page. "She has your smile."

Maggie seized the book closer, studying her mother's face with a hunger that made her weak. Emily Rose stared back at her across time, her fair skin smoother and younger than her daughter's and framed by black hair cut in a bob reminiscent of Jacquelin Kennedy's. The shape of her face reminded Maggie of her own, and she unconsciously traced the line of her jaw as she continued to scan every detail. She noted that Emily's nose was longer and more classically beautiful than her slightly uptilted one, and her eyes appeared darker, almost black.

"She's lovely," Maggie breathed, and felt tears gathering.

"Like mother, like daughter," Adam said, and squeezed her hand briefly.

"No, no. She's magazine-quality beautiful."

"And what do you think you are? Suitable only for the shopper's guide?"

Maggie shook her head wonderingly, beaming into his eyes. "I've found her! I've found my mother!"

"Yes, you have." He looked as if he wanted to gather her in his arms but didn't dare. Abruptly her ecstasy died.

"Why didn't they publish addresses? Is paper that expensive?" She lifted another volume, then another. "Here's 1962. Maybe she was attending then, too." Pages whirled by.

Adam silently lifted 1964 toward him and turned to the back.

Taut moments passed. "Nothing!" Maggie cried.

"Maggie," he said, his voice full of promise. "Here she is again. And this one has addresses."

She snatched the book and saw another view of Emily, her face tilted away from the camera, eyes lifted upward as though viewing a distant dream. She appeared pensive, her faint smile mysterious.

"She looks sad. I wonder if she was thinking of my dad, or if she even knew him then."

"I wouldn't read too much into that pose." When Maggie sent him a questioning frown, he added quickly,

"She might have been thinking of him, of course, but it's apparent the photographer instructed all the students to look that way."

He gestured toward the photographs she had ignored. Every face on the double-paged spread gazed into the unknown. Momentarily cross at the theatrical photographer, she decided her mother still looked secretive, then wondered why she was trying to romanticize an affair into a doomed, star-crossed love story. She had not been so generous with Zack's adventures.

Because it was my mother and father, she admitted to herself. *And I want my birth to mean more than an unfortunate accident.*

She flipped to the index and searched. "Auburndale," she said, her voice trembling. "193 Jack Seminole Lane. Do you know where Auburndale is?"

"Vaguely. I'll find out."

While Adam went to search for the librarian, Maggie discovered a row of copy machines in the basement and fed coins into it, experimenting with contrast until she made the sharpest copies possible of her mother's photographs. By the time she finished, Adam had returned with David, and both men were talking as they waited beside the bookshelves.

"David has been giving me directions to Auburndale," Adam told her as she handed the remaining yearbooks to the librarian.

"It's easy as pie," David said, stacking the books beside the others and locking the glass doors. "Take Interstate 4 until you get to the Auburndale exit, then follow the signs. It's less than an hour away from here. You'll wiggle around a couple of lakes and housing developments, but you won't get lost. If you do, call this number." He pulled a business card from his pocket and scribbled on the back. "My ex-girlfriend lives right outside Auburndale. We're still friendly, so she won't hang up on you."

"That's kind of you," Maggie said, accepting the card.

"Nah." His eyes lingered on her. "If you need anything else, my number's on the other side."

Trying not to notice Adam's raised brows, she thanked David and moved toward the elevator, the photocopies gripped carefully in her hands.

"It appears you've made a conquest," Adam said as they buckled into the rental car moments later.

"Don't be silly. He looked younger than Carter."

Adam started the engine. "I don't know about that, but then I haven't seen Carter in a long time. Age didn't seem to matter to the librarian. Or maybe he thought you were younger. You do look young, you know." He paused, then added hastily, "Not that you're not. Young, I mean."

"I'm not interested in librarians," she said, feigning a fascination in the passing scenery. "Or anyone."

Adam made no answer. The silence grew heavy.

Maybe I shouldn't have said that. But it was the truth. Wasn't it?

Maggie drummed her fingers on her knees and told herself to relax. She watched for signs to the interstate, but Adam didn't need her help; he spotted them before she did and followed smoothly. Within minutes he drove the Escort onto the busy highway, accelerating drastically in order to keep up with right-lane speeds, the car whining in response.

"Lots of traffic," she commented.

"True," he said.

She dashed a covert look at the speedometer. "Everyone's going really fast."

"That's the way it is here. Go fast or get out of the way."

"I guess it's all the tourists."

"Probably."

She stared at him. He did not look angry, but the purposeful way he kept his profile to her meant something, as did his ping-pong responses to her conversational overtures. Strange how his silence buckled her emotions into a knot. Strange and disturbing. He exerted no hold over her. She had enough on her mind without worrying about him.

"Was it something I said?" she asked crisply.

"Pardon?"

"You seem unusually quiet," she explained, knowing there was no need for explanation; he knew perfectly well what he was doing. Men were maddening, every last one of them. Why should Adam be different?

"Sorry. I'm concentrating on driving." As if to illustrate, he glided around a station wagon crowded with children, then back into the flow of the right lane.

"That's good. I'd hate to think I'd said or done anything to offend you."

"Of course not."

"Great." She laced her fingers together. "I'll be quiet, too. I don't want to disturb your concentration."

"Thanks."

"No problem."

He cut her a glance. She slanted her eyes at him without turning her head and saw the grim line of his jaw weaken. As their gazes held, he almost smiled.

"Back at the library..." he began reluctantly, then stopped as if he did not intend to continue.

"Yes?" she prompted.

"I hope that comment wasn't directed at me."

"What comment?" She softened her voice, fearing she knew the answer.

"That remark you made about your not being interested in anyone."

"Oh, *that*. I didn't mean anything." But she had.

"Because I don't want you to think my being here is because I'm *interested*. Not in that way."

"Oh, no, I didn't think that," she lied.

"My only motive is to help."

"I know, Adam. Since we first met, your compassion is one of the things I've admired most about you." She averted her head. She was only making things worse.

"It's not that I don't find you attractive, because I do. I mean, I would if it weren't for—"

"Allison," she said, nodding, hurrying him along because she hated this conversation and the way it made her heart pound. "You're grieving for her, as you should be."

"Yes, I am, and of course there's Beth—"

"Both of you are grieving, yes," she said quickly.

"Not that you would be interested anyway." He responded as swiftly as she. "You've made it plain how you feel about a relationship because of your divorce."

"Right. Zack killed that part of me." But why, then, did she listen so intently to Adam's every word, as if her future, her very life, depended on what he said?

A tractor trailer truck, speeding out of the way of a red Corvette, wedged into their lane, and Adam hit the brakes. He appeared unaware of the discourtesy and chuckled humorlessly.

"Besides, we've been down that road before," he

said, faking cheerfulness. "Didn't work then. No reason it should now."

It was her turn to be silent. She felt scalded. Sick. Remorse pumped through her body. She fought the eruption, her arms crossing, fingers clawing at her ribs. And then the tears came. And the desperate, silent sobs. Ashamed, she turned her back to Adam.

"Maggie?"

She heard the disbelief in his tone and the concern. He never stopped, did he? No matter what she'd done, he had never stopped caring. She wept harder.

"Maggie, what's wrong?" He sounded devastated and fearful for her. Nearly blinded by tears, she felt the car veer to the right and up an exit ramp.

"No, don't pull off, I'll be okay," she said thickly without turning. Adam could not see her like this. It was bad enough he knew she had broken down. He didn't need to view her ravaged face, the way her nose shined strawberry red and her eyelids swelled when she cried.

"This is our exit," he said simply.

Oh, she thought. *We're going to my mother's house, or what once was her house. And maybe we'll find someone who knew her.* Somehow it didn't seem as important as before.

Adam drove the car into the parking lot of a restaurant and stopped, leaving the engine idling. He turned toward her, placing one arm across the back of her seat. With his other hand, he reached into his pants pocket and offered a handkerchief. She took it gratefully, wiping her eyes and blowing her nose with as much dignity as she could.

"I'm sorry," she said.

"Don't apologize for crying. You've been through a

lot these past few weeks. The tension must be unbearable. You need the release.''

She gave a short laugh through her tears. "I'm not sorry for crying.'' Her smile died. She was finding it hard to breathe. "I'm sorry for—for what I did to you, all those years ago.''

Adam did not pretend to misunderstand. Pain flickered briefly in his eyes. "Water under the bridge, Maggie. You did what you had to do. It would've been a mistake to go on with the wedding after you realized you didn't love me.''

She could not let him believe that. "I never said I didn't love you.''

"No, I guess not.'' He smiled faintly. "As I recall, your note said you were confused about your feelings. But I read between the lines.''

Then you read wrong. "I was a mess, Adam. Mom and Dad were pleased with you—especially Mom. Life with her became easier during the years you and I dated, and especially after we became engaged. She seemed happy with me for the first time in my life. I wasn't sure if marrying you was my decision or hers.''

"Maggie, who's to say it wasn't for the best? Look at what God gave us both to replace each other. Can you imagine life without Sam? And what would I do without Beth?''

"That's the other thing,'' she said, almost angry. "You are so devout, and I...'' She averted her eyes. Across the parking lot, an elderly man and woman emerged from a recreational vehicle and linked arms as they strolled toward the restaurant. "I saw myself becoming my mother—I mean, Rhonda. Running to church every time the doors opened. Listening to boring sermons I'd heard twenty times before. Cooking myself frazzled for the weekly potluck suppers and baking dozens of cookies for Wednesday night youth meetings. I couldn't buy into it. That just wasn't me, Adam!''

The sorrow in his eyes wounded her. When he ran the back of his hand along her cheek regretfully, she wanted to weep again.

''Well,'' he said, struggling for a light tone, ''it could have been worse. I might've worn that gaudy-looking tuxedo—do you remember insisting on the blue frilled shirts to match the bridesmaids' gowns? You could have changed your mind while I was standing in front of everybody. At least we were able to call most of the guests ahead of time and post signs on the church doors for the ones we missed. I didn't have to look anyone in the eye and tell them in that lounge lizard costume. People wouldn't have known whether to laugh or cry.''

He was trying to make the disaster less than it was, when she knew what it had cost him. He was breaking her heart.

''Not only did I leave, I left the cleaning up for you,'' she said miserably.

''Actually, Rhonda made most of the calls.''

''Did she? I never knew.''

''No, you got out of town quick, didn't you? Where did you go? I always wondered.''

''I stayed with my friend Janice until college started. Her parents had a summer home in Vermont. I had to escape, even though it meant forfeiting my parents' support for school. Mom would have made my life a horror. I don't think she's ever truly forgiven me.''

''Sure she has.''

She shook her head. In the sudden quiet, broken only by the hum of the engine and passing trucks on the highway, she asked tremulously, ''Have you?''

His hand felt like velvet on her cheek. She leaned into the caress, then straightened with embarrassment as he moved his fingers to the back of the seat.

"I thought I had," he said. "But I guess I wasn't aware how much our breakup still hurt. Thank you for speaking, Maggie. You've melted an old grudge that needed to be gone. I have closure now."

Closure. She heard the sound of steel doors clanging shut. That was what she wanted, of course. But she felt strangely heavy when he guided the car back into traffic.

Chapter Eleven

Auburndale was a typical Florida town, which would fit into a single one of Maggie's New York skyscrapers, Adam thought as he drove west on Highway 92. Almost every building and house was one-storied and made of block, including the flat-topped shopping centers. Grass and trees looked sunburned and tired; puddles of sand skirted every road. They passed a canning plant for a major orange juice company. He didn't care to imagine why it exuded a rotten smell. Typical, typical, all of it, yet this subtropical town, like so many he had seen in Florida, exerted its own hot, moist charm.

After asking at a service station, he easily found Jack Seminole Lane. He was conscious of Maggie's tension as they drove a short way down the four-lane road, the numbers rapidly growing higher. When they reached the address given in the yearbook, he slowed, checked the number again, then drew to the curve. The motorist behind honked his horn and swung around their car with tires squealing.

"It can't be," Maggie murmured. "Tell me this isn't the right number."

Adam caught himself reaching for her hand and pulled back. "I'm sorry, Maggie."

"We're at a dead end." She sounded curiously unmoved. "All of this has been for nothing."

He gripped the wheel. "Don't give up now. We're just getting started."

After driving along the shoulder at a crawl, he turned into the parking lot and guided the rental into a slot. Beside him, Maggie stared at the maroon-bricked building, its federal blue shutters and white pediment, an oddly pleasing adaptation of colonial American architecture. Auburndale Seminole Bank, declared the tall, impressive sign in front.

"Adam, I don't see what use—"

"It never hurts to ask," he said decisively, and unfastened his seat belt.

The interior of the bank looked passably elegant with its burgundy-and-navy color scheme, although the mahogany furnishings, reproductions all, spoke more of Queen Anne England than early America. The office was moderately busy with customers one and two deep before a row of brass-railed teller stations. On the opposite side of the room, three women and one man worked behind desks scattered at discreet intervals, each with two wing chairs flanking the customer side. Adam nodded toward a well-preserved lady dressed in a tailored suit at the desk nearest the doors. When Maggie did not respond, he lightly nudged her in that direction and tried not to think how hopeless and broken she seemed.

The woman, who was clicking long, ivory nails across a computer keyboard, glanced up and smiled brightly. "May I help you?"

Adam smiled back, an apology in his eyes. "We need some information unrelated to banking, I'm afraid." She tilted her head inquiringly. "Some time ago, a house was located on this property. We're looking for the owners. Any chance someone here might remember?"

"Oh my, that's a tough one. I've only worked at Seminole since the early nineties, when my oldest started at FSU and it was either work or starve, you know what I mean?" She waited for Adam's nod. "I think the bank was built in the eighties sometime." Her gaze drifted across the room. "Why don't you ask Jerry Doty over at the middle desk? You can't miss him. I think he's been here longer than anyone."

Adam thanked her and walked forward, pulling Maggie along as if she had suddenly gone blind. But Jerry Doty, whose nameplate declared him to be a vice president, could offer little help.

"The bank was built in 1985," he said in the slightly flattened accent of the native Floridian. "That's when I transferred to Auburndale from Sarasota. I vaguely remember some talk about a house being demolished on the site, but that's all I can tell you. You could check at the courthouse."

Disappointed, Adam dared not glance at Maggie. "That's worth a try, although I'm not sure they can help us. We already know who owned the house. We're trying to find out where the owners are now."

Jerry Doty glanced from Adam to Maggie and back. "Are you detectives?"

"Family," Maggie said. "I'm trying to trace my roots."

"I see." The vice president studied her, tapping an expensive pen against a leather desk blotter. "I know who could help you. Our president, Buddy del Ray. He's at a conference this week, but he'll be back next Monday.''

''Monday,'' Maggie repeated, her tone desolate.

''I'll write down the name,'' Adam said. ''We can call him from Chattanooga if we don't find any other leads.'' He thanked the man, shook his hand and guided Maggie from the building.

''Our timing may be off, but that doesn't mean you won't find your mother,'' Adam began, but she shook her head, walked to the south edge of the bank and peered around the corner. He followed her tentatively, meeting her halfway when she reversed direction.

''There's some older homes down that road,'' she said, striding to the northern side. ''And others over here. That was a good idea you had, Adam. Maybe somebody will remember.''

The old Maggie had returned. Adam willingly let her take the lead as they walked from house to house, business to business. Considering the greetings they received at some of the residences, he felt as welcome as a vacuum cleaner salesman. The humiliation was worth it so long as Maggie recovered her spirits. Given their lack of success, he couldn't guess how long her determination would endure.

He was finding it difficult to keep his own motivation going. The midafternoon sun burned through his shirt and threatened to set his scalp on fire. He began to worry about sunburn, always a problem with his light skin. Not only that, but Maggie's apology had reopened old wounds, and he had to be careful not to let her know. She felt bad enough already. He had not lied when he spoke about the old hurt dissolving, but he imagined the scar would be tender awhile. Especially since he fought a constant temptation to touch her when he knew it would be the worst thing possible.

"This place is incredibly full of transients," she said in exasperation after one young woman, toddler twins clinging to her knees in the front yard of a trailer, explained she had moved from Minnesota last year and didn't know a soul except her neighbor to the left. "It's probably not worth the change, but I'm going to call the number the librarian gave me."

They were approaching a convenience store, and while she went to the public phone near the highway, he promised to buy a couple of soft drinks. Inside, a trio of ceiling fans stirred the sluggish air but did little to cool the building. One of the overhead fluorescents flickered. Adam nodded to an elderly lady behind the counter and headed for the cooler at the back. Grabbing a cola and ginger ale, he brought them to the cash register.

"Hot day for it," declared the woman as she punched in the numbers. Her husky voice and the puckered lines circling her lips betrayed many years of smoking. "I been watching you two walking along. What you doing, selling something? Because I ain't buying, I'll tell you that right now."

Adam explained briefly.

"Is that right? Well, you've come to the right place. I've lived in Auburndale all my life, and I remember there was a Wilkerson family on this road at one time. Don't know much about them, but I knew the brother and his wife. They're dead now, but the son still owns the family business. I hope he gave his folks a discount, but I doubt it."

A moment later, Adam met Maggie halfway across the parking lot. Before he could relate his discovery, she launched into an energetic tirade.

"I never heard such a ditzy female in my life. She had call waiting, and in the few minutes we talked she received two calls. She kept switching back and forth and calling me *Mark*. I thought I had the wrong number, because she said she'd never heard of any David. But then she gave me a message to tell him he's a creep and not to call her anymore."

Adam flashed a perfunctory grin and blurted, "I think I've found Emily's cousin."

Wilkerson's Funeral Home had been built on a gentle rise overlooking a lake. With manicured lawn and sculpted topiary, the two-story brick building fit discreetly into its neighborhood of expensive, aging homes. When Adam slowed to park in the circular drive, Maggie almost leapt from the car.

After Maggie gave a shorthand version of why they were there, a kind-eyed receptionist ushered them into Charles Wilkerson's office. Despite her eagerness, Maggie could not help noticing the luxuriousness of his workplace. What seemed to be an acre of plush carpeting led to a massive teak desk, behind which sat the owner and proprietor. As they approached, he stood with practiced elegance, the quiet lighting of the room casting a warm glow on his skin. Charles Wilkerson was a large man, both in height and girth, but his precisely tailored suit made him impressive rather than overweight.

"Mandy tells me you're my second cousin?" he asked as he shook Maggie's hand, then Adam's. Though he spoke pleasantly, she noticed a suspicious light in his eyes. Maybe he thought she was going to ask for a loan. Or a free coffin. After she told her story, rapidly and succinctly before he decided to throw them out, the suspicion changed to interest. He settled into his chair and motioned toward the love seat opposite the desk.

"So you're the secret," he said, his voice low and rumbly as thunder. He would make an outstanding bass if he sang, Maggie thought with excited irrelevance. "I've always wondered what really happened to Emily Rose. She was about ten years older than me and way too young to die. Aunt Felicia and Uncle Harold let on it was diabetes, but Daddy knew something was up when they had Cottonwood do her service." Cottonwood, he explained, was a funeral home in Frostproof, a town about sixty miles south.

"Can you tell me anything about her?" Maggie asked eagerly.

He leaned back in the leather chair and tapped the side of his nose reflectively. "I was only eleven or twelve when she died, and you know how kids are, especially boys. They don't study grown-ups much, and to me she was an adult. I remember her as pretty in a dark way, a lot like you, Mrs. Gould. She was fun and liked to laugh. But that's about all. Maybe you should ask her sister."

Maggie's heart almost quivered to a stop. "My mother has a sister?"

"You didn't know? I'm sorry I can't tell you Cousin Nancy's last name. She's been married more than once and I've lost touch. The last I heard she'd moved to Georgia."

"You don't know her address?" Maggie asked, dismayed.

"No, but they might at the nursing home. Aunt Felicia and Uncle Harold moved to Twin Towers Retirement Center in Winter Haven. He died about three years ago. I know because we did the interment."

"My grandmother is still alive?"

He assured her this was so. Winter Haven was less than five miles to the east, he told them, and easily reached via Havendale Boulevard. As he continued giving directions to the center, Maggie watched his mouth move with horrified fascination. How could he live so near and know so little? Didn't he care about his relatives?

She could not help asking, "When did you see my grandmother last?"

"I guess it was at the funeral. I'm sorry to tell you Aunt Felicia doesn't remember whether she has visitors or not. We've never been a close family, not on that side. My wife's people are another matter, but you're not interested in them."

What luxury to have so many relatives one could dispose with half of them, Maggie thought as they took their leave of the funeral director. He made no overtures to continue their relationship, not even for the length of dinner, and she returned to the Escort feeling deflated.

Less than a half hour later, her spirits began to rise along with the elevator she and Adam ascended in one of the twelve-story "towers" at the retirement center. The nurse accompanying them had explained this building was dedicated to guests needing full-time care, whereas the other provided hotel-like service to its healthier residents.

"You've never visited Miss Felicia, you say?" the nurse asked. "That's strange behavior for a granddaughter. I'm not trying to offend you, but I have to call it like it is. I see these lonely old people day after day. Nobody visits them, nobody cares. It's like their whole life amounted to nothing. They don't so much die as fade away."

The elevator doors slid wide, and a nurse's aide walked in. "Have you been scolding again, Ruth?" he chided. "I heard you before the doors opened." He swept a glance over Adam and Maggie. "Don't pay her any mind. She chomps on everybody."

"I'm sure she's right," Maggie said. "But I'm afraid I live too far away to visit." Maggie could see no reason to relate her story to everyone in Florida, and Adam remained obligingly silent.

"Yeah, yeah," Ruth said. "That's what everybody says."

It suddenly seemed important to win the nurse's approval. "Will it disturb my grandmother if she doesn't know who I am? Can she speak at all?"

"She doesn't get upset too easily, so I imagine whatever you say will be all right, within reason. And yes, she can talk when she wants to, but you won't be able to make sense of it unless she's having a really good day. That doesn't happen much anymore."

Ruth led them a short distance down an immaculate, tiled hallway bordered with rooms and opened the door to one labeled Iris. "Afternoon, Miss Felicia," she said loudly. "You have visitors."

Maggie clutched Adam's arm in abrupt panic.

Misunderstanding, he whispered, "Do you want to go in alone?"

"Not a chance," she answered softly.

Felicia Wilkerson sat on the edge of her bleached pine bed, her back turned to the door. She appeared transfixed by the panorama outside the room's picture window. Maggie followed her line of vision and saw a horizon uncluttered by buildings or mountains. In the foreground, sailboats moved lazily across a lake while a speedboat, a slalom skier attached, plowed trails in the water. In the distance sprawled the small city, its businesses and homes liberally softened with clusters of trees. No wonder her grandmother stared.

Slowly, as Maggie and Adam approached, Mrs. Wilkerson turned her gaze toward them. Not a spark of interest lit the dreamy haziness of her eyes. For all its lack of expression, her face commanded attention. It was the face of old aristocracy, Maggie thought. A high forehead; heavily lidded eyes; long, straight nose; lips thin and wide; a noble chin with only a slight sagging of the flesh beneath. Felicia Wilkerson's features seemed too strong for beauty, but in her youth she must have been striking. She was striking now, even with gray curls clipped short and permed, the style so many elderly women adopted. Instinctively Maggie felt that, given the choice, her grandmother would wear her hair long and swept up to display her elegant neck. And instead of the cotton gown and duster that puddled around her knees, she would hold court in a satin kimono or silk pajamas.

But Felicia apparently no longer cared about such things. Her world had diminished to a single room with its picture-postcard view of the outside. Whatever she had been, whether good or bad, was gone now. Although Maggie could see nothing of herself or Emily Rose in this woman, her heart constricted with pity.

She pulled a chair directly in front of her grandmother. Adam stood a few feet away, propping his weight against the deep windowsill. Maggie introduced Adam and herself in clear tones and hoped the old woman would not feel Maggie's anxiety and become alarmed.

Greetings made, Maggie searched her mind for a gentle way to explain their connection. As seconds ticked by, no way suggested itself, and Mrs. Wilkerson's eyes sought the window again. Her brow puckered as if she were annoyed at the barrier Maggie presented.

"We've never met before," Maggie began awkwardly, "but I feel as though I know you." That was not precisely true, but she had to start somewhere. "Do you...have any grandchildren?"

The old woman remained silent. This was the wrong approach. Maggie glanced desperately at Adam, but he shook his head slightly. Thanks for the help, she told him with her eyes.

"Do you think about your children sometimes?" she continued. "Nancy? Do you remember her?"

No response. Maggie moistened her lips.

"Emily Rose? Can you tell me about your daughter, Emily Rose?"

This time, Maggie imagined she saw a flicker in her grandmother's eyes, but still the old lady said nothing. Frustration pounded through her, followed by grief. She seemed destined never to know about her mother. This pathetic woman could tell her nothing. The aunt would remain elusive, merely a first name she could not trace. She thought of her only remaining options, lawyers and detectives, and wanted to weep. She had to make a connection on some level or return to Chattanooga feeling like a failure.

She studied her grandmother's dispassionate face for a moment, then cradled her hands. Felicia grimaced at the intimacy but did not try to pull free. Cheered by this small victory, Maggie began to speak. She told her grandmother about her life; who she was, how carefully she had been raised, the beautiful son—Felicia's great-grandson—she loved. She spoke simply as she would address a child, with short sentences and few details. When she finished, the room vibrated with quiet. Intensely aware of Adam's stillness beside her, Maggie felt her heart pulse in her ears as she waited.

After one moment stretched into two, she thought, *How pointless to continue to hope there will be a reaction. Felicia Wilkerson is an empty husk.* Overwhelmed with sadness, Maggie stood and kissed her grandmother's forehead. As she passed by Adam, she felt his hand at her back as he joined her. His touch was welcome; she needed the comfort.

"Em-i-ly."

At the doorway, Maggie spun to face her grandmother. Again, the old woman uttered the name, her voice sounding rusty with disuse. Maggie rushed to Felicia's side and crouched in front of her, stroking her grandmother's hands encouragingly. Felicia began to rock back and forth. Rather than seeming upset, she appeared comforted by the name she repeated like a mantra. Finally, after multiple entreaties, Maggie accepted there would be nothing more. Eyes glistening, she touched Felicia's shoulder and whispered goodbye.

In the hallway, Maggie saw the compassion in Adam's face and unabashedly headed for the comfort of his arms. Resting her cheek on his chest, she drew courage from the strong beat of his heart, the feeling of power in his body.

She was so tired, tired of being alone.

"Is everything all right?"

Blushing like a schoolgirl caught necking in the parlor, Maggie broke away from Adam and saw the nurse Ruth making her way down the corridor with a tray of medications. "She wasn't very lucid," Maggie told her.

"Like I said, she has her good days and bad," the nurse replied. "If you'd visit more often, you might have better luck."

Maggie could hardly bear the look of condemnation on Ruth's face. "I can't."

The nurse shrugged. "There's nothing I can do, either. Everybody has their own lives to live." She began to move past them.

Adam stepped in her direction, and Ruth paused. "Does Felicia's daughter ever visit?"

A brief downturn of golden eyebrows. "Oh, sure. She comes a little more often than you two, I'll give her that. Once a year without fail at Christmas. You must be a real close family." She turned to Maggie. "Wait a minute. Don't you know? Aren't we talking about your mother?"

"My aunt," Maggie said, and found herself explaining the circumstances of her birth all over again.

"I wish you'd told me before," Ruth said when she finished. "I didn't mean to sound ugly. My husband tells me I pass judgments too fast, but I accuse him of the same thing. We have to keep each other straight."

"You wouldn't happen to have her aunt's address on file, would you?" Adam asked.

When Ruth hesitated, Maggie held her breath. "We probably do," the nurse said, "but I don't have the right to give it to you. I'm sorry."

"Could you at least tell me her last name?" Maggie begged. "I understand she's remarried several times."

"I don't see how that would be a problem. I don't even have to look it up, because the name is so distinctive. We're Civil War buffs at our house, thanks to my husband, so you'll be able to see why I remember it. The last time I saw Miss Felicia's daughter, she called herself Nancy Lincoln."

"That gives us a start." Maggie glanced at Adam.

"Wonder how many Nancy Lincolns there are in Georgia?"

Ruth regarded her for a moment. "A lot more than you'll find in Savannah, I imagine," she said innocently. "I've always wanted to go to Savannah. From all I've heard, it's a beautiful place. Even the name sounds good."

Wordlessly Maggie grabbed Adam's hand. Ruth saw the look in her eyes and smiled.

"I hope you find her," she said, "I'll be praying that you do."

"Thank you," Adam said. "I believe God has already used you to help us."

Maggie couldn't help wondering if he was right. So much had happened today, so many minor miracles, that she could almost—*almost*—sense a guiding hand at work. The feeling was imaginary, of course. It had to be.

But Adam was real enough. Without his help, she would have given up in frustration. She might never have met her grandmother or found out about her aunt. How was it that he came back into her life at precisely the moment she needed him most? And what forces had been at work to make a man with his qualities of integrity and selflessness?

Who could form a man like Adam?

The question worried her as they made their way back to the car. She found her gaze returning to his strong features again and again. When he looked at her inquiringly, she flashed an embarrassed smile and glanced away.

Chapter Twelve

After booking rooms at a motel, Adam and Maggie parted to prepare for dinner and make phone calls. After unpacking her clothes, Maggie took a deep breath and lifted the phone receiver. Only when the metallic recording repeated Nancy Lincoln's number did she relax. She had been certain it would be unlisted.

Fingers shaking, she began to dial. *She won't be home.* The phone rang once, twice, a third time.

"Hello?" said a feminine voice.

"Oh. Hello. Is this Nancy Lincoln?"

"Yes," returned the voice, inflecting the syllable with caution. *She thinks I'm a salesman. Hurry and say something before she hangs up!*

"I'm not selling anything," Maggie said with a nervous chuckle. "I—I'm…" *I'm what, besides ruining this conversation?* "Let me make certain you're the Nancy Lincoln I'm looking for. Is your mother's name *Felicia,* your father's *Harold?*"

"Ye-es." She sounded more guarded than before.

The phone became slippery in Maggie's hand. "And—and you had a sister named Emily Rose?"

A brief pause. "Who is this?"

Maggie swallowed. "I'm Emily's daughter." Tears flared as she whispered the words.

"Emily never had any children." Angrily she demanded, "What are you trying to pull?"

"Nothing! I just want to find out about my mother—"

"What are you after? Money?"

"No! Please, you don't understand. Until last week I thought the woman who raised me was my mother. But then I found out Emily was my *real* mother—my birth mother, I mean—and I've come to Florida in search of who she was. I wanted to contact my relatives—"

"Well, search somewhere else. My sister is gone, and she never had children. I won't have anyone blackening her memory!"

The phone went dead. "But I have to know for my son's sake," Maggie told the receiver. "I have to know."

She brushed moisture from her eyes and walked to the window, lifting the curtains. *No more tears.* She had wept enough today to last a lifetime.

Dusk was falling over the neon-lit island. The windows of the restaurant beside the pool revealed a healthy crowd with plenty of families with children. Good. Not a hint of glamour there, just the promise of average food and plenty of it. A pit had opened in her stomach, and she had to fill it with something. She closed the drapes, grabbed her overnight bag and headed for the bathroom.

More than an hour later, renewed if not cheered by a long, hot shower, she was putting the finishing touches to her makeup when a knock sounded at the door. Seeing

Adam through the peephole, she let him in and motioned toward the table and chairs.

"Wow," he said, sitting as directed. "Are you sure you want to be seen in public with this farm boy, city girl?"

Applying a lightly tinted moisturizer to her lips, Maggie eyed his reflection in the mirror. He was wearing jeans and a white golf shirt, his damp hair curling over the collar in back. "You look fine, Adam." He looked wonderful, but she knew better than to say so. "Did you go shopping?"

"Had to. Either that or wear the same clothes every day I'm down here."

"That's right. You didn't know you'd need a change of clothing." She pulled a wide belt from the suitcase and cinched it at her waist. Moving back to the mirror, she adjusted her dress above and below the belt, turning to see if the material fell gracefully.

"I didn't know I'd need a bathing suit, either," he added, his eyes shifting away when she caught him looking.

"Did you go for a swim? I'm envious. I didn't think to bring a suit, either."

"I know where you can get one cheap."

Maggie frowned into the mirror. "That's all right." This was not a pleasure trip, not in any sense of the word. "I just washed my hair."

"That's what they all say," Adam replied lightly, standing as she collected her purse and card-key.

Outside, the fresh coolness of the evening air swept over them. She felt relaxed suddenly, almost cozy despite the unfamiliarity of her surroundings. For one wild moment, she wanted Adam to drape an arm around her shoulders as they walked. She wanted to burrow against his chest as she had at the nursing home.

Before she could act on her crazy impulse, she said hurriedly, "I called my aunt."

"Did you? I was afraid to ask. But you don't look pleased. Your conversation didn't go well?"

"You could say that." Maggie looked down, becoming absorbed in descending the steps. "She hung up on me."

"Oh, Maggie," he groaned. "Why?"

"She figured I was after money or something, I don't know. She was very suspicious. Maybe she thought I was a lunatic."

A boy trotted by them wrapped in a towel, water dripping from his hair and skin. He greeted Adam and grinned as he passed.

"Hi, Justin," Adam returned. "We raced in the pool," he explained to Maggie. "He beat me every time." They walked quietly for a moment. "You're not letting this little setback with your aunt discourage you, I hope."

"It doesn't feel like a little setback." She had been foolish to imagine God was guiding her search. Arriving at the restaurant, she paused as Adam opened the door. "I think it's over as far as what I can do. When I save some money, I'll hire someone to find out more."

"It doesn't have to be over. When the plane is repaired, we'll fly home via Savannah, that's all."

Seeing the hostess approach them, Maggie did not answer immediately. She followed the middle-aged lady to a booth near the salad bar. After they were seated, the woman distributed menus and promised a waitress would be coming soon. While Adam began to read, Maggie ignored her bill of fare and leaned forward.

"Would that be possible? To fly to Savannah?"

"Why not? Savannah International is a Mode C airport. That means it's not too big for us to land. I know, because John takes his family to the east Georgia coast every couple of years."

"But what if she won't see me? What if I can't find her address?"

"Most communities print addresses in the phone book. We'll find her somehow, don't worry."

"But if she refuses to let me in her home..."

Without looking up, Adam said, "That's when being as wise as serpents and harmless as doves comes in."

"What's that supposed to mean?"

"We don't tell her you're coming. You simply show up. Nobody could turn you away from their doorstep."

That remained to be seen, Maggie thought, but her spirits rose. After placing their orders, Maggie said in a rush, "Have I told you how much I appreciate what you're doing for me?"

"No more than five hundred times," Adam said.

"I have to admit I'm glad something went wrong with the plane—as long as it was minor, I mean. Without you, I would have given up when I saw the bank."

Adam unrolled his silverware. "No, you wouldn't. You've always been resourceful." In spite of his protest, he looked pleased. "Let's get some food. I'm hungry enough to eat this table."

When they returned with loaded plates, Maggie took a bite of meat loaf, then stopped chewing as she noticed Adam's bowed head. She waited until he finished to swallow.

"Have you called Beth yet?"

"Um." He flinched around a mouthful of fried chicken. "Wish you hadn't reminded me."

"Adam, you mean you haven't? What time was she expecting you to return?"

"No time, really. I told her I'd call this evening."

"I hope she doesn't believe you've crashed."

"No, I'm sure John will think to tell her about the plane." A worried look entered his eyes. "Pretty sure. Like I said, she wasn't expecting me at any certain time." He broke a roll in half and spread butter on it. "I'll call as soon as we're done with dinner."

"I'm phoning Johanna's to speak with Sam, too."

"Do you plan to call Rhonda, as well?"

"Yes, of course."

They ate in silence for awhile. At a nearby table, a toddler in a high chair emitted a piercing squeal and shook his drinking cup, dislodging its cap. Grape juice streamed over his tray and T-shirt and puddled on the floor. The young man Maggie assumed was the father groaned loudly; the mother stood, seized the child and headed for the ladies' room, her expression harried.

"I wonder why my grandmother let Dad take me," Maggie said.

"You can ask that after listening to power lungs over there?"

She was not amused. "You'd think after losing her daughter, Felicia would want to save anything that belonged to her, especially her daughter's own child. I know I would, if the child were Sam's."

"Maybe your grandparents felt they were too old to raise a baby. They might have had health problems. That would explain the move to the retirement center."

"Maybe," Maggie said slowly. "Or it could be they blamed me for her death."

"That would be rather Middle Ages of them."

"People can't help how they think."

"Maggie, are you trying to make yourself feel bad? Is this somehow becoming your fault?"

"I suppose it's possible my mother didn't get along with her parents," she continued, as though she had not heard him. "An illegitimate child in those days brought shame on the whole family."

"You can ask Aunt Nancy these questions."

"If I get the chance."

Adam put down his fork. "Listen to me, Maggie. You've been through some hard times recently, and finding out about your birth hasn't made things easier. But in one day you've discovered a grandmother, a cousin and an aunt you never knew you had. *In one day.* I don't know about you, but I consider that pretty successful."

"Well, maybe, but——"

"*And,* I happen to believe success breeds success. I feel certain you're going to find what you need. Now, you can think what you please. You can take the blame for something you had absolutely nothing to do with or imagine every negative thing that can happen to hinder your search. *Or* you can be thankful for what's been accomplished and look forward to what will come."

He lifted his fork and stabbed a cucumber. His face was flushed.

After a moment, Maggie spoke. "Adam..."

"What?" He still sounded angry.

"Would you be interested in splitting a piece of hot fudge cake?"

After seeing Maggie to her room, Adam returned to his and phoned the Covingtons' number. He and Maggie had agreed it would be best if he called Beth first, before Maggie spoke with Rhonda. Beth answered on the second ring.

"Dad!" she cried after he greeted her. "What took you so long? I've been trying to reach you for hours. Mrs. Rhonda showed me this great recipe for making chicken and dumplings with lasagna noodles instead of rolling the dough out like Mom used to, and I was hoping you'd join us for dinner. We already ate, but there's some left. Honestly, it's the best thing I've ever made. Are you hungry or have you eaten?"

Guiltily Adam told her he was sorry to miss her cooking, then explained about the plane and his extended stay in Florida. A long silence fell from his daughter's end of the line. Finally she spoke.

"How long will you be there?" Her tone was cool, but not as angry as he'd expected.

"Only one or two days," he assured rapidly. "We'll be back as soon as the plane's fixed." There was an uncomfortable pause. He wished he could relate the reason for their trip to his daughter, but it wasn't his story to tell. "Oh, and, Beth? We'll be taking a very fast side trip to Savannah on our way home."

"Savannah," she repeated.

"Yes." His collar was getting tight. "Maggie wants to visit a relative there."

"Oh, really?"

Adam sensed the phone lines freezing. He heard a whispered conference in the background but couldn't make out the words. Beth must have had her hand over the mouthpiece.

"Mrs. Rhonda's here with me. She wants to know if she can speak with Maggie."

"Oh, she's in her room, and I'm in mine." There was no need to talk so loud, he guessed, but he wanted Beth to understand every word he said and what he meant in between the words. Kids could imagine anything these days. "The last thing she told me before saying good-night was that she planned to call Rhonda."

"I'll tell her."

"Thanks, Beth. And give Rhonda my best."

"I will."

"And, Beth? I want you to know how much I appreciate your staying with her."

"You already said that before you left."

"Yes, and I'm sorry about this—leaving you alone. I didn't have any idea the transponder would go down."

"Seems kind of strange, actually."

It seemed strange to him, too, come to think of it. John was meticulous about maintenance. A person could almost think God meant him to stay with Maggie. But maybe he shouldn't be reading everything as a miracle. "Well, stranger things have happened," he said, forcing a chuckle.

"I guess so." He wished she wouldn't sound like a robot imitating his daughter. "Something pretty strange happened here today, too."

Glad she volunteered something, he murmured encouragingly.

"Jake Browne was waiting for me at my car after school." She could not have said anything that would upset him more. She knew it, too, because she didn't wait for him to react. "Yeah, Jake told me you'd been to visit him at work last week. I think it's interesting you didn't mention it to me."

I was hoping I wouldn't have to, that maybe he'd leave you alone after our talk. "The conversation didn't go very well, I'm afraid."

"That's what he said. I want you to know it's pretty humiliating that you'd do a thing like that. I'm not a baby."

"I know. To tell you the truth, I'm sorry I went." *Especially since it didn't do any good.* "But I wouldn't have done it if I weren't concerned about you."

"Yeah, I see how concerned you are."

He stared at the print of a vase of flowers over the television and counted to five. "Well, now that you've brought up the subject of Jake Browne, what about his painting?"

"You mean the one on the back of the garage?"

"That's the one." His heart missed a beat. "You're not saying there are *more* paintings, are you?"

"Not yet. It was fun posing, though. He's a great artist, isn't he, Dad?"

Adam's jaw set. "Exactly when and where did this artistic adventure take place?"

"I forget. Didn't you say Mrs. Gould is going to call Mrs. Rhonda? I guess we'd better get off the line."

"Beth, he is way too old for you—"

"We'll talk when you get back," Beth went on breezily. "When you and Mrs. Gould get back, I mean."

"Beth, I forbid you to see him—"

"Bye, Dad. Nice talking with you."

"Beth—"

Click.

Adam slowly replaced the receiver. So much for long-distance parenting. He paced to the bathroom, changed into his damp swimsuit, grabbed a towel and hurried to the pool. No one was there, and he was grateful for that. He dived in and swam several furious laps. When tiredness calmed his muscles, he turned and did slow backstrokes, moving only enough to keep afloat while he stared at the dark sky and prayed.

Chapter Thirteen

Maggie and Adam met for breakfast the next morning in the motel's restaurant. They ate leisurely, having nothing to do to fill the day aside from shopping for forgotten items. Over his second cup of coffee, Adam suggested they visit one of the many tourist spots in the area.

"I'm not talking about the biggies that will make us feel guilty we don't have our kids with us," he said when Maggie asserted she was not there to vacation. "I'm thinking of someplace to help pass the time. Someplace peaceful."

Studying his tired face, Maggie weakened. "What did you have in mind?"

"There's a garden area in Lake Wales called Bok Tower. It's not far, and I think you'll like it."

Less than an hour later, she and Adam were strolling across well-kept pathways while the carillon tolled its haunting notes from the tower. Maggie saw beauty everywhere: Technicolor flowers, grass so green it almost hurt the eyes, dignified old trees bearded with moss.

When they tired of walking, she and Adam sat on a bench and watched the other tourists pass by.

"Allison wanted to come here," Adam admitted after a while, "but we never seemed to have time. She'd visited as a child and hoped I'd get to see it. Now I can understand why."

"It's very lovely," she said, although the fact he'd taken her instead of his wife made her uneasy.

Adam sighed and stretched his arms along the back of the bench. "It's so quiet here you can almost touch it. There's a sacred feel to the place, don't you think? It reminds me of some cathedrals I've visited."

Highly aware of his fingers brushing her shoulder, Maggie said nothing, although she nodded agreement.

"I needed this," he continued in a contented tone of voice. "My call with Beth last night didn't go well, but I won't bore you with that."

"I'll bet she misses you, unlike a certain son who shall remain nameless. When I spoke with him last night, he begged me not to come home yet. He and Andrew are building a tree house."

Adam shook his head sympathetically. "Children."

"Ungrateful wretches," she added.

"But what can you do?" He shrugged helplessly.

"Not a thing. Love them and be prepared to get stomped."

"My mom used to say I'd never understand what a parent goes through until I had my own kids. She was right."

"My mother used to say the same thing." Maggie's grin faltered. "Rhonda, I meant."

"I know," he said softly. "She's your mother, too, isn't she?"

I thought I had resolved this. So why does the word

mother *keep sticking in my throat when I think about Rhonda?* "You haven't told me how your mom is," she said, carefully changing the subject. "Did she ever remarry?"

"No, and I don't think she will. But it's not for lack of opportunity."

Adam's father had been killed in a car accident while Adam was still in college. Now he launched into a series of anecdotes about his mother's suitors over the years that sent Maggie into gales of laughter. Because Mrs. Morgan continued to live in Texas in the home where her only child had spent the first decade of his life, Maggie had only met her once. She remembered a petite, vibrant woman with an outrageous sense of humor. She'd liked her immediately.

"With all those boyfriends, why hasn't she married again?" Maggie asked, catching her breath. "The magician sounded interesting."

Adam's smile became pensive. "She says she can't. She still feels married to Dad."

Maggie's eyes lingered on his face as she wondered if he felt the same about Allison. She would not ask; it was none of her business. But when they stood and ambled toward the exit, it seemed the most natural thing in the world that their hands bumped together, then joined.

They stopped at a roadside café for lunch, both of them ordering salads. While waiting for their food to arrive, Adam used the pay phone to call about the progress of the plane.

"The part came in overnight," he told Maggie when he returned to the table. "They're working on it as we speak. We have a choice. Either wait until tomorrow, or start heading back this afternoon. If all goes well, we could be in Savannah by five. Then again, the mechanics might have problems, and we'd be stuck in Orlando overnight.''

''As much as I don't trust that plane, I think we ought to give it a try. I know you're anxious to get back to Beth.''

Adam nodded, although he didn't look too happy. ''And you're eager to meet your aunt.''

But that isn't all, Maggie thought. *I have to get away from you. Holding your hand felt too good, and I don't like the turn my thoughts are taking.*

The plane was ready when they arrived and the weather favorable for flying. During the flight to Savannah, Maggie said little. Adam seemed no more willing to talk than she. When they landed, she headed for the first phone she saw and scanned the directory. To her vast relief, Nancy Lincoln's address was listed.

Since they would need a car only for that afternoon, Maggie decided to splurge on a Taurus. She had noticed how cramped Adam was in the Escort. He looked pleased at her choice. As he drove through the neat squares of the city, Maggie drank in the lush gardens, immaculate streets bordered with trees, well-kept buildings and, without wanting to, the steady procession of tourists wearing T-shirts, shorts and jeans, and carrying camcorders. If not for them, she could imagine she'd slipped into an earlier time, when the South was prosperous, aristocratic, genteel, but hiding a dark legacy.

Am I like that?

Her gaze drifted sideways. There were no hidden facets in Adam; she would stake her life on it. If he saw a need, he offered his help without complaint and without bragging about it. If he was angry or disappointed, he didn't plot revenge. When he laughed, the humor came from his heart, not from a desire to flatter or act the sycophant.

From the time she first knew him, he had been like this. As a teenager, she thought him wonderful, but not exciting enough, not *dangerous*. As an adult, she knew him for what he was. A hero. But he was not *her* hero. Even if he could forgive her for the past, his religious faith stood between them like an impenetrable barrier.

Braking for a traffic light, Adam returned her stare with a curious smile. She smiled back, then turned away. She could not look at him.

Adam *lived*. He was the most fully alive person she had ever known.

And she had traded his faithfulness and vitality for…what? A whisper of trouble, a misty haze of glamour that was only an imitation of the real thing?

No wonder the music died.

"We're here," Adam said, and pulled to the curb in front of a brick two-story.

Like the other compact mansions on either side of the street, Nancy Lincoln's home was set well back from the road. The house, designed in the Georgian style, looked to be decades old but had been maintained well. Shrubbery of varying heights edged the drive and sidewalk leading to it, and a terraced riot of flowers surrounded two imposing oaks in front.

"Your aunt must have a very green thumb—no, a green hand. Either that or a gardener."

Maggie took a deep breath and reached for the door. When Adam made no move to exit, she asked, "Aren't you coming?"

"Not unless she invites me. Given your lukewarm reception on the phone, I doubt she'll be happy to see me. Your first meeting should be private anyway."

"I guess you're right." It was ridiculous to feel abandoned, but she did.

The walk to the entrance pulled slightly at her calf muscles, the upward incline feeling more elevated than it looked. The double doors, painted a deep red, loomed before her. She punched the doorbell without allowing herself to hesitate and heard Westminster chimes reverberate through the house in response.

The door opened to a chained crack, and a woman peered outward.

"Who is it?"

Maggie recognized the throaty, throbbing voice of her aunt from last night's phone call. "Are you Nancy Lincoln?"

"I know who I am," she said, sounding peeved. "What I want to know is, who are *you*?"

Maggie did her best to look harmless. "We spoke last night. My name is Margaret Gould, although I'm usually called Maggie."

"Yes, and I'm usually called before I'm visited. You're that person claiming to be Emily Rose's daughter, aren't you? I thought you said you were in Florida."

"I was, but I flew here this afternoon to meet you." If she would take down the chain and open the door just a little wider, Maggie might be able to see what she looked like.

"Well, you have a lot of nerve, I'll say that."

"I know I should have called, but I didn't think you'd let me come if I did."

"You'd have been right."

"Please talk with me. I've visited your mother in Winter Haven and your cousin in Auburndale, but I didn't learn much about Emily Rose. I have to find out about my mother. I hope you can understand that. Not only for my own curiosity, but for health reasons. My mom—the woman who raised me—said Emily Rose had diabetes. I have a little son. It's important for us to know our genetic background.''

The older woman was silent for a moment. "Is Cousin Henry still running that funeral home?''

"Henry? I thought his name was Charles.''

"It is. I was checking to see if you knew. You can't be too careful, you know.''

Maggie agreed fervently. Surely the woman would let her inside now.

"Who is that man there in the car?''

"He's a friend, my pilot.''

"I don't want him coming inside. I don't know him from Adam.''

Maggie stifled a nervous laugh. "He'll understand that.'' With sudden inspiration, she repeated her aunt's earlier words. "You can't be too careful these days.''

"No, you can't.'' Her eyes raked over Maggie. "I don't keep money in the house.''

"Mrs. Lincoln, I'm not after anything except information.'' She had never met a more suspicious woman. Moving jerkily with growing anger, she opened her purse and pulled out copies of Emily Rose's yearbook pictures. "This is all I have of my mother. I deserve more, don't you think?''

After one long, searching glance, the woman unhooked the chain and opened the door. Maggie slipped inside before her aunt could change her mind. The foyer was impressive with a curving staircase, an opulent chandelier hanging from a two-story drop, a curving balcony leading to what she imagined were bedrooms. Downstairs, several wide doorways led to a living and dining room, and straight ahead, a spacious room with a plump sofa, love seat and armchair with matching ottoman surrounding a massive fireplace. It was to this place Mrs. Lincoln led her, after snapping shut some half-dozen locks or more.

As she walked, Maggie's aunt quizzed her about the date and location of her birth. Her voice was engagingly husky, her vowels rounded with a Southern accent that made Maggie wonder as to its origin. Eastern Georgians spoke like that, not native Floridians, which was what she assumed her aunt was; but it fell charmingly on the ears whether faked or not. Maggie answered her queries as she sat on the love seat and Nancy settled on the sofa, then began to speak of her father's affair and the secret she had recently discovered.

As she spoke, she searched for a resemblance to Emily Rose in the woman across from her. Nancy's eyes were a dark blue like her own, her face attractive in spite of a threading of wrinkles around mouth and eyes. Other than the shape of her eyes and the angle of cheekbones, she saw little of her mother in Nancy. She was several inches shorter than Maggie, her figure thickening but still shapely. Now that her guarded expression was fading, she looked to be one of the most feminine women Maggie had ever met; the kind of woman who bathed in scented bubble baths, showered herself in perfume and spent hours carefully preparing hair and makeup. Not a hint of gray marred Nancy's short, dark hair. Here she was in her own home at six o'clock on a weekday evening, dressed in an elegant floral dress, hose, heels, earrings and a pearl necklace, apparently on the chance someone might happen by. Abruptly Maggie remembered her manners.

"Were you on your way out?" she asked.

"No." Nancy hurried on, seemingly very interested

in her now. "Do you mean to say your father's wife raised you as her own? I can't believe any woman would do such a thing. I wouldn't."

With a twinge, Maggie admitted she didn't believe she could have, either.

"I think I remember him," Nancy said. "Your father. Lyle and I—Lyle was my first husband—were living in Sanford during most of the time Emily Rose attended Bellen." Her hands moved expressively as she talked, and Maggie was hard-pressed not to watch them. "I paid a surprise visit once. Not on purpose, but I had gone to Orlando to shop and simply decided on the spur of the moment to visit Emily Rose's apartment. There was an older man with her. They were having tea, dear, nothing shocking. But I *thought* something was going on when he rushed off. And Emily Rose was simply too full of explanations, if you know what I mean. He was her professor. They were working on a project. Blah, blah, blah, blah, blah. I didn't believe a *word*."

Tremulously Maggie said, "Then you *do* believe I'm her daughter."

"I'm willing to accept the possibility, although don't expect to receive any money from my sister's estate or my parents'. They ran through a lifetime of savings in two years at the retirement home, and Emily Rose was a student and never had anything anyway. What you see around you is due to marrying well and hiring a marvelous investment broker. Don't expect me to put you in the will, either. I have my pet charities, and I plan to live a long time."

Maggie closed her eyes. "Mrs. Lincoln, please. I don't want your money."

"All right, all right," she said, waving a hand and laughing a little. "I simply wanted to clear that up in case you had any fantasies from some movie or other. Better to be safe than sorry. Besides, you do look like her a little bit, or I wouldn't have let you in the house. But it's more than simply looks. I see my sister in the expressions running across your face." She clapped her hands angrily. "I could just shoot my mother for hiding this from me all these years! She must have been so ashamed. But oh, it does my heart good to think Emily Rose is living on in you."

Glowing, Maggie said, "You don't know what it means to me—meeting you, finally speaking with someone who knew my mother, especially someone so close to her." She hoped she wasn't going to cry again. "What can you tell me about her?"

"Oh, my, my. What can I tell you about Emily Rose? It's been so long. She was far too young to die, you know. In my memory, she'll be a young girl forever. Although, of course, that was what she was. Oh, she had personality, she did. Ten young women could enter a room at the same time, and some might be prettier than my sister, but it was Emily Rose who caught the eye. She had charisma, that certain something."

Not wanting to miss a word, Maggie slid to the edge of her seat.

"That, of course, explains why she was always in trouble," Nancy added.

"Trouble?"

"With our parents." The older woman looked past Maggie and fiddled with her necklace. "Oh, Emily Rose was no angel. Not that she did anything really *bad*, but she simply drove Mother and Father to distraction with her sneaking out at night and coming home late from school. It was always to see boys. Emily Rose was quite popular. Oh, yes, very popular."

Nancy's eyes narrowed thoughtfully. "Mother wanted her to be serious about her studies, but Emily Rose knew what she wanted out of life. She wanted to find a husband who would care for her, to cherish and provide her with a good life. That's all either of us ever hoped for." She laughed and gestured at the room. "It's ironic that I achieved what *she* deserved more than I. We had a bet going in our teens as to which of us would marry first and best, and who would get to join a country club before the other. I was older and got to the altar before her, but you can be sure she wouldn't have been far behind—if she had lived."

Of all the things she had anticipated hearing about her mother, good or bad, this was not one. Nancy was describing the type of woman Maggie scorned most— someone who used a man for a meal ticket.

"But she was going to school when she met my father. She was a graduate student," she argued.

"Why, naturally she was, Maggie. What better place to find the sons of rich men than an exclusive college? I think your father must have been an accident. I don't mean to speak lowly of your papa, dear, for I'm sure he was as wonderful as could be. But Emily Rose aimed higher. At least, I thought she did. A couple of months after I saw her and your father, Lyle and I moved to Miami. I don't suppose I ever saw her alive again."

Maggie felt her face flush. "If she was only looking for a wealthy husband, why did she have me?"

"Well, now, that's an interesting question. Abortions weren't so easy in those days, but they were possible. You've made me think, Maggie. Perhaps she did love your dad and thought she could make more of him than he was. She couldn't have wanted the quiet academic life. That wasn't her at all. Yes, it could be she was determined to have him. If so, then getting pregnant would've been the logical thing to do.''

Maggie stared. "Exactly what are you saying?"

"Oh, don't get huffy." She clapped her hands together. "How much you look like Emily Rose right now! She was always getting mad at me. But you don't need to get angry. It's an old, old story—trapping the man with a child."

"But my father was married."

Nancy looked perplexed. "Why should that have bothered Emily Rose? Should she consider the feelings of a woman she'd never met?"

Maggie debated this in silence. "Dad never would have left us. Not his family."

"Nobody knows what another person will do," Nancy said shrewdly. "Especially when you're talking about a man."

"He loved my moth—stepmother. You never saw them together. You can't make that kind of judgment."

"And I'm not trying to," she said, throwing up her hands. "You asked about my sister, and I was doing my best to tell you how she thought and did. I can't help it if you don't like what you hear."

"You're right. I'm sorry." Maggie didn't want to offend her only source of information, but disappointment nearly choked her. "Do you have any pictures of her?"

With an exaggerated cry, Nancy assured her she did and exited to search for the family photos. Returning a few minutes later, she laid a stack of photograph albums on the coffee table. Maggie turned pages while Nancy rambled about summers at Sanibel Island, cotillions they had both attended, boys Emily Rose had dated.

Mindful of the time and Adam waiting in the car,

Maggie broke into her aunt's chatter. "What about her diabetes?"

"You know, that's an interesting thing. The only other diabetic person in our family was a great-aunt on my father's side. And Emily Rose was perfectly healthy until she died. I guess it must have been her pregnancy. Some women contract the disease when they're expecting, I've heard. And that explains a lot to me. I always have wondered how she could suddenly get diabetes and die from it like that. If I had known pregnancy was involved, I could have slept better in those early days."

"Do you have children?"

"Gracious, no. Staying married is hard enough without the friction a child causes, although I don't mind petting a baby now and then. But as to changing diapers and waking up in the middle of the night for a squalling infant? Not me!"

So much for cousins, Maggie thought. "I'd better go," she said, rising. "My friend is waiting."

Nancy, bubbling now with Southern charm, urged her to stay for a cup of tea. When Maggie refused, Nancy removed several photos of Emily Rose from the album and gave them to her niece—shots of Emily Rose as a baby, a little girl, a teenager and a young woman standing alone at the end of a pier. Gratefully Maggie took them, then supplied her address and phone number when asked.

"I didn't know it would be so much fun to have a niece," Nancy said. "Now I'm going to check on you to see you're who you say you are. And don't you dare be mad about it. If I find out you're not pulling a fast one, I'd like us to get together again soon."

Maggie expressed her willingness and finally made

her way from the house to the car. She slid into the seat and apologized for making Adam wait so long.

"No problem," he said, watching her. "I slept a couple of hours, jogged three miles, wrestled a groundhog, ran under the sprinkler and had a cracker sandwich, so I wasn't bored. Now only one of those was the truth— you pick. How was it in there?"

"Like going to a banquet and coming away hungry," she replied.

They stopped for dinner at a small restaurant on the edge of the city. With its simple frame exterior and stained-glass windows, the eatery resembled a church, and Adam wondered if maybe it hadn't been once. After taking seats in a booth, he ordered grilled chicken and Maggie asked for coffee and a wedge of black-bottomed pie topped with chocolate-chip ice cream.

"A woman after my own heart," the waitress said as she walked away.

"You sure you don't want whipped cream and chocolate syrup with that?" Adam asked with raised brows. "How about some cake?"

"The pie should do for starters," she said, resting her elbow on the table and cupping her chin. "I need a lift."

"Well, if that combination doesn't raise you up, we'd better hire a crane." Her smile was feeble, and Adam felt moved to touch her arm briefly. "Don't be sad, Maggie. Your aunt's recollections are over three decades old. People reconstruct memories all the time. You've seen the studies—no two people remember exactly alike. Why do you think there are four gospels? Nancy's perceptions are her view of the truth, her interpretation— no more than that."

"My mother must have been so...shallow."

"She was young," he said softly.

"Growing older hasn't helped Aunt Nancy's development."

"She's probably projecting her own personality onto Emily Rose."

"I don't think so, but thanks for the kind words."

She swept smoky eyes over his face, her expression thoughtful. He had noticed her doing that a lot lately, looking at him as if seeing someone different inside his skin. It puzzled and excited him, but at the same time alarmed him. If she was becoming as attracted to him as he was to her, they had a problem. And it was not the kind of problem he could pass off as a joke.

"You are the most compassionate person I've ever known," she said quietly.

He almost jumped, so intimately spoken were her words. Despite the direction of his thoughts a second ago, his first reaction was to drawl, "Now, ma'am, you're makin' me blush—"

"Don't Adam." He saw the seriousness in her eyes and ground to a stop. "I'm not playing. I really mean it."

His heart began to accelerate. "Well, thanks, Maggie, but I don't deserve such praise."

"You deserve a lot more than that. I wish..." She waited as though hoping he would prompt her, but he could not help her. Not now. "I wish I had *really* known who you were...back then." She laughed dryly. "Maybe you were right about my mother's youth. I shouldn't condemn her lack of character and poor decisions, not when I made so many mistakes myself at that age."

Their eyes locked. Adam could hardly breathe.

Father, help me. She was reaching out to him, and it

took all his strength not to circle the table and grab her—
Maggie, the woman he had loved his whole adult life.
If she had only felt this way before he'd met Allison, he
would have—no, that wasn't fair. His late wife was not
the problem, and neither was Beth. Among the delights
of heaven, would sweet Allison resent him remarrying?
Hardly. And Beth could not resist Maggie forever. But
if Maggie had lost her faith as she claimed, they were
not compatible.

Or were they? Could they make it anyway? One part
of him cried *yes!* But he knew better. His belief in God
meant more than a philosophical disagreement or a pref-
erence for contemporary furniture over antiques. God
had woven Himself into every cell, every bone and cap-
illary of his body. He could no more exist apart from
faith than he could separate from his skin. And living
with a woman who didn't recognize or accept her need
for that same truth would drive a wedge between them
no earthly love could heal. And it would hurt Beth.

There was hope, though. Although the ultimate decision was between her and God, he would do everything
to help Maggie regain her faith. He resolved to be there
when she needed him, to pray for her constantly. But as
a friend. Nothing more was possible at this point. For
now, he must tread lightly to preserve Maggie's pride
and not, please God, to hurt her. Aching inside, he
prayed for courage to deny himself what he wanted most
in this life. He had not felt such pain since Allison's
slow dying.

"We all do things we regret," he said slowly. "The
important thing is to go on, not live in the past." He
fingered his fork. "That's what Beth and I are trying to
do, with God's leading." That was enough. She knew
what he was talking about; she'd heard the verse about

being unequally yoked together. Still, he swallowed hard before adding, "You and Sam have a bright future together, I know you do."

By the way her eyes flickered and moved away, he knew she had not missed the point. His heart felt heavy enough to drop through his shoes. When he spotted the approaching waitress, he brightened with the relief of a man stranded on a desert island.

"Here comes your sugar fix," he said heartily. "I guess you don't have to worry about diabetes anymore."

"I never knew to worry about it until this week, but I need to find out if the type of diabetes my mother had will make Sam more likely to get it."

She sounded normal, not on the verge of tears as he had feared. Maybe he'd overestimated her feelings. But she spoke little after they began to eat, and half her pie remained on the plate when she placed her napkin on the table.

The parking lot's gaslights flamed to life as they walked from the restaurant. "What's your pleasure, Maggie?" Adam asked as he unlocked the passenger door. "Shall we press on to Chattanooga? I'm experienced with night flying."

"Aren't you tired?"

"Not especially." She looked disconsolate as she sat in the passenger seat, and he felt compelled to lean downward, one hand lingering at her open door. "But I'm not in a hurry, either."

"We'd be pretty late getting in. I'd hate to wake up Mom and Beth."

"That's true, and it's a school night. Why don't we stay over? We can set out early tomorrow."

In agreement, they drove to a motel near the airport and booked rooms. After saying good-night to Maggie,

Adam walked next door, shifted his department store bag containing a last change of clothing, removed his card-key and entered. He saw the usual double beds, both looking to have mattresses no thicker than pie crusts. A card above the television proclaimed movies could be rented for a small fee. His eyes roamed onward and snagged at the unexpected door beside the metal clothes rack.

The desk clerk had given them adjoining rooms.

"Swell," he muttered. Nothing like knowing the love of your life was sleeping only a few feet away. *Father, what are You thinking? Is this a test? I might not be strong enough to pass it.* And then he thought, *Face it head-on. Don't try to ignore it.*

He went to the door and knocked. "Maggie, it's me."

Seconds later he heard locks moving aside. Opening the door, she gave him a sober, inquiring look.

"I thought if you were planning on calling Rhonda tonight, we might as well make one call do for both. Why don't you come in, and I'll phone?"

She agreed without enthusiasm, walked to the aisle between the beds and sat on the edge of the bedspread. He took the opposite bed and reached for the telephone. Their knees almost touched. She looked so lost and alone sitting across from him.

Maybe *facing it* hadn't been such a great idea. The quicker he got her out of this intimate place, the better. He tore his eyes from her face and stared at the buttons on the phone. Long seconds drifted by.

"You know what?" he said, forcing a laugh. "I've forgotten the number."

"Why don't you let me dial?" she said, and pulled the phone toward her. "No, keep the receiver. Beth will answer before Mom can."

She was right; his daughter answered on the first ring. Before he could do more than utter her name, she interrupted breathlessly, her voice shaking.

"Dad, where have you been? I've been waiting and waiting for you to call. I've tried the airports and everywhere I could think to get in touch with you."

"Hold it, honey. Calm down—"

"It's Mrs. Rhonda. The ambulance took her to the hospital a couple of hours ago. I'm so sorry, Dad!"

He looked into Maggie's anxious eyes and felt his stomach fold into a knot. "Don't cry, baby. Take your time and tell me what happened."

By the time he hung up, Maggie's face was ashen. "It's not Sam, is it?"

"No, Maggie, but it is bad news. I think we'd better leave tonight after all. Your mom's had a stroke."

Chapter Fourteen

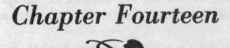

By the time they landed in Chattanooga, it was past four in the morning. While Adam fetched his Riviera from the lot, Maggie called the hospital. Rhonda Covington was holding her own, the nurse told her. And yes, she could see her briefly. Intensive care allowed exceptions to their hours in cases like these.

On the nearly empty, well-lit city streets, Adam's car gulped the miles between airport and hospital. Maggie's palms were moist, and she could not keep still. "I should have known this would happen," she said as Adam raced through a series of green lights. "She kept having dizzy spells. I shouldn't have left her—not so soon."

"You couldn't have known. The doctor told you she was all right."

"I was supposed to take care of her. That's why I came down here."

"Maggie," he said in a firm voice, "you are not responsible for her stroke. Stop blaming yourself."

She started to protest, then stopped. Burdening Adam with her guilt accomplished nothing, but she could not help feeling Rhonda's illness was her fault. Since coming to Tennessee, she had argued, questioned and confronted her mother countless times. She had not considered the toll such friction would take on the health of a convalescing woman. Not to mention her search for her biological mother. How badly that must have hurt.

"I need to call Johanna and Carter," she said numbly as Adam swerved into the entrance of the sprawling, eight-storied hospital. "Beth wouldn't have known to do that."

"Why don't you visit your mom first? If she's doing well, you might want to let them finish a decent night's sleep."

Adam dropped her off at the front and went to park the car. Inside the enormous lobby, Maggie checked with the young woman at the information booth and discovered that intensive care was on the fourth level. She scurried to the elevator, then down shining tiled floors to a forbidding set of closed doors leading to intensive care. She buzzed and stared intently through the window at the two nurses behind the desk. They both looked in her direction, and one lifted a hand indicating she would be there in a moment. Maggie nodded and bit her lip.

"Mrs. Gould?"

She turned, startled, and saw Beth emerging from the visitors' waiting room. Beside her was the pastor of her mother's church.

"Beth! You should be home in bed!"

"I couldn't," she said, her eyes welling with tears.

The pastor squeezed Beth's arm and extended a hand toward Maggie. "Mrs. Gould, I'm James Dixon from Parson's Ridge Bible Church. We met last Sunday."

"I remember," Maggie said, shaking his hand. "It's

good of you to come, both of you, but I'm here now. You should go home and get some rest.''

''Appreciate the concern, but Beth and I have been nodding off now and then, haven't we, girl? The waiting room is equipped with comfortable sofas and recliners.'' He inclined his head toward the open doors, and Maggie glanced within, seeing a large room with several clusters of people taking advantage of the cheery, overstuffed furnishings; some sleeping, others whispering softly. ''Besides, we had to be near Mrs. Rhonda. She's a very special lady.''

''It's all my fault,'' Beth said in a hollow voice.

''I want you to listen,'' the pastor said. ''I never heard such carrying on in my life. We're all in God's hands, little girl, and only He knows what's best. We've got to remember He's in control, and His timing is perfect.''

This was precisely the sort of thing Maggie didn't want to hear right now. Beth lowered her head, seemingly no more cheered by his words than she was. Down the hall, the elevator doors slid wide, and Adam emerged, spotted them and headed their way. Behind Maggie, the door cracked open.

''May I help you?'' the nurse asked.

''I called about my mother, Rhonda Covington?''

''Oh, yes. You can come in for a couple of minutes, then I'll have to ask you to wait until the next visiting time which will be at nine-thirty in the morning.''

Maggie slipped past the doors and followed the nurse. Patient rooms were glassed-in cubicles surrounding the nurses' station, which was like a hub in a square wheel. Her eyes moved restlessly over the sleek counters backed with monitors and other incomprehensible equipment. A few nurses, male and female, moved in and out of patients' rooms, most of which were shielded by vertical blinds. Maggie's mouth was dry, her breathing quick. None of this seemed real.

She questioned the nurse as they walked: Was her mother going to be all right? What was the extent of the damage? But the woman told her only that Rhonda was stable, and she would have to speak with the doctor in the morning.

Rhonda's room was directly opposite the doors, on the far side of the central station. The nurse walked in first, saw Rhonda's closed eyes, then gestured for Maggie to enter while pressing a finger to her lips. Maggie watched the woman leave, then tiptoed to the head of the hospital bed and forced herself to look down.

Rhonda's face was unnaturally pale. Electrodes ran from her heart to a monitor that beeped softly at each beat. Intravenous fluids dripped into the vein inside her elbow. Her curls had flattened against the pillow, and Maggie felt a ludicrous urge to find her comb and fluff it.

There were so many things she wanted to say to her mother, but she didn't dare wake her. She scanned Rhonda's small frame, which was draped with a thin white blanket. Maggie gently straightened the coverlet over her toes. Rhonda's feet were frequently cold. Maggie often told her to wear socks, but her mother declared nothing looked tackier with a knee-length gown than a pair of booties. She could almost hear her saying it, and for one wild second she wanted to laugh.

Her hysteria faded. She hoped her mom wasn't aware of what she was wearing now. The nubby hospital gown had been washed so many times, the color in the printed flowers had nearly all faded away.

Rhonda sighed then, and her eyelashes swept down,

then up. Maggie, plastering a bright look on her face, returned to the head of the bed.

"Hi, Mom. I hope I didn't wake you. What's going on here? Can't I leave you alone for a minute?"

Rhonda's lips moved as if trying to smile. She muttered something that sounded like Maggie's name, then a procession of unintelligible words. Hearing herself, she frowned in frustration, her eyes bewildered and lost.

"Don't try to talk," Maggie said swiftly, her heart shattering. *Look cheerful. Don't let her see how bad this is. Not yet.* "You'll be better soon, but right now you need to rest. The nurses won't let me stay with you long, but I'll be outside in the waiting room. I'll come back every time they let me, okay? And I'm going to call Johanna and Carter, so don't you worry about a thing. The most important step is for you to recover your strength. Please close your eyes, Mom."

To her surprise, the older woman obeyed. Maggie stroked Rhonda's brow and bent to kiss her cheek. "I love you, Mother," she whispered, and blinked slowly to contain her tears. When Rhonda's breathing grew even, Maggie crept from the room.

Returning to the waiting lounge, she saw Adam sitting on a striped sofa with an arm around Beth, who clutched a tissue and stared downward. The pastor had pulled a straight chair closely to them and looked to be speaking earnestly. He broke off when he noticed her approach.

"How is she?" Adam asked.

"I don't know," she said miserably. "Her speech is garbled, and she seems confused."

The minister rose and offered his seat. "I had an opportunity to speak with Dr. Stallbart earlier." As he spoke, he moved another chair beside Maggie and sat.

"He said the stroke seems to have affected both sides of the brain, but it's early days yet."

"That doesn't sound good." Maggie heard anger in her voice.

"He said it might mean she'll avoid paralysis in one side or the other," Reverend Dixon responded kindly. "On the other hand, some patients have difficulty re-learning coordination, especially as it relates to walking, dressing and feeding themselves."

"You mean she might not be able to walk?"

"Like he said, it's early days yet. You'll be able to talk with him in the morning. He might know more then."

"I should have been home earlier," Beth said dully.

"Beth had an unexpected meeting after school," Reverend Dixon explained. "She's bound and determined to make this whole thing her fault despite all I say to the contrary."

Adam hugged her to him. "You did the best you could, Beth. You called the ambulance, waited to get in touch with me, then stayed at the hospital like an adult. I'm proud of you."

Maggie leaned toward the girl. "If anyone's to blame, it's me. I shouldn't have left, not when I knew she was ill."

Beth looked at her briefly, then away, as if unable to meet her eyes. "When I called her after school there was no answer. I thought she was in the bathroom or something. I remember being irritated she didn't have an answering machine. Why is it old people never buy answering machines?"

"Beth," Adam soothed, patting her shoulder.

"Well, what if she got scared when she didn't hear

from me? What if she thought I was in a wreck, and that made her so upset, she had a stroke?''

"Now you're talking foolishness.''

"Dad, the doctor said there's a medication that might have made the stroke go away, or almost. But she had to get here quick enough for it to work. I didn't make it!'' She began to cry.

Maggie could not bear her tears. She sat on Beth's other side and took her hand. "Please don't think anyone blames you for this. I accept full responsibility. In fact, I want to thank you for staying with my mother and taking such good care of her.''

Beth stared at their intertwined fingers, flashed a look of regret at Maggie and then, as if she didn't want to hurt her feelings, slowly removed her hand. Flinging both arms around her father, she buried her head on his chest and sobbed.

A little before noon on the following day, Johanna arrived to relieve Maggie at the hospital. By mutual agreement, she had left Sam and her children at home with Sid, who had taken off the rest of the week to help. Before Maggie left to grab a few hours' sleep and a shower, she and Johanna went downstairs for lunch in the hospital cafeteria.

"You haven't been able to contact Carter yet?'' Johanna asked, picking at a plate of fries. Her haggard face was stamped with shock, mirroring Maggie's feelings.

"I've told the university, and they're sending someone to the dig. Apparently his cellular is out of range. They assured me he'd know by nightfall at the latest.''

"Good.'' Johanna shuddered. "I'm wondering if I can do this. I just want to run for the hills. I can't stand the thought of Mom being helpless.''

"You *can* do it because she needs you," Maggie said firmly. "You'll be fine. You're better at nurturing people than I am. But I know that you'll have to get back to Sid and the children eventually. And Carter can't stay. His dissertation depends on his being at the archaeological site in Mexico. He can't waste all those years of study. Not when he's so near getting his doctorate. I understand I'm the one who is most free to stay with Mom, and I want you to know I will."

"Oh, Maggie," Johanna said, her eyes filling. "You don't have any idea how you've relieved me."

Maggie covered her emotions by taking a sip of iced tea. "It's the least I can do. She's stood by me forever."

"I'll take care of Sam as long as you need."

"Thanks, but after Mom's stabilized, I want him here with me. I'm dying for him already. I can stay with him during the day and get a sitter in the evenings." She planned to call Beth. The girl needed a shot of confidence, and surely Maggie's entrusting her son to her care would restore her faith in herself.

After the sisters parted, Maggie drove home in her mother's Mercury. The day was heartlessly beautiful, the sky a blue dome accented by faraway strokes of white clouds. There was a suspended quality to the air, as though this part of the earth, tilting away from the sun, ached at the cold barrenness to come. Flaming maples and burning oaks lined the roads and blanketed the mountains. Soon the rains would pour and the leaves drop, sentencing her to a colorless winter that she knew would seem like an eternity.

Why, God? Why my mother, and why now?

She received no answers as she turned into her mother's driveway. There never were any, she told herself as she entered the silent house and closed and locked the door.

But what do I expect, a voice from above? If that happened, I wouldn't believe it was God talking, I'd have myself committed.

For the first time in years, the possibility that she was being childish entered her mind. She decided not to think about it.

Her body longed for the comfort of a hot shower and rest, but she couldn't stop herself from walking through room after room and remembering. This structure, a simple matter of wood and plaster and concrete, seemed alive with the personalities it had sheltered: her charming, dreamer father; bossy Johanna; careless and kind Carter; and rebellious Maggie. But more than anyone, Rhonda had imprinted her stamp on the house; and now it seemed lonely, having lost its heart.

But not for long, she assured herself. Rhonda would be back. Maybe she'd never be as strong as before, but she *would* return.

Maggie lingered longest in her mother's room. She smoothed the wrinkles from the bedspread and hung up a dress thrown over a chair. Pausing at the desk, she straightened a stack of stationery and put it into one of the drawers. She spotted her mother's journals lying temptingly in their cubbyhole. No, she would not touch them. From their childhoods, Rhonda had taught her children to honor each other's privacy, especially in the matter of diaries. All the Covington women had kept them at one time, and Maggie often spied Rhonda writing in hers.

She turned from the room, walked upstairs and took a steaming, heavenly shower, lathering her hair with extra shampoo and massaging her scalp for longer than was probably good for it. By the time she toweled dry and pulled on a nightshirt, she was reeling from exhaustion. Ignoring her damp hair, she collapsed under the covers and fell asleep almost instantly.

The sound of pounding awoke her. She sat up, viewed the darkened room with confusion and looked at the clock. It was almost eight. Poor Johanna! She jumped from bed and pulled on a robe. The knocking was not a figment of her dreams; she could still hear it. She ran downstairs in her bare feet.

"I'm coming, I'm coming!" she shouted to whomever was there. Peering through one of the windows edging the door, she recognized her brother. She unlatched the lock with shaking fingers and flung her arms around his neck, nearly falling over the luggage at his feet.

"Why didn't you call me?" she cried, looking over Carter's shoulder and seeing a cabdriver leaning against his car. "I could have picked you up."

"You think I didn't try?" Carter said as he released her. "I finally got through to the hospital and Johanna told me you were here. I wanted to get my clothes home and clean up before I see Mom. I figured the reason you didn't answer was because you were asleep. You always could sleep through a hurricane."

"That's not me you're describing, it's *you*," Maggie returned. She was so delighted to see him, she could almost forget the reason he was here. "Did Johanna say how Mom is doing?"

"She's about the same," he said soberly. "Say, do you have twenty bucks for the cabdriver? He won't take my credit card."

Same old Carter. Maggie ran to get her wallet. After she paid the man, she followed her brother up the stairs to his bedroom, bringing him up-to-date on their mother and sketching over the past two weeks. Remembering Rhonda's reluctance for anyone to know the circumstances of Maggie's birth, she hesitated before telling him, then went on. Johanna already knew the truth; it didn't seem right to exclude Carter.

He emptied his bags while she spoke, stopping her with a question now and then. She chattered brightly, as though nothing that happened had hurt her. For the moment she felt no pain because Carter was there. That was the effect he always had on her; he was like a human shock absorber. She knew other people felt it, too; in all his life he had seldom wanted for companions.

As she talked, he sat across from her on the other twin bed. "This is a real shocker, Maggie." He leaned forward and propped his forearms on his knees. "I can only imagine what you're feeling."

"I felt angry at first," she admitted, "and betrayed." She searched for words, finding it hard to explain. "But now I feel guilty for resenting Mom. If only I hadn't been so *obvious* about it. Why couldn't I suffer in silence?"

"Oh, *Mom*. I thought you were telling me how you felt about Dad."

Funny. Her father had caused the worst crisis in their family thus far, but it was her *mother*, a woman not related to Maggie by blood, who received the lion's share of her emotion. Was that because her father was dead and not able to defend himself? She didn't think so.

It must have something to do with her mother's central role in her life—in the lives of all her children, she decided. To think of home was to think of Rhonda. Maybe it wasn't the same in all families, but she recognized it for truth in this one.

"I've forgiven Dad," she said. "It's hard not to forgive someone who's responsible for bringing you into existence."

Carter started to say something. Maggie could almost hear him thinking, *Dad didn't bring you into this world; God did.* Fortunately, he remained quiet; one of the things she appreciated most about him was that he kept his religion to himself.

"I'm not surprised you feel guilty about Mom, since she's sick," he said finally. "On the flight, I was busy going over my shortcomings, too, like how long it's been since I wrote, and why didn't I come down last Christmas. I guess it's natural to feel guilty when someone you love becomes ill. But we'll have time to put things right, because she *is* going to be okay." The words were as much an appeal as they were an assertion.

"I think so."

"Good. Have you got anything to eat? I want to get to the hospital as soon as I can."

They went downstairs, and Maggie put an individual-sized serving of her mother's stew in the microwave and broiled a couple of slices of French bread in the oven. Carter found a bowl of leftover salad in the refrigerator, drizzled oil and vinegar over the greens and sat to eat.

At precisely the instant the microwave's timer dinged, Johanna entered the kitchen, followed by Adam. Maggie dampened an urge to fling a dish towel around her uncombed hair, then wondered how she could worry about how she looked at a time like this.

"I knocked but no one answered," Johanna explained as she enveloped Carter in a big hug. "Adam came to visit Rhonda and was nice enough to bring me home."

"Then I'd better go and change," Maggie said, easing toward the doorway and not meeting Adam's eyes, as if that would make him not look at her. "We shouldn't leave Mom alone."

"I just talked with the doctor before I left the hospital," Johanna said, moving aside while Adam and Carter greeted each other with a handshake. "Her blood pressure has stabilized, and they plan to move her to a regular room tomorrow. If she keeps holding her own, the doctor says she might be moved to the convalescent wing pretty soon."

"That *is* good news. Well, if you'll excuse me…"

To her dismay, Adam accompanied her to the foot of the stairs. "How are you holding up, Maggie?"

Better than I look, I hope. "I'm all right."

"If there's anything I can do…"

"Thanks," she said, meaning it. "You've already done more than anyone could ask." She started to move up the stairs, then paused. "How's Beth?"

A troubled look came into his eyes. "She's taking it rather hard. I didn't know she felt so close to Rhonda."

"Please tell her no one blames her."

"I have, countless times."

"It must have been a terrible shock, finding Mom. I hope it hasn't reminded her of…" She trailed away, wishing she hadn't spoken.

"Of Allison's death?" he finished for her. "I thought about that, and I'll bet you're right. On the other hand, Beth often has an overdeveloped sense of responsibility." His eyes cooled. "Except in her choice of boyfriends."

She smiled and glided up the stairs with as much dignity as she could in a ratty robe that exposed legs with a bad case of five o'clock shadow. *You're such a good actress,* she told her reflection in the bathroom mirror. *No one would guess you've discovered you love Adam even though he rejected you. Keep smiling and treating him like he's nothing more than a good friend, and maybe one day you'll believe it.*

Maggie would enjoy this, Adam thought as he settled into his seat Friday evening to see *Our Town*. Then he told himself to stop thinking about her. Given Rhonda's condition, she didn't have time for high school plays or anything else. He had to get out of the habit of wanting to include her in every facet of his life anyway. There was no future there. None. Not unless God intervened in her heart, and he prayed for that daily. He knew he couldn't persuade her to believe with words. She'd heard all the sermons and had read the Word from childhood. All he could do was live what he believed and pray she would come to God in her own way. But it frustrated him to feel so helpless.

The lights dimmed. A crumpled program soared overhead. Saul Danbridge, English teacher and director of the play, walked to center stage. A few whistles sounded, followed by shushing noises from the scattering of adults present. Mr. Danbridge told a few facts about the play and announced two cast changes. While he spoke, the chatter gradually diminished. He exited to thready applause.

When the curtains parted, Adam felt a pit open in his stomach. Usually he enjoyed watching Beth perform, but tonight he didn't have a clue what to expect. Since Rhonda's stroke, she had moped around the house like a black cloud, and all the prompting in the world couldn't make her talk to him. He tried and failed to imagine her throwing off that mood to perform well.

But from her first lines, Adam saw only the character Emily, not his daughter. Beth was good—more than good. He couldn't help noticing how quiet the audience became when she spoke. She held the eye, and he felt certain his evaluation had nothing to do with fatherly pride.

When the play ended to firm applause, he slipped backstage. He arrived to a confusing mash of heavily made-up teens going in all directions and talking excitedly. He discovered the girls' dressing room but didn't dare walk inside, so he found a space against the wall and waited. When he saw his daughter's friend, Jackie Parker, exiting, he called to her.

"She was here like a minute ago," Jackie said, her big brown eyes ringed with a raccoon's share of eye liner. "I saw her leave the dressing room. Maybe she left already, you know? We have a cast party tonight at Mr. Danbridge's house."

Sinking inside, he thanked her and walked to the exit, stepping around knots of exuberant teens, dodging props and boxes and tangled cables. Outside, the night was crisp and comparatively quiet, although he could hear departing theatergoers laughing and engines revving around the side and front. Surely Beth had parked back here. He scanned the rows of cars for hers and felt a shot of relief when he spotted pink near the far corner.

His eyes narrowed. Beth was standing beside her vehicle, talking to someone straddling a motorcycle. There could be no doubt who that someone was.

As he drew closer, he read her body language: arms crossed, head tilted at that angle he had come to dread— her angry look. With joy, he realized that expression was directed at Jake Browne. As he watched, Jake reached for her arm, and she jerked free and stepped back. Adam's stride quickened.

"Beth, what's going on?" he called while some distance away.

Both young faces turned to him with surprise. His daughter pinkened and looked down for an instant. "Nothing, Dad. Jake came to the play. We were just talking."

Adam walked beside her. "Is that right?" he asked softly. "What did you think of the performance, Jake?"

Browne's eyes turned several degrees chillier. "Not bad," he said after a moment. "For high school." He made the words sound like a curse.

"That's a real compliment coming from you, since you're an artist," Adam said. "Naturally you're more sensitive to the nuances in Wilder's play and expect greater depths of characterization than the average observer."

"Dad," Beth said miserably.

"You like to hear yourself talk, don't you, *Dr.* Morgan?"

Beth's eyes widened. "Jake!"

"All the professors talked like you where I went to school. Like they just couldn't get *enough* of themselves."

"So, you've walked the halls of ivy?" Adam asked in a cozy tone of voice.

"Yeah, for one year. Surprised? Bet you thought I was a high school dropout because I've got dirt under my nails."

Something elemental and nasty twisted inside him. "Not because of the dirt, no." When Browne's jaw tightened, Adam felt a glow of satisfaction. "Why only one year? Surely college wasn't too much for a tough guy like you."

Browne started the motorcycle and gave Adam a cold

look. "I had enough—" he revved the engine, fortunately drowning out a few words "—to last a lifetime." He glanced at Beth. "See you around sometime, kid."

While Browne drove off like a black knight overdosing on testosterone, Adam fought an urge to shout. That sounded like a parting line if ever he'd heard one. His elation faded when Beth began to cry. He put his arm around her shoulder. She leaned against his chest and said something he couldn't quite understand.

"What was that, honey? I'm a tight Dad?"

She giggled tearfully. "I said you were right, Dad."

He still couldn't believe he'd heard her correctly. "What?"

"About Jake being too old for me, or at least not right for me."

"Well," he said, squeezing her shoulder for want of something to say. Had he lived long enough to be told he was right about something by his child? He hadn't been this happy in a long time. *Thank you, Father, for protecting Beth. In spite of my incompetence.* Since Allison's death, he had made one blunder after another. Most of the time, he didn't understand Beth's emotions at all. The girl needed a mother's insight and guidance to handle these delicate issues.

And he needed a wife.

Maggie.

A sudden suspicion clouded him. "What made you change your mind? He hasn't—he didn't hurt you in any way, did he?"

She stiffened and stepped back. "He always treated me with respect. Jake's not as bad as you think. He really isn't."

"All right, I'll accept that. But you've decided he's not right for you for some reason."

"He wanted to finish college, but he ran out of money." She seemed determined not to tell him what he wanted to know.

"Lots of students run out of money." He had worked every weekend and summer to fund his way through school, and it had taken him five years to repay his loans after he graduated.

"His mom was sick, though, and he had to look after a younger brother. And he never knew his dad."

"Really." It sounded like a plot out of Charles Dickens to him.

"Yes, really," she said with a look of resentment for his disbelief. "He's still working to send Jared through Vanderbilt. His brother's studying to be a doctor."

"Jake sounds like a real humanitarian. So why is it you don't like him anymore?"

"I still like him," she said in a small voice. "It's just that he's so…I don't know. Bitter, I guess. He hates God, and he hates the church. I mean, it's not like I try to shove spiritual stuff down his throat or anything, but every time I mention something about our youth group, he calls me a little girl for believing. Dad, I've mostly had good experiences at church, but so far as I can tell, he hasn't had *any*. How do you get through to someone like that?"

Adam stared at his daughter. "I don't know. All I can say is that I'm very proud of you for worrying about him but knowing when to quit."

"I can't take his anger anymore. He makes me feel bad all the time—for him, mostly. But…I'm going to miss him."

"I know you will, honey." He opened his arms wide and held her while she wept for the loss of her first love. Remembering the pain he'd felt when Maggie left him, he felt his heart swell with tenderness. And something else that surprised him: concern. For Jake.

His old love and Beth's were worlds apart, but they had one thing in common. Neither seemed able to accept the love that God offered them. Adam might not know what to do to help Maggie, but he believed he could do something for Jake if he had told Beth the truth. And maybe in the scheme of things, Maggie would be blessed. Acts of kindness tended to ripple outward to touch more lives than one ever dreamed. He had often seen it in his life, and he believed it to the marrow of his bones.

Jake's problem was certainly worth a call to his old friend, Ted Masoner, a full professor at Vanderbilt now. The thought made him smile. Time to call in a favor.

Chapter Fifteen

The decorators of the hospital had done their best to make an antiseptic environment warm and cheerful, Maggie thought on Sunday morning as she hurried through the hall toward her mother's room. Floral wallpaper in shades of mauve, celery and cream lined the walls, broken by a white chair rail. The floor tiles, white with a green border, sparkled like polished marble. In the small waiting areas near each set of elevators, visitors' chairs, although small and anchored together, were upholstered in coordinating tweeds. Still, there was no mistaking this building for anything than what it was: a place of pain and terror. Even for those who found healing here, or those who brought home new lives to cherish, there was that.

In her mother's case, she feared little good could come at all. But she was allowing Rhonda's depression to affect her, and she mustn't let that happen. They had to remain optimistic—Johanna, Carter and herself—otherwise her mother might give up entirely. That's what Dr. Stallbart had told them.

Life was starting over for Rhonda. Already the nurses were forcing her to use her hands and move her feet. Maggie could not help feeling protective in the face of her mother's defenselessness.

Arriving at Rhonda's private room, she took a deep breath before entering. In the second she paused, an aide exited with a breakfast tray bearing the remains of a plate of eggs, grits and toast. Her mother had barely made a dent in the food.

Johanna, pushing the button to lower the incline of the hospital bed, looked relieved to see Maggie and greeted her with the overbright tone all of them had mysteriously adopted when in Rhonda's presence. Their hospital voices, Maggie thought.

"You should see how much better Mom's getting at feeding herself," Johanna added. "She ate most of her grits this morning."

"Did you, Mom?" Maggie walked to her mother, refusing to speak of her in third person. Rhonda sent her a soft look, then turned her head. Maggie fought the knot in her throat and bent to kiss her cheek. "I hope they put enough butter in them. That's the only way you could get me to eat grits when I was little—butter and salt."

Rhonda blinked but gave no other indication she had heard. Maggie and Johanna exchanged a long glance.

"Dr. Stallbart says she'll be ready for the convalescent wing tomorrow," Johanna said cheerfully. "Isn't that good news?"

No, Maggie said silently. *Good news would be Mom at home baking and primping and driving herself to church. Having to learn how to walk again was not something to get excited about.*

"She's really making wonderful progress," Johanna said with a pointed look at her sister.

"Yes, you are, Mom," Maggie said softly after a second's debate. "Wonderful progress."

Rhonda closed her eyes.

With a tender expression, Johanna took her mother's hand. "I'll be here again tonight, but I can't tomorrow. I have to get back to Sid and the kids. I will return next weekend, though. I promise. Carter's going to remain a few more days, but then he has to go back to Mexico. The good thing is Maggie's going to stay. You won't be alone."

Johanna bit her lip, waiting for a response. *Waiting for absolution,* Maggie thought. As if she needed her mother's understanding for leaving; as if she had any other choice. In the past two days since Rhonda was moved from intensive care, they had often told her of the looming departures, fearing her memory might not be functioning properly. No one wanted her to become surprised or upset, or to feel abandoned. But as always when comments were directed at her, she hardly reacted. The momentary opening and closing of her eyes might mean anything. Since the very first hours when the extent of her stroke became apparent, she had "turned her face to the wall," as Carter so succinctly put it.

Nodding toward the foot of the bed, Johanna gently set her mother's hand on the coverlet and walked a distance away. Maggie followed.

"I'd better go home and get some rest before I pack," Johanna said quietly. "I won't need much because Mom was quiet last night, but the nurses kept waking me up." The siblings had divided hospital time into shifts so that Rhonda was never by herself.

"We need to talk about what's going to happen with

Mom." Maggie started to speak, but her sister hurried on. "Maggie, I know you've volunteered to stay with her while she's in the hospital, but what about later? We're talking months of recovery and, let's face it, she might not ever be able to live alone again. She could stay with us, but I know the kids would get on her nerves. I think we'd better start looking at assisted-living places."

"Aren't you missing something?" Maggie whispered acidly. "Don't you believe Mom should be consulted about where she's going to spend the rest of her life?"

"Of course I do, but I already know she won't want to live anywhere else but at home. I can't imagine you wanting to stay with her indefinitely, nor will Carter. We all have our lives, don't we?" She didn't pause for an answer. "That's why I say we have to start considering what's in her best interest."

Maggie heard the ring of truth in her sister's words, but all she felt was fury. "Let's take it one step at a time. Maybe she will make a full recovery. I can stay for as long as necessary." She heard her words with a sense of shock and added with less conviction, "It's not as if I have a job to lose."

Johanna's smile threatened to swallow her face as she said her goodbyes and left. Maggie's worried thoughts returned to her mother's state of mind. Rhonda had never seemed so lifeless, not even at her husband's funeral.

She walked to the opposite side of the bed, closer to her mother's face. For a full minute or more, she studied her in silence. She seemed smaller beneath the covers, and the faint lines in her cheeks looked sharper, as if she had shrunken inside her skin.

"Mom, I know you're not asleep."

Slowly Rhonda's eyes opened. The desolation of her

expression ripped Maggie's heart. *What are you going to say to her?* Maggie thought frantically. *Cheer up. Things could be worse?*

God help me to know how to encourage. If you're there, please.

Her mind boiled with fragments of ideas. Nothing took shape, no insightful words surfaced. She wanted to scream with frustration.

"I am so angry," she said at last, and clutched Rhonda's hand in a fierce grip. "I don't understand why this has happened to you. It doesn't make any sense. You don't deserve to be lying here. Somebody horrible might. A murderer, maybe, or a child abuser. Not you."

Maggie blinked, but the tears fell anyway. She snapped one of the hospital tissues from the bedside table. It felt like sandpaper on her cheeks.

"What's happened to you isn't fair, but you're needed, Mom. No one can take your place. You can't give up. You have to fight."

Rhonda's chest moved in a sigh. Her mouth twitched slightly, but her eyes remained downcast. *She probably wishes I'd leave her alone,* Maggie thought with sympathy. *Sorry, Mom. No chance.*

"I haven't had a minute to tell you about my trip to Florida," she continued. "I found out a few things about my birth mother. Her sister gave me some pictures of Emily Rose."

She paused, recalling her sadness at the questions Nancy Lincoln had stirred in her mind concerning her mother's character. The whole matter seemed to have occurred a lifetime ago, and to someone else. She could hardly remember why finding out about her birth mother had seemed so important.

"What I said a minute ago, about your being

needed?'' Maggie's voice softened to little more than a whisper. "No one needs you more than I do. I want you back, Mom. I miss your advice about how to raise Sam. I miss our arguments. You're the one person who really knows how to put me straight.''

She pushed her free hand, the one not clinging to Rhonda's, through the bars of the hospital bed and stroked her hair.

"I need your forgiveness for the million times I've hurt you.''

The hand within Maggie's moved. Rhonda lifted her eyes.

"I need my *real* mother. I need *you,* Mom.''

A single tear fell onto the pillowcase. Maggie rose and threw her arms around the beloved woman who had raised her.

Shortly before four that afternoon, Carter peered around the hospital door and found Maggie reading in the imitation-leather chair at the foot of the bed while Rhonda slept. With his computer carryall slung over his shoulder, he walked softly to her.

"What's going on here?'' he whispered. "One of the nurses stopped me in the hall and said Mom ate almost all her lunch and that she's been exercising her hands and trying to talk.''

"She's had a good day,'' Maggie said, her gaze resting warmly on the huddled form in the bed.

He smiled confidently. "I knew she'd come back. That's our mom!''

"She sure is.''

"Well, hop up, girl, and give me the good chair so I can get some work done. You'd better scoot home before Johanna cooks everything in the house. She's sure Sid and the kids haven't had a decent meal since she left, and I guess she's trying to make up for it. I imagine you're anxious to see Sam, too.''

"Does a nurse wear white?" Maggie joked, rising.

"Oh, Mag," Carter said when she stood to almost his eye level. "You got a call this afternoon. From Zack.''

All her ebullient feelings of the day dropped like a stone. "What did *he* want?''

"He wondered why you hadn't gotten back with him about Sam." Carter carefully avoided her gaze.

"Does he really think we have anything to discuss?''

He gestured helplessly as if to say *Not my fault.* "He said he'd given you more than a week to think about sharing custody but that he was running out of patience. Said he was going to the lawyer tomorrow. But when I told him about Mom, he promised to give you more time. Maggie.'' Carter's big, brown eyes appealed to her. "Are you sure you're taking the right stand on this? I know he didn't treat you well, but has it occurred to you Zack may have changed? Or that Sam has plenty of positive role models around him?''

Maggie's emotions churned with hostility and something she feared to name. For the first time, she was beginning to doubt herself.

"You're meddling," she mumbled at last.

"I know I'm a bad brother," he said, grinning. "But what would you do without me?''

"Oh, for pity's sake. I have to help Johanna." With a rush of affection, she planted a kiss on his cheek and walked from the room.

At home, however, as she helped Johanna with supper—paring potatoes and putting them on to boil, setting the big walnut table in the dining room—her disquiet about Zack continued. Only when Sid arrived with his vanful of children and Sam ran into her arms did she come back wholly to herself.

She hugged her child's sturdy little body and showered his cheeks with kisses until he squirmed to be set free. Around her, Johanna's children greeted their mother with exuberant hellos and embraces, then directed their attention to Maggie and her son, whom she soon realized they regarded as a pet. In turn, she received dutiful hugs from Andrew and Tim and shy ones from the girls, Sara and Sandi. It had been years since she last saw her nieces, and she felt saddened that time and distance had prevented a closer relationship from developing between the families.

"I missed you, too!" Sam declared over the bedlam, when she took him in her arms again. As if to deny his words, he peered past her shoulder to see what his cousins were doing. "When is Grandma coming back? I want her home now. Does she hurt?"

Her boy was compassionate, she thought with pride. How many children his age would worry about their grandmothers?

Sam did not cry or make a scene when Johanna and her family left, as Maggie feared he might. But when they had the house to themselves, he ran from one activity to the next, dragging toy after toy from his bedroom to the kitchen as if he could not bear being by himself. Feeling his frenzy as if it were her own, she picked a pathway among trucks and books and matchbox cars and hurried to refrigerate the perishables before he exploded. The dishes could wait until his bedtime. Right now he needed a mother's comfort. She drew a warm bubble bath, let him soak with his rubber toy, dressed him in fresh-smelling cotton pajamas and snuggled beside him in bed for a long session of reading. When at last he fell asleep, she left his room, sighing in relief at disaster averted.

Over the next few days, her hopes that Sam would revert to his old self were dashed, especially when the time came for Carter to depart. The three of them had slipped into a comfortable routine—she spending mornings and a small portion of the afternoon with her mother while Carter stayed with Sam, then switching positions, with her brother remaining at the hospital until early evening.

During the times Carter kept Sam, they bonded in a way she never expected. She didn't realize the full intensity of it until Wednesday evening, the night Carter planned to return to Mexico.

"Sorry, buddy," Carter said. "I have to go."

"You don't *have* to go," Sam said, anger fueling his tears.

"Yes, I do, guy. But I'll come back as soon as I can. I promise."

Murmuring comforts, Maggie pulled Sam into her own arms. Again he stiffened, forcing her to let him slide to the floor.

"Nobody *has* to go! You just *want* to!"

"It's my job, Sam." Carter had never sounded so patient, Maggie thought, or sad. "Grown-ups have to work. You don't want me to starve, do you?"

"You could stay here. Grandma would feed you."

"But that wouldn't be right. We've talked about this, haven't we? You know I have to finish my work."

"No!"

There was no reasoning with him now, Maggie saw, and she gave Carter a quick embrace and nudged him toward the door. He kissed the top of Sam's head and shot Maggie a look of regret as he slipped outside. As he did, Sam uttered a cry of rage and flew up the stairs.

He needs a father, Maggie thought helplessly, following him. *If only Zack were more like Adam.* Adam was the kind of man who remained loyal to his loved ones. He would never have caused her pain or left his son. He was a true family man. How could she have made such a mistake? How had she missed him?

Chapter Sixteen

Anxiety gnawed at Maggie's stomach as she watched Beth stack towers of wooden blocks on the coffee table. She had brought a laundry basket full of toys to the parlor, and the girl was attempting to engage Sam's interest in something. So far Beth had made racing noises with his toy cars and set up for a game of Candy Land. Sam wasn't biting.

"Oh, I know you'll like *this*," she said, lifting the fire truck from the basket. "It's your favorite."

Sam flopped facedown on the sofa. "Don't want to play with that old thing."

Beth sent Maggie a quizzical look, as if to say, *What's happened here? Is this the same boy I baby-sat before?*

It was Thursday afternoon, the day after Carter's departure. Dressed for the hospital, Maggie lingered, hoping she wouldn't have to leave Beth with a tearful or angry child. Thankfully the girl didn't seem daunted; she'd probably dealt with worse. At least Maggie hoped so.

"You're sure Mrs. Rhonda is better?" Beth asked suddenly, relegating Sam to the back of her attention.

"She has therapy every day, and they're teaching her to walk and speak, and to feed and dress herself, too. She's improving quickly."

"That's good." Beth looked as if she meant it. "It's so sad she's going through this. I don't know how she can stand it—learn how to do everything again, I mean, just like a kid."

What a caring child, Maggie reflected, feeling almost comfortable with her. She hoped the girl's concern didn't mean she still felt responsible for Rhonda's collapse. Interesting how her attitude toward Maggie had mellowed; perhaps Adam told her they were finished.

Not that they had ever begun.

"You know, Beth, my mother had the warning signs of a stroke before I left, only I was too stupid to recognize them. Her dizzy spells and headaches were big clues, but even Dr. Stallbart ignored the symptoms. Maybe because there was nothing he could do to prevent the stroke from happening."

"I know what you're trying to say, but I still wish I'd been here sooner that day."

Beth didn't look up from the blocks as she spoke. She was building a pyramid, and Sam began to watch.

"And I wish I'd never left. But until somebody invents time travel, I guess we'll have to accept what happens as best as we can."

Beth smiled weakly and turned to Sam. "Have you decided what you're wearing for Halloween, big boy?"

As Sam's face brightened, Maggie moaned. "Halloween! It's tomorrow, isn't it? I forgot."

"Oh, no problem," Beth said eagerly. "I have lots of costumes at home. Mom made them for an outdoor nativity scene years ago, and I keep them in the attic for kids to play in when I baby-sit at my house. Sometimes I take them to church. There should be a few costumes his size. Shall I bring them over tomorrow night? I mean, you do allow him to go trick-or-treating, don't you? I could take him.''

Sam had caught her enthusiasm, finally. "Can I, Mommy?''

The little glutton; mention candy and his mood improved eighty percent, child of his mother that he was. She nodded, smiling, and gathered her purse and keys from the hall table.

"Would you like to be an angel or a shepherd?'' Beth was saying as Maggie waved goodbye. "We could glue on a beard and wrap your head in a towel, and you could be Moses dividing the Red Sea!''

Beth was a natural with children, Maggie thought, considerably relieved as she drove to the hospital. After-school traffic was thick, and by the time she reached her mother's room, one of the aides was rolling a cart of supper trays from the service elevator.

Rhonda lay curled on her side facing the window when Maggie entered, and she softened her footsteps as she circled the bed. Her mother's eyes were closed, her skin like parchment, her chest moving in shallow breaths. With a shock of concern, Maggie stepped closer. Rhonda opened her eyes, a spark of recognition transforming her pallor. Maggie returned her smile and bent to kiss her forehead.

"I hope I didn't wake you. Are you feeling all right?''

Rhonda nodded, a look of concentration on her face. She muttered a word that Maggie interpreted as "tired.''

"You're tired?'' Maggie repeated, hating how she'd fallen into the habit of restating everything Rhonda said, but it was the only way she knew to be sure she understood. "Did they work you too hard in therapy?"

"Ha-a-rd."

The dietary aide entered with Rhonda's tray, and the women exchanged greetings. While Maggie pressed the button to raise the bed, the aide rolled the table into place, lifted the insulating lids and left. Maggie settled into the bedside chair and leafed through a magazine she had bought yesterday. She knew Rhonda didn't like to be watched while she ate. Maggie found it painful herself, so she pretended an interest in the recipe section. After a few moments, Rhonda clattered her fork to the plate and sighed, letting her head fall against the pillows.

Maggie was up in an instant. "You're not finished yet, are you? Look, you haven't eaten your Jell-O, and it has fruit. And your beef stew! You need to eat to get stronger, Mom."

Rhonda leveled her a look of exasperation. And no wonder, Maggie thought, hearing herself. She was talking to her mother as she would a child.

At that moment, Rhonda's hand flopped on the tray and grasped the fork, holding it out to her. "He-eh-elp."

Maggie shook her head. "Oh, no, Mom. The nurses insist that you feed yourself. I want to help, I really do, but they say training will…" Maggie paused. Rhonda had squeezed her eyes shut and was again struggling to speak.

"No sh-p-o-on."

"No spoon? They didn't give you a spoon? Well, no wonder you can't eat! Who eats soup and Jell-O with a fork? I'll get you one, Mom. I'll be right back."

Before she reached the door, Rhonda said, "Mah-gee. To-o-o ti-i-rud."

Maggie saw it was so. She debated a second, then

gave her mother a conspirator's look. Stealthily she closed the door to the hall and glided to the bed. Lifting a forkful of Jell-O toward her mother's mouth, she hesitated dramatically.

"You have to promise not to tell," she said.

She was treated to a wide, genuine smile. "You—er go-o-d gi-rr-el."

Maggie lowered her eyes quickly. "You're a good girl, too, Mom."

"You don't know how much I appreciate this, Ted. I owe you a steak." Adam's smile grew tight, as though Ted Masoner might suspect something if he let it go. "Oh, you, too? A grilled chicken salad, then."

Adam hung up the phone and stared at the serene Monet print on the opposite wall. When they first returned to Chattanooga, Allison had given it to him for his new office. Monet was one of her favorites, she once told him, because he painted the world she saw without her contact lenses.

He wished his world was like the painting: soft with misty edges.

No, he didn't. He wouldn't mind taking a vacation, though—not from his life, but from himself.

He looked down and rubbed his aching temples. Ted had confirmed that Jared Browne was a second-year medical student at Vanderbilt. The young man planned to be a surgeon and was near the top of his class academically. And yes, his brother, Jake, was footing the lion's share of the bills. Amazing the drive that can come from nothing, Ted had concluded.

Amazing, indeed.

Adam scraped back his chair and walked to the glass overlooking the showroom. A man and woman were browsing through the software section; Harry was watching them surreptitiously. Adam crossed his arms and stared outward. From here, he could see through the windows at the front of the store to the sunny afternoon outside. Leaves were falling from the trees dividing his parking lot and the shopping strip next door. He failed to receive his usual rush of pleasure at the sight.

It was natural for a father to protect his daughter from a man like Jake Browne, he soothed himself. Any fool could see the danger.

But had he ever offered him a kind word? No. Everything that slithered out of his mouth had been snide or demeaning. And he had to admit that he'd wanted to hear Jake had lied to Beth in order to impress her. No wonder Jake was bitter, if he kept running into people like Adam.

I'm no better than a Pharisee, looking on the outside of the cup instead of seeing what's in it. Jake had sacrificed, or at least delayed, his own dreams for his brother's. He knew few who would be willing to do that, Christians or not.

Forgive my pride, Father, he prayed. *Help me see how to make it right.*

You already know, his heart told him. *And while you're at it, what about Maggie? How long are you going to abandon her?*

Feeling heavy and light at the same time, he returned to his desk and picked up the phone.

Adam waited until nearly seven before he drove to the hospital. He had a hard time finding a parking spot; both lots were full. He finally left his car at the mall a mile from the hospital. It was a pleasant walk beneath fog-wreathed streetlights. Half-nude cherry and pear trees, clinging stubbornly to their leaves through the mild fall, lined the road and threw skeletal shadows on the sidewalk. He breathed the sharp air into his lungs and wondered if he would ever want to live anywhere else but in this beautiful city. When he strode into the hospital lobby and to the elevator, he felt invigorated and ready for anything.

His bravado faded when he reached Rhonda's floor in the convalescent wing and saw her closed door. No telling what might be going on in there. He knocked tentatively. After an uncomfortable few seconds, Maggie opened the door. The instant shock in her eyes, although quickly masked, made his heart skip a beat.

"Oh. Adam." Somehow she avoided looking directly at him. "Mom's asleep. If she knew you were here, she'd want me to wake her up, but she's really tired tonight."

He held up a restraining hand. "No, don't wake her. I came to see you. Of course, I wanted to see Rhonda, too, but I'll visit another day when she's awake." A look of hesitancy came into Maggie's eyes. "I've come to apologize," he added with a tantalizing lilt in his voice.

That got her attention. "For what?"

He glanced at a passing nurse. Behind her, an old man dragging an attached IV on wheels crept down the hall. "Look, could we go to the lounge for a minute?"

She cast a reluctant glance over her shoulder, then nodded. They walked in silence to the waiting area adjacent to the elevators. To his disappointment, he saw the room was occupied by a middle-aged woman and an older lady sitting separately. He led Maggie to seats as far from the women as possible and hoped they were as involved in their magazines as they appeared.

"I'm sorry I haven't been around lately," he began awkwardly.

She looked surprised. "Adam, you don't need to apologize for that. I know you're a busy man, and I don't expect—"

"I've been avoiding you."

"Oh."

"Yes." He smiled ruefully. "There's a reason for that. When we were in Savannah, you said something to me, and I don't think I responded very well. I might have sounded…abrupt. I wanted to make sure you understand what I really feel."

"I think I already understand," she said uncomfortably.

"Do you? It's very important to me that you do. I don't want to leave it to chance. Some things have happened lately that taught me I don't know as much about people as I thought. And with your mom lying down the hall unable to communicate what she feels, it's finally getting through my mind how vital it is to be honest with the people I love."

For what seemed a long time, she searched his face in silence, then shifted her eyes. He waited, watching her beloved features with hope.

"There's no doubt in my mind that I love you, Maggie. But in the past few days I've had to come to terms with something that I don't like to think about. I have no right to push my own beliefs on anyone, or to expect you to make a choice in life that doesn't come naturally to you. So, even though my first inclination is to tell God, 'I want Maggie, and I want her *now!*' it may be we're not meant for each other after all. Frankly I find that hard to believe, having loved you most of my life, to the point that I couldn't forget you even while I was married to a wonderful woman.'' Maggie stirred as if to protest. ''No, let me finish. This needs to be said, and then we can put it all to a decent burial and go on. I thought I'd gotten over you, because when Allison fell ill, she became the focus of my life—for the first time, I'm ashamed to say. But from the moment I saw you at the airport, I knew nothing had changed, even though I fought and denied my feelings as strongly as I could. All that aside—if it's not to be, I can live with it. But I don't want there to be awkwardness between us. I can't imagine life without at least having your friendship, Maggie.''

The waiting room pulsed with quiet. Adam glanced over his shoulder; as if choreographed, the women's gazes returned to their magazines. He shrugged, one side of his mouth raising in an ironic smile. The smile faded when he saw Maggie's eyes were bright with tears.

''Oh, Adam. I can't imagine not being your friend, either.''

He reached for her hands and they sat quietly for a moment.

''What are your plans, Maggie? Will you remain in Chattanooga while your mother recovers, or are you going back to New York?'' He didn't breathe as he waited for her answer.

''I've promised my family I'll stay until Mom gets better.''

''And then?''

She shook her head, looked down at the floor. ''I don't know. I'm not planning too far in the future these days.''

''I wish you'd move back permanently.'' When her gaze flew to his, he said quickly, ''It may be selfish of me, but I'd like it if you lived here. A fellow appreciates having his *friends* around him.'' He saw her struggling to hold back her tears, and his voice grew tender. "I'm not fooling you for a second, am I? I'm asking you to stay because I want you to give us a chance, Maggie. A second chance. We have a lot of differences between us, and one major one that needs to be resolved before we can move forward. But if you're in New York, there won't be a remote possibility of any kind of resolution between us." He swallowed, geared up his courage. "What do you say, Maggie? Do you think it's worth a try?"

She dashed tears from her eyes. "I can't promise anything."

"I'm not asking for promises."

"Then...I do think it's worth a try, Adam. More than worth it." He didn't believe it was possible to be happier than he was at that moment, but she made his heart soar when she added falteringly, "Would you pray for my mother?"

He did so, softly and gladly, tightening his hands around hers.

"I wish it was that simple for me," she said, when he finished. "The kind of faith you have."

He raised his brows. "Who said it was simple?"

Chapter Seventeen

The following Sunday, after an inner debate, Maggie took Sam to church. She sat alone in her mother's favorite pew while Beth led Sam to children's church. When Adam met her gaze from his seat in the choir loft, she felt as shy as a nineteenth-century maiden. After the service, hundreds of people, or so it seemed, greeted her and asked about Mrs. Rhonda. Was there anything they could do? Did Maggie need dinner brought? The ladies' brigade would be happy to put her on the list. Embarrassed at their generosity, she thanked them all but said she and Sam were managing.

Adam spoke to her briefly, a friendly sentence or two, nothing more. She watched him walk away with a sense of loss. Since his visit with her at the hospital, thoughts of him shadowed her every activity, every moment of the day.

Unlike him, she had been too immature to recognize real love when it had first entered her life. And during the past weeks, though, she had acknowledged to herself what a fine man Adam was and what a great father he'd make for Sam, she had felt too confused, too bitter to admit that she needed him *for herself.* She loved Adam for all that he was—for his character, his quirky humor and gentle eyes, his bewildered but caring manner with his daughter. She loved him for his strength. For the way he'd never forgotten her in spite of her behavior toward him. She loved him for loving her after all these years, for never giving up.

But as fast as her love expanded, so did the realization that she could hurt him again. A man like Adam would never be content with a woman who didn't share his faith. Until she found peace one way or the other, she didn't feel free to tell Adam about her feelings for him. She would not put him in the position of making a choice between losing the woman he loved or marrying one who didn't trust in his God.

After the weekend, Maggie settled into the routine that was becoming her life. Beth came every afternoon after school and refused to take a day off. Maggie appreciated her constant cheerfulness with Sam, who was not the easy charge he used to be.

Rhonda continued to show improvement, although less dramatically than before. Her chronic tiredness became a matter of increasing concern. On Thursday evening, Maggie cornered one of the nurses, Debbie, a pale, intense woman who took unsentimental but effective care of her patients.

"Fatigue is not uncommon," the nurse said. "A stroke is a terrible shock to the system. But if you're worried, you should ask Dr. Stallbart."

If I could ever find him, Maggie thought, and returned to her mother's room. In the time she'd stepped out, Rhonda had fallen asleep again. She could go home, she supposed, but it felt too early to leave. She eyed the recliner at the foot of the bed with longing. Keeping Sam occupied, especially in his more demanding state—how she regretted letting him stay with Johanna!—and sitting and worrying about her mother for hours every day was taking its toll. She walked soundlessly to the chair, leaned back as quietly as she could and slipped into slumber within minutes.

She didn't know how long she slept. But when she opened her eyes, the sky had darkened to black. The room was shadowed except for the night light over her mother's bed. Maggie blinked, her eyelids feeling scratchy. Blearily she checked her wristwatch. A little after nine-thirty; she should think about leaving.

Some company she'd been tonight. She pushed to a sitting position and frowned when the chair squeaked. Surprisingly, Rhonda had awakened and was watching her. At least it seemed so at first; as Maggie drew closer, she saw the older woman's eyes carried a bewildered expression, almost as if she were in pain.

"Mag-gie?"

Maggie realized instantly that this was the sound that had awakened her. Her mother had been calling. Her heart began to pound. "Mom! What's wrong?"

The surprise in Rhonda's eyes deepened. "Mag-gie?"

"I'll get the nurse." *Don't panic.*

Rhonda reached out and clasped Maggie's wrist. "Sta-ay."

"All right, all right, just let me push the button—"

"No-o-o."

She froze, mesmerized by the beatific expression on her mother's face.

"Do…you…see…?"

Her skin prickling, Maggie slowly turned her head.

Nothing out of the ordinary behind her. "See what, Mom?" she whispered, turning back.

The light in Rhonda's eyes began to dim. Her lids lowered.

"Mom? Mom! Oh, no." Frantically she pressed the nurse's call button. No answer. She tore into the hall and made eye contact with Debbie, who was emerging from a room two doors down. "Nurse! Come here! Help!" She rushed back to the bed and seized Rhonda's hand. No answering squeeze of the fingers comforted hers. She leaned over the rail and pressed her cheek against her mother's cooling one, cradling her shoulders.

"Don't go," she cried. "Please, *please*, I need you!" *Mother.*

The nurses and the doctor on call did what they could, which wasn't much. Rhonda had signed one of those forms requesting that no heroic measures be performed to resuscitate her. Maggie hadn't known. Sitting in the dimly lit room beside her mother's body, she wondered when that business had transpired. Perhaps at the time she fractured her hip. Maybe before. She could not understand why her mother hadn't been willing to fight harder.

Maggie was waiting for Adam to pick her up. Silly thing, really. She could have driven herself home, but Nurse Debbie had insisted she call someone. When Maggie refused, she'd demanded a name. Without thinking, Maggie had responded, "Adam Morgan," and Debbie made the call herself.

The nurse meant to be kind. First she'd tried to get Maggie to wait in the lounge, saying she shouldn't be in the room when the van came from the funeral home. When Maggie declared she wanted to stay beside her mother, the nurse had offered to sit with her. But Maggie preferred to be alone.

Out of respect, the door to the hall was closed, and the room was very quiet and strangely peaceful. The only sound Maggie heard was that of her own heart breaking.

"Why did you have to go, Mom?" she whispered. "Just when things were finally getting right between us, you had to go and leave.

"Oh, Mom." She closed her eyes. "I wonder if you're in heaven now. Are you and Dad together again? Was that who you saw, at the very last? I wish you could tell me."

It wasn't fair. Rhonda had given and given, and for what? A daughter who had spent half her life fighting and resenting her?

None of it made any sense. Why did anyone care about anything?

She thought of Sam and her fierce love for him. She recalled Adam saying that faith was a choice. She could hear him asking, "Can you force love?"

Maggie slowly removed her hand from her mother's and cradled her head against the sheets.

"God? Are You there?" In the silence, her tears began to fall. "Because if You are, I need You."

She breathed in sharply. In the dark cave of her arms, she could hear her heart beating.

"I don't know why it's so hard for me to believe. But I've really lost my way."

Like a long-held breath, verses began to repeat in her mind—verses she had memorized long ago, as a child. "I am come that they might have life, and that they might have it more abundantly. He hath shown thee, O man, what is good; and what doth the Lord require of thee, but to do justly, and to love mercy, and to walk humbly with thy God?''

She could feel the words pushing shoots of hope through her soul, a whole network of them, running, crisscrossing, digging deeper and deeper and taking root. Sobs racked through her, and she thought it might be the pain and ecstasy of new growth.

''I'm sorry for running away from You so long. Deep down, I always knew You were there. It's just that I was angry, and bitter. I guess I wanted to punish You because I didn't like the way things were going in my life. Please forgive me. Please...take me back.''

Slowly a sense of peace flooded her heart. She felt bathed in forgiveness.

She began to smile through her tears. ''Thank You, Father. Thank You for loving me...in spite of myself.''

A hand fell on her shoulder. She whipped around, but it was only Adam, not an angel, or God Himself as she had halfway feared. *Only Adam?* His eyes were streaming, a world of compassion and joy shining through. Maggie rose and melted into his arms.

It was almost midnight when Adam and Maggie pulled into the Covington driveway in the Mercury. The porch light was on, the house dark except for flashes of lightning behind the sheers; Beth had to be watching television.

''Why didn't I call Beth?'' Maggie said, her voice thick, sounding as if she had a cold. ''She must be worried out of her mind wondering where I am.''

She turned her face toward him. Tears had washed away her makeup, and her nose looked pink. Smudged mascara ringed her swollen eyes. Adam, wishing he could embrace her again, touched her hand briefly. No one had ever appeared more beautiful.

"I should have thought to call, not you," Adam said. "Under the circumstances, I think she'll forgive us."

With his arm around her waist, Adam walked with Maggie to the door. The second she opened it, he let his arm fall to his side. As they entered, Beth sprang from the sofa.

"Thank good—Dad! What are you doing here?" The color receded from her cheeks. She put one hand on the sofa, as if for support. "What's wrong?"

"I'm afraid we have bad news, honey," Adam said.

Beth stepped back, shaking her head. "No. Oh, no. It's Mrs. Rhonda, isn't it?"

Maggie moved forward but stopped a few paces away from her, looking unsure as to whether she should get any closer. "I'm afraid so."

"She's dead?"

"The doctor said her heart just…stopped." Maggie swallowed. "She went very peacefully. No pain."

Beth sank to the sofa. She leaned forward and cradled her head on her knees. "I knew it. I knew this would happen." Her shoulders began to shake.

Adam exchanged a look with Maggie and went to sit beside his daughter. "Honey…" Her reaction perplexed him. He knew Beth had been fond of Rhonda, but her grief seemed extreme. He patted her back, feeling helpless. "Try not to take it so hard. She lived a long, full life and loved the Lord."

Beth turned her head angrily, her hair sliding over her eyes. "You don't understand. This is my fault!"

"It is not your fault!" Adam said in exasperation. "I've told you that ever since she had the stroke!"

Maggie touched her shoulder. "No one could have

stopped what happened. If you had seen her face, you'd know she was ready to go. It was her time.''

Beth clenched her fists on her knees. ''I should have been here that day. I didn't have a meeting after school.'' Her knuckles whitened as the words ripped from her. ''I was with Jake.''

Adam felt a flush spread from his neck upward. ''What did you say?''

''We were already breaking up, but he wanted to talk to me, to change my mind, I guess. So after school we rode his bike to the river and hung around there for a long time. I knew I wasn't supposed to see him. That's why I did it. I went because I was mad.''

''Mad at me?'' Adam asked. ''For taking Maggie to Florida?''

She nodded. ''And staying longer than you said. I thought you were making up reasons to be with her. I was afraid the two of you were...you know. Starting to be a couple. Now that I know you're just friends, I feel even more awful.''

Maggie sent him a quick look of caution, a look Beth intercepted. The girl hesitated a fraction of an instant, then went on. ''I don't blame you if you can't forgive me, Maggie. If anyone had done that to my mother...I just want you to know how sorry I am.''

''And I want you to stop feeling guilty,'' Maggie said with such earnestness that Adam looked at her curiously. ''Losing my mother is terrible—for me. But, Beth...for her, this is a gift.'' Her voice grew hushed. ''Just before she died, she saw something, or someone. It transformed her. I've never known what to think about near-death or after-death experiences. I don't know why some people have them and some don't. All I can say is, Mom looked happier than I've ever seen her. As much as I need her, I can't wish her back. Not from that.''

Beth stared at her intently. Adam thought he saw a wisp of hope in her eyes. After a moment, he said, ''It's late. We'd better go. If you'll let me, I'd like to come tomorrow morning and help with the arrangements. Is there anything we can do for you tonight? Make some calls?''

''Thanks, Adam. I'll phone Johanna and Carter early tomorrow morning. They may as well get a night's sleep. They'll need it.''

He pressed her hands and then, because he couldn't help himself, kissed her cheek. Closing the door behind himself and Beth, he led the way to his daughter's car and stopped at its trunk.

''Give me the keys,'' he said. ''I'll drive. We need to pick up my car at the hospital.''

Beth pulled a key ring from her pocket and handed it over without comment. Adam folded himself into the driver's seat and adjusted it as far back as he could. He bumped his head on the visor and suffered in silence as he started the engine and pulled onto the road.

''Are you very mad at me, Dad?'' Beth said when the quiet became unbearable.

He kept his eyes on their curving descent, feeling relief as he always did when he reached the main highway. ''You mean because you disobeyed me and then lied about it?''

''Well, when you put it like that... Am I grounded?''

Adam turned onto the four-lane road, then changed lanes to pass a truck. Beth's car roared with the effort. ''I think you've punished yourself enough for this one.''

''Thanks, Dad.'' She fiddled with the radio dial, found nothing to her liking and flipped it off. ''You and Maggie. You're more than just friends, aren't you? The way you looked at her tonight reminded me of how you used to look at Mom."

Although she kept her tone even, he sensed the pain behind her words. "How would you feel if that was true?" he asked gently. "Now that you know Maggie better, does the thought of me loving her still make you angry?"

For a long time, long enough to get his adrenaline pumping, she stared at the passing traffic. "I have to say it bothers me. Maggie's nice, but she's not my mom."

"I understand." He patted her hand and wanted to say more, but now was not the time. In spite of his sorrow at Rhonda's passing, hope was rising. Tonight, Maggie had accepted the Lord. Surely nothing stood between them now. But he shouldn't presume. Maggie had surprised him before. Besides, she had some grieving to do before changing her life.

We all do, he thought, cherishing Allison's memory with feelings of sweetness and loss.

Chapter Eighteen

After Adam and Beth left, Maggie checked on Sam. He lay in a tangled heap on her sister's bed, his lips parted slightly. How could she explain his grandmother's death to him? He was only four. Would a funeral traumatize him?

She turned and walked from the room. Sleep was impossible. She wanted her mother. She descended the stairs, entered Rhonda's bedroom and flipped on the light switch. Her eyes moved over the familiar furnishings. How many times had her mother polished those carved bedposts? That the bed and everything in this room should survive her was a crime.

Her glance fell on Rhonda's rolltop desk. Her mother's Bible, a concordance and three red volumes stood on the shelf inside. Beside them was a cup lettered Mom that Maggie recognized as a gift from Johanna on a long-ago Mother's Day. Would it be wrong to read her diaries? She had always wondered what her mother was writing about. She'd just skim a few pages and then, if

Rhonda's thoughts seemed too personal, she would lay the books aside.

Guessing the journals were in chronological order, Maggie reached for the third one. She turned to the first page and saw Carter's name written in her mother's graceful script. Maggie flipped through the pages. Letters—all of them letters to Carter, tracing his life. She closed the book and reached for the middle one, hardly daring to hope.

"Maggie," said the first page. She dropped it and reached for the first book. "Johanna."

Oh, Mom.

Maggie carefully restored Johanna and Carter's journals to the shelf. Tenderly she took her legacy to the chaise lounge, wrapped herself in the afghan Grandma Covington had knit many years before and began to read.

On the first pages, Rhonda related the story of Maggie's birth, but no mention was made of her hurt at Philip's unfaithfulness. In the next sentences: hope for the baby she could not help loving. Months, then years, flew by, Rhonda reflecting upon significant and not-so-significant events in Maggie's life.

As Maggie entered her teens, the tone of Rhonda's letters began to change. She wrote of battles and an increasing sense of gloom that she was failing to influence Maggie in the right direction. Evidently Rhonda, too, had questioned God's purpose.

Maggie paused, rested the journal on her chest and rubbed her eyes. The bedside clock read 3:12. She was finally sleepy, but no way could she stop. She went back to the book.

A brief time of hope flowered in the letters as Maggie and Adam dated and became engaged. Hostility flowed when Maggie ran away, and then a long break, marked only by the date of her wedding to Zack and Sam's birth, duly noted without comment.

The next letter was Rhonda's last, written only weeks ago. In it her mother confessed that she had indeed invited Maggie to her home because she hoped the time had come for Adam and Maggie to reunite. When she reached the final paragraphs, Maggie sat up, the afghan slipping unnoticed to the floor.

> Of all my children, you are the most like me (which is odd for reasons you now understand, if you hold to the genetic theory of personality). Perhaps that's why I've expected so much, hoped so much from you. This hope—and my fears for you, as well— caused me to make many mistakes. The greatest one was your marriage to Zack. I should have accepted him, flaws and all. But I couldn't.
>
> You see, Maggie, we're alike in another way. Before I married your father, I loved a man much like Zack—charming, irreverent, exciting to my naive eyes. But, unlike you, I chose to reject his proposal, although it broke my heart. Even after I committed to Philip, I couldn't forget him.
>
> Now that I'm old, I have to ask myself if I wasn't a little jealous that you decided to follow your heart. Perhaps it was this ugly emotion that led me to feel too much vindication when your marriage disintegrated. I beg your forgiveness for it and hope you will remember the good days as well as the bad.

Maggie raised her eyes to the bed where her mother had spent so many of her last weeks. She felt relieved in a way she didn't fully understand, although certainly there was comfort in knowing her mother was human. As to forgiveness, there could be no question. Maggie only wished she'd known in time, so that she could hold Rhonda and say, "There's nothing to forgive."

During the next three days, visitors poured into the house carrying consoling words and casseroles, cakes and salads. The phone rang constantly. The house swelled to its fullest occupancy and beyond. Johanna and her family arrived, Carter flew in and Sid's parents came. Adam was an almost constant presence, attending to details when the family became too overwhelmed.

On Saturday afternoon, however, Maggie sat alone downstairs. Adam had gone to his store to relieve his employee, who was to attend a wedding. Sid and Johanna were shopping for groceries with their children, and Carter and Sam were sleeping upstairs. When she heard a knock at the door, she sighed. The funeral of a loved one seemed a peculiar time to have to entertain thousands of people, many of whom she'd never seen before.

But when she opened the door, she recognized all too well the man on the porch. Her heart dropped. Zackary, dressed in khaki pants, a sports coat and tie, stood at the threshold bearing an expensive-looking planter overflowing with greenery. He extended it toward her.

"Hello, Miss Margaret. I heard about your mother and came to tell you how sorry I am."

She took his gift reluctantly. "Thanks."

He flashed his million-dollar grin. "Could I come in a minute? Just a minute. I promise."

With a stony glare she slowly moved aside.

"I appreciate it, I really do." He settled on the sofa,

riding one arm across the top. His jacket fell open to reveal an elegant white shirt that hugged his tight stomach and chest. He made a smiling gesture toward the nearby chair. "Why don't you sit down?"

"Thank you, I prefer to stand."

"Whatever you like, Miss Margaret. I'm not one to argue with you." He gazed around the room, tapping his fingers on the sofa back. "So. How are you getting along?"

"I'm getting along all right, considering. How are you getting along?"

He laughed. "Fine, just fine. Thanks for asking. Where's Sam?"

"Upstairs. Asleep."

He made no effort to hide his disappointment. "Oh. Guess he needs his little nap."

"Yes, he does. Definitely."

"Is he getting along all right? I mean, are you both okay? Financially, I mean. I wouldn't want you and the child to want for anything."

"Mom left her house to me."

That gave him pause. "Did she? I am surprised. Guilt finally got to her, I guess."

"No, she left all of us comparable bequests. Carter received some stocks Dad had for decades. Johanna inherited the cabin and acreage in North Carolina."

"Well, well. You've got a place to live, but how about food and clothes? Looks like you could use a new dress, honey. If you need a job, my offer to put a word in the right set of ears still stands."

Thanks, but no thanks, she thought. *The last thing I need is to be beholden to Zackary Gould.* "I don't have to work right away. Mom left some money—not a lot, but enough to live on while I decide what to do. There's been too much change in Sam's life lately. He needs me. I'm thinking of staying at home until he's old enough to go to school."

"I don't know, Miss Margaret. Sounds too domestic for you. You can't bottle yourself up like that. You'll explode. You're too smart."

"Not too smart to know what my child needs."

His beautiful eyes turned smoky with the kind of look that used to send her heart into somersaults. "I wonder if that's true."

She turned away. *Is this my first test, Lord? Why are You starting at the doctoral level instead of kindergarten? This one's too hard.*

"Rayne and I would like to help you. A small child can be hard to handle during a funeral. Why don't you let us take him for a few days?" He saw her skeptical expression. "All right. You know, and I know it's Sam I'm thinking about. Maggie...I don't want to go to court with you. I'm aware I haven't done right by you, and I see the stress you're under, what with losing your mama and all. I've decided to wait and give you more time. But please, *please* give it your full consideration. Try not to let your thinking be clouded by how much you hate me. Think of what's best for our child."

His yearning tore into her soul like spikes. A bloody battle began to rage inside.

Let him go. Sam doesn't belong to you anyway—he belongs to God.

But this man—the things he did to me! He deserves nothing but my scorn.

Like a whisper in her ear, she heard Adam's voice saying again. *Is it possible to force love?* Sam did need his father. He craved him, if his allegiance to his fire truck was any indicator. If she tied her son to her side, wouldn't he come to resent her?

She had acted almost as badly toward Adam as Zack had to her. Adam had let his bitterness go. She could, too. Every pulse of her forgiven heart urged her to do the right thing. And wasn't that how God spoke to His children?

"All right," she said, the words tearing from her tongue. "Take him for a few days. If it works out, we'll talk."

She had never seen him look so ecstatic. He grabbed her in a spontaneous embrace, which she endured without returning, then tore up the stairs yelling for Sam, telling him Daddy had come to take him for a visit.

"Ashes to ashes, dust to dust," intoned Reverend Dixon from the pulpit of Parson's Ridge Bible Church on Sunday afternoon. The church was filled with mourners; even the balcony was packed. Rhonda's body lay within her closed white casket in front of the altar, surrounded by roses and lilies and carnations. The organist played uplifting hymns quietly and well; Maggie had seen to that, paying for a trained musician.

She watched everything through a haze of tears. When the pastor finished, friend after friend filed into the pulpit to give brief eulogies: a middle-aged woman who had been touched as a child by Rhonda's Sunday school class; an elderly man who spoke of Rhonda's sense of adventure in their seniors' group. Everyone, it seemed, loved Rhonda.

The time came for the family to say their final words. Johanna, adrift in tears, elected Sid to speak for her; and he did well, even causing laughter when he related the story of his wedding to Johanna. In detaching the bride's ring from the ring bearer's pillow, the best man had dropped it, the golden circle rolling down the aisle like a runaway horse. Rhonda had leapt after the ring, ending her search halfway under a pew.

Carter spoke movingly of his mother's acceptance of him and how much it meant in forming his character. His father had wished his boy to excel in sports, but Rhonda recognized his love for knowledge and encouraged it.

Maggie had asked to be last, and now it was her turn. She didn't know if she could do it, but she had to try. Beside her, Adam, sensing her nervousness, squeezed her hand and winked.

The walk to the pulpit seemed to take forever. When she finally stood behind it, she ran her eyes across the many faces watching her, lingering at her family's pew—Johanna looked uncomfortable, as if she didn't know what to expect—then on to the coffin. Fresh tears misted her eyes, and she blinked them away. She could cry later.

"I've listened to the wonderful words of the people who spoke before me, just as you have," she began. "They praised Rhonda Covington for her generosity, her selflessness, her virtuous and honorable life. All that's true of my mother, of course. But not one person has talked about the *real* Rhonda Covington. Not the one *I* knew.

"*My* mother could be irritable. She was unfair sometimes. When I was young, I thought she was too strict. I still think she was too strict."

There were uncomfortable stirrings in the congregation. Johanna's expression sharpened. Adam smiled bravely, but his eyes were wary. *Dear Adam, I'm sorry, but I have to say this.*

"Mom and I were estranged for several years because of our own stubbornness. Those were wasted years. We both missed a lot. She almost missed knowing her grandson entirely."

Behind her, Reverend Dixon cleared his throat. She heard his legs uncross. Maybe he planned to throw her from the pulpit.

"What I really want to say is that my mom was not a saint. And I'm glad she wasn't. I couldn't begin to hope to be like her if she never made the kind of mistakes we all make—the human kind.

"And I do hope to be like her, because I've found out more about the *heart* of my mom during this past month than I knew in all the years before. And I'll tell you this. If I can show half the love she showed, if I can be half as compassionate and forgiving, then I'll have gone a long way toward becoming the kind of creature God calls us to be."

Trembling, she moved her gaze from her mother's casket to Adam, who shot her a beaming look of approval. Johanna was wiping her eyes, Sid nodding and Carter giving her a discreet thumbs-up. Then, as she continued to stand there, her family—her very *dear* family, and she was ashamed to put them through this without warning, but she hadn't been sure she could do what she planned—began to show varying amounts of surprise. And poor Adam, with Beth beside him. Maggie caught them exchanging puzzled glances. Did he know what he was getting into, loving her? Perhaps this would give him a good idea.

When the organist began the introduction to "Amazing Grace," Johanna's lips parted as she realized what was about to happen.

Strength, Lord, Maggie prayed, and fastened her gaze

on Adam's. He was her lifeline. Her rock. Without him, without his powerful love, she wouldn't be standing here. Perhaps she wouldn't have found her way back to God, and how could she have borne this loss without feeling the Lord's comfort? She didn't know what the next days would bring, but of one thing she was sure. She belonged with Adam. She sent him a promise with her eyes and saw an answering light in his.

The introduction ended, and she opened her mouth to sing. To her vast relief, her voice sounded strong and sure, the notes flowing from her like golden messages of love to God, in praise of her mother.

Chapter Nineteen

What a strange Thanksgiving, Maggie reflected a few weeks later as the family gathered around her mother's large table for the afternoon meal. This year had brought vast changes into her life. She thought briefly of her biological mother, who would forever remain a shadow to her. She remembered her dad, who should be carving the turkey at the head of the table, not Sid. And how was it Johanna came to be sitting at Mom's place at the foot? The Franklin children were loud replacements for the three who used to wait with quiet eagerness for plates to be filled. Of those three grown children, only two were present; Carter had been unable to leave his work. And strangest, perhaps saddest of all: Sam was missing. He should be here but instead was with his dad in Atlanta. Zack and she had worked out a custody arrangement between them. Sam was to stay with his father on alternating weekends, at Thanksgiving and Easter, and for two weeks every summer. But that meant he could be with her at Christmas, a voice reminded her. And look at Adam and his daughter, precious additions to their gathering. They seemed at home at her mother's table, as if they had always belonged there. Even Beth appeared happy, although Maggie occasionally caught a glimmer of the old resistance in her eyes. Adam and Beth filled a void in her life that she hadn't known was there.

The faces around the table changed and always would; she could not set any moment into time like a photograph. But she could be thankful for what she had, which was bounteous beyond measure and more than she or anyone like her deserved.

She wondered how she had failed to see it before. Existence was to be savored—every good moment, every bad moment. Each life that intersected hers was to be cherished and made better; every action and work to be done with her best effort and for God's glory.

After Sid gave the blessing, the table began to bustle with activity; bowls of vegetables passed from hand to hand, followed by the platter of sliced turkey and two baskets of Johanna's homemade wheat rolls and banana bread. Conversation flowed as freely as the food. Inasmuch as they could over the children's chatter, Johanna and Sid extended themselves to be gracious to Adam and Beth.

"Have you decided about college yet?" Johanna asked the girl during a rare lull.

Beth wiped her mouth with her napkin. "I'm still debating. I'm looking for a small college with a good education program."

"So you're planning to teach?" Sid asked.

"Yes, I like little kids."

Johanna passed the Jell-O to Andrew, who was clamoring for more. "Are you going to try for a scholarship?" Her sister was always competitive academically,

Maggie remembered. She had been a tough act to follow in high school.

"I guess so, although Mom left more than enough for my education. Oh, that reminds me. Dad, I can't believe I forgot to tell you, but Jake Browne came to see me yesterday afternoon while you were at work."

Adam, who was cutting a bite-sized portion of white meat, paused. Maggie felt his apprehension like a cool wind. "Oh?"

"Yep." Glancing around the table, she explained, "Jake used to be kind of my boyfriend, but now we're just friends. Anyway, he wanted to say goodbye. You're not going to believe this, Dad, but his brother got a scholarship big enough to pay his way through med school."

"Did he?" Adam said, visibly relaxing.

"Yeah, isn't that great? That means Jake can use his savings to go back to art school. He's moving to New York this weekend so he can get settled before the January semester gets started."

"God is good," Adam said sweetly. Maggie stifled a smile.

"And the best thing is, the scholarship came from an anonymous donor. It was given in memory of an exceptional woman of God, Jake said, with the intention of showing His love to the next generation. Wasn't that something?"

"I'll say," Sid commented. "I like the anonymous part. It adds mystery."

Beth agreed. "What makes it even more special is that…well, Jake's not a believer. He's never had a good thing to say about God or the church before this. Not that he's shouting in the aisles or anything, but I could tell he was kind of reeling from the surprise. Maybe it'll make a difference. I don't know.''

The adults murmured their pleasure at this news—all except Adam, who forked a large mouthful of fried corn into his mouth and chewed industriously. He was looking especially detached from the conversation, Maggie thought. Maybe he was afraid of showing how glad he was the young man was moving.

After the meal, Adam and Sid washed dishes while Maggie and Johanna cleaned counters and foiled and stored enough leftovers to make the most ardent turkey lover ill. Beth went outside with the children, but it wasn't long before they all trooped back, cheeks blooming with cold. She ran upstairs to play with the two boys while the rest of the overstuffed diners settled into the parlor to watch a football game. Before long, Sid was snoring on the sofa, Johanna was reading a mystery she'd brought from the library and Sandi and Sara were working on a five-hundred-piece puzzle at the kitchen table.

"Anyone for a walk?" Adam asked.

Johanna looked from him to Maggie. "Too cold for me."

"I'd love to," Maggie said. "I'll get my jacket."

When they stepped outside, the frigid air shocked Maggie's skin and lungs. Thanksgiving wasn't supposed to be this cold, she thought grumpily. Not in Chattanooga.

Adam tucked her arm in his and led her down the porch steps. "Alone at last," he said.

"Finally. It gives me the chance to tell you how wonderful you've been these past few weeks. I don't know how I could have gotten through any of it without you."

"Thank you, ma'am. There's a lot more where that came from."

She smiled. They had reached the road and were walking along its edge, beside the woods. The few houses along this stretch all had extra cars in their driveways. The thought of families and friends enjoying one another warmed her.

Adam seemed disturbed by her silence. "It has occurred to me that I might be taking too much for granted. You've never really said—" he cleared his throat "—what your intentions are concernin' me, ma'am."

Maggie gave him a mischievous look. "How's Beth taking it? Your spending time with me, I mean."

"She's coping. I've promised not to go too fast. She needs time to heal. We all do." He patted her hand. "Those were not the words I wanted to hear, Maggie."

"No?" With a wicked smile, she pulled him behind a thick oak tree and backed him against it, caging him with braced arms. "How's this, then? Adam Morgan, I love you, every inch of you, inside and out!"

"Why, ma'am, this is so sudden, Ah have to think of mah reputation—"

"Hush, you." She reached her arms around his neck and kissed him thoroughly. It wasn't, she discovered, so cold out after all.

Taking a shaky breath, Adam gazed down at her in humorous appreciation. "You've definitely compromised me," he said, forgetting his accent. "I guess you're going to have to marry me now."

A grin lit her face, then faded. "Adam, are you sure? It won't be easy living with me, especially in comparison to Allison. I have a temper, you know."

"Is that right? I'm glad you told me before it was too late." They laughed companionably. After a moment,

Adam looked thoughtful. Musingly he said, "People don't change all that much. God works with what He has, but He doesn't do personality transplants."

Maggie blinked. "My goodness, am I that bad?"

"What? Oh, no, Maggie. I was thinking about *me*. Aside from the usual wear and tear, I'm not all that different than I was twenty years ago."

Understanding dawned. "I hope you aren't worried—please don't think for one second that I would repeat old history." That he might believe so made her want to cry. "I was wrong for leaving you, and I've regretted it all my life. But I have to disagree with you. In some ways, you *have* changed."

"I don't know about that. I've never lived in the fast lane," he warned, as if that were a consideration that bothered her. "I'm pretty much set in my ways."

"You're pretty much set in *good* ways. But even you have mellowed, Adam. When we were kids, you tried to make me believe as you did. I felt like I was being forced to follow God because that was what you wanted. Combined with the pressure from Mom, I felt…stifled, I guess. But now you've allowed me to come to Him in my own way, in my own time. You made it plain where you stood, but you didn't push. That was exactly what I needed and I'll always be grateful to you for it."

He beamed and covered her hands with his. "Don't thank me for what God has done. Think of all the richness in our lives despite the bad things. You had some good years with Zack. My life will forever be blessed by Allison's influence. And our children. Thank God for them, for the beauty and joy they bring. If there is one thing I've learned in the past twenty years, it's that nothing is ever wasted with God. He brings goodness to everything."

Maggie felt tears welling in her eyes. *Thank you, Father. Thank you for bringing this wonderful man into my life.* Laughing lightly, she declared, "My real concern is how will *you* be able to stand living with *me?* You know it's hard for me to conform to things when I can't see the reason for them. Like bake sales, for instance. How many hours do women spend shopping and baking and selling, when they could give the same amount of money without all that work and probably make a better profit?"

"Hmm. Are you sure you don't feel that way because you're afraid no one will buy your cookies? Because I will, you know."

"Thanks a lot." Her face grew serious. "There's something else. I still have questions. There's so much I don't understand, and I've got a long way to go, faithwise. Are you going to be able to stand fifty years or whatever of me trying to figure things out?"

He appeared to think deeply. "Well, Maggie, it's like this. God's been so good to me, I figure I owe Him something back. And sacrificing myself for one of His most rebellious children seems like a good way to do it."

"Adam Morgan..." she warned.

"Oh, and I guess I'd better mention this, too," he continued. "I can't imagine living without you. It would be like this." He waved his hand, indicating the leafless trees, brown grass, gray sky and the chill surrounding them. "Winter. Forever winter."

Naturally this called for another kiss. After a delightful interval, Maggie pulled away, her heart hammering against her ribs, the November air seeping through her clothes. She shivered, and Adam wrapped one arm around her shoulders, pulling her close to his warmth. They walked on.

Like this, Lord, Maggie sang silently, feeling music pour into her greening heart like welcome rain. *Together.*

* * * * *

Dear Reader,

Writing isn't easy for me. I have author friends who produce twenty pages of perfect prose daily while I'm sweating out five—and that's on a good day. So why do I do it? As soon as print began to translate into images in my mind, I was hooked. I love to read, and I love to write. And also, if the truth be known, the only thing that *does* come easy for me is eating chocolate-covered caramels—not a wise vocational choice.

The mind can be a self-willed sponge, soaking up what it sees, hears and smells into long-term memory. To paraphrase Paul a bit, the things I would remember, I do not, but the things I would not, I do. I believe we do well to monitor what we offer our minds.

That's why I'm excited about the Love Inspired line— entertainment with something extra. Not that everything we read or watch has to have a spiritual message, but it's comforting to know it's out there when you need it.

Like the act of writing, maintaining faith isn't easy. I won't add the obvious: "in today's world," because it has always been hard. Writing this novel has been a delightful spiritual voyage for me, for through Maggie Covington Gould's honest, hard questions, I've explored a few of my own—and maybe some of yours. I hope the answers she receives bring comfort to your heart.

Lovingly,

Marcy Froemke